Alan Carmichael

the Reluctant Thief

Pen Press Publishers Ltd

First published in Great Britain by
Pen Press Publishers Ltd
The Old School Road
39 Chesham Road
Brighton BN2 1NB

ISBN 1-905203-97-7
ISBN-13 978-1-905203-97-0

Printed and bound in the UK

A catalogue record of this book is available from
the British Library

Cover design by Jacqueline Abromeit

For G, W, and C.

For reasons that they will not remember.

The Reluctant Thief

Alan Carmichael was born in 1957. He studied mathematics at Bristol university, and lives in London.

He no longer works in the computer industry.

Well
something's lost
but something's gained
in living every day

Joni Mitchell

Part I

one

It is in the re-telling that importance becomes clear. Tim Scott knew this as he flew thirty thousand feet above the Atlantic. It is in the re-telling that beginnings and endings emerge. And his old life, he saw, ended that afternoon.

A strong mid-May sun, Mozart in the background. The wine carefully chosen and chilled.

Or perhaps it ended during a single minute of that afternoon. Or in the time it took for his friend to utter one word.

A name.

"Sanjay," Pete said. "Do you remember Sanjay?"

Tim listened and closed his eyes, and his stomach seemed to go into freefall. For a second he felt his face burning, and then it passed. He opened his eyes and smiled at the others. He wondered whether they had noticed.

"Sanjay. Of course," he said quietly, and he recalled perhaps the only one of all their friends who even as an undergraduate seemed already to have crossed over from boyhood into the adult he would remain for the rest of his life. He remembered Sanjay's Italian suits, the gelled and faintly effete hairstyle, the hint even then of an executive portliness that might have come from too many extended lunches. And he recalled a memory once erased, the two of them in his car, a long, cold night, a long night of driving, and then a grey dawn, and both of them staggering out of the car in disbelief. The fear of what they would find. The mess on the front bumper.

Later he would try to re-imagine his life as it was before.

Or even the way it had been just minutes earlier.

They sat outside on the patio. Pete's wife had prepared a

table. Three children were playing hide-and-seek at the bottom of the garden. They talked of their careers, for they had not been in touch since their university years. Perhaps they had never been close, and when they ran into each other the Friday before Tim had hesitated. But that day he decided to take a gamble, they stopped to chat, and Pete invited him over the same weekend.

His friend had become a journalist working in the crime section of a national newspaper, and he discussed some of the cases with which he had a close connection. He talked about villains, conmen, yardies, crime families, he discussed policemen, lawyers, judges, the whole panoply of skilled and well-paid professionals that society has assembled to regulate the activities at its fringes. His wife, a lawyer, added a few stories of her own, and Tim listened open-mouthed at the world they described, a parallel universe of brutality, intimidation, degradation, with stories of pain and despair, which ran so close to his own, and yet in the normal run of things intersected so rarely with his comfortable existence, a life of work, friends, commitments of routine and pleasure, of afternoons like this, which drifted along in a haze of sun and wine.

He looked across at Pete and Janice's children twenty feet away, at that moment quite removed from the world of their parents, and as he gazed at them, the three of them running, tumbling, laughing, screaming, the thought came to him that they seemed almost perfect, that they were brushed with the fineness of the new, of the as yet uncompromised, as if they were an advance party of a new species who would populate a brighter, fresher world, where the continuous wearing down and shading into grey that most accept is their fate in life would instead be for them a thing of history, a memory from a grimier and less certain past. Perhaps, for once, Tim was touched with the sense of optimism that all parents have for their children. He felt surprised at its warmth.

Janice followed his gaze. "How is...?"

"Imogen," Pete nudged his wife.

"How is Imogen? It's a shame she couldn't make it."

"She's very busy," Tim said. "She's rehearsing today."

"Did you two get together at university?" Pete asked.

"Soon after."

They sipped their drinks.

"Who do you still see, then?" Pete said. "Who else do you see from the old gang?"

They talked of old colleagues and friends. Which among them had succeeded. Which had failed.

Sanjay.

"Do you remember Sanjay?" Pete had asked. And for a minute Tim's world seemed to fade as the past shimmered and threatened. He may have said something in reply. He knew the others were listening, he knew they were still there, their lips were still moving, but he could not make out a word they said, until, as if breaking surface, conversation suddenly began to take shape around him once more.

"We met him," Pete was saying. "Two, three months ago. Up town. We were there for the sales."

"He had a rather glamorous lady on his arm," Janice said.

"He was standing there, dressed in black, carrying all these glossy shopping bags with Parisian names on them," Pete said. "With this somewhat over made-up woman next to him."

"I thought at first he was the chauffeur," Janice said.

"We only spoke for a few moments," Pete added. "As they waited on the pavement outside the shops."

"They were waiting for a limousine to pick them up. A *limousine!*"

"He said he was a senior accountant or something," Pete said. "Chief Financial Officer, he called it."

"She was very elegant. She was wearing a rather immaculate trouser suit. She said it was one of her own designs," Janice said.

"He was always big on titles. He said he was with some West End property company."

"She gave me her card," Janice said.

"It was all so Sanjay," Pete said. "Discreet, stylish. Faintly corrupt. I don't know why."

"Here." Janice said. "I still have it. It's in my bag."

"I don't think he even told me his company's name."

"Here. Here it is," Janice said. She handed the card to Tim.

Tim read. *Vicky's. Couture.* His voice seemed finally to emerge from somewhere deep.

"That's Sanjay," Tim growled. He cleared his throat. "I guess you can always tell," he said. "You can always tell how people will turn out."

But perhaps that's wrong, he thought. *Perhaps you can't.*

two

"We kill. We kill every day. And at night, we listen to Beethoven. That's what makes us what we are. That's what makes us superhuman."

General Mannfred von Essler, 1943. Warsaw.

Michael Palmer chuckled to himself.

The muscles around his eyes relaxed slightly, and he became aware of his reflection in the plate glass window, a ghostly superimposition on the city skyline at which he had been staring for a quarter of an hour.

I must be losing my touch, he thought.

He walked over to his desk, and pressed a button.

"Patti, hold all calls for half an hour."

"Yes sir."

Superhuman.

He moved over to the bookshelf and spent a minute trying to find the quotation, and then, failing, turned back to stare outside.

He wondered what his uncle would have thought about the numbers coming in from Moscow.

"I trust you, Michael," his uncle had once said. "We all do. Just one word of advice. Stick with what you know."

And then, another time. "Listen to Bernie, Michael. Just listen to what he says."

Bernie. Something he had said. Why had it popped into his head at this moment? After all these years. He looked out of the window at the balcony on the narrow ledge, and watched a pigeon picking a careful path on the metal rail. As his eyes followed it, he made a mental note to remind the office cleaners to have a look out there. The balcony was covered with bird shit. He would tell them, they should be laying down some poison. The birds were so tame, they no longer even bothered to move when he shook open the blinds.

Bernie Stubbs. Michael remembered the pub where he had met him for the first time. He was twenty-two when his uncle had introduced them. It was after a meeting, a business meeting. Some Americans. He had waited in reception, watching as his uncle showed the men to the lifts. Three men, sleek, with briefcases and identical dark suits, they said nothing as they waited for the doors to open. As soon as they had gone, his uncle had turned to him and punched the air. Fifteen minutes later they stood at the bar inside a pub, his uncle studiedly extracting notes from his wallet. He handed two of them to Michael.

"Get the round in. Order an extra beer. We'll be over at that table in the corner."

Michael looked across and saw a man watching them expressionlessly. Stiff, bulky, uneasy in a tight grey jacket and slacks. When Michael walked over a few minutes later with a tray of drinks, neither his uncle nor the grey man looked up or interrupted the flow of conversation. He watched the two men as they talked quietly for ten minutes, and wondered what his uncle saw in him. So unlike the Americans.

"I'm off. I have some entertaining to do. Across town. Here. Buy yourself some more drinks."

His uncle left more notes on the table and put on his coat. Michael hesitated, but the man picked up his empty glass and waved it towards him. An hour later, and he began to open up about Belfast and the Falklands.

There was something that Bernie had once said. It wasn't that night, but later, when they knew each other better. Was it in the same pub? How long ago, fifteen years? Michael could not recall, and yet the words themselves came crashing back into his mind. *Never forget how it feels.* He took a sharp, deep breath and walked towards the sliding doors. He pulled them open and stepped on to the balcony. The pigeon regarded him for a moment, and then started pecking at the metal rail on which it stood. It hopped forward two paces. *Listen to Bernie*, his uncle had said. Vermin, Michael thought. The pigeon flapped its wings, but then settled back on the rail. Michael moved slowly towards it.

His uncle had relied on Bernie for ten years. The business had grown in that time, and Michael with it. The American connection worked well. Perhaps too well. His uncle was already eyeing up golf courses in Florida and talking of slowing down a little. Michael began to collect his own team around him, especially when many of the old guard disappeared, some into various jails around the country, others, after occasional disagreements with competitors, right off the face of the earth. The economy was booming, and Michael began to see that the borderline between some of the City's sharper practices and the lines of business traditionally favoured by his own colleagues and associates was becoming ever more blurred, that this frontier was increasingly being fought over by lawyers and accountants rather than the men with bad breath and tattooed arms that his uncle had employed. And also, society was loosening up, and some of the businesses with which his people had traditionally been involved had shifted across, sometimes without anyone realising, from under- to over-the-counter, from top to middle or even bottom shelf. He looked on amazed as the payments to various Special Branch officers became unnecessary, as his shops began to advertise in the press and open up in the high street, as a new wave of porn film directors began to move up into television and the mainstream and a kind of kitsch respectability.

Those remaining from the old guard had time on their hands.

One day, Bernie asked Michael to meet him for a drink.

"Time for me to move on, mate," Bernie said. "I need to get back into the field."

"What will you do?" Michael asked.

"Africa, I reckon. Down South. A few of the lads from the regiment are there already. There's always a war going on. They pay good money for guys like me."

That was the last time Michael had seen him, until, years later, he got a call for a few grand to help fish him out of an Angolan jail. But that night they argued over their beers, discussed payoffs and old times, and at the end of it Bernie had got up and walked out. For a while, Michael had worried and began to look for a replacement, but it came to him that things had moved on, that new methods were needed, and after a time he began to forget about it. Had that been wise? Perhaps he had moved too far.

Never forget how it feels. Something Bernie once said. Where had it been? The same pub? It must have been a year or two before that final meeting. Bernie talking.

"I remember our first day after we'd finished six months of basic. A bunch of us recruits. Still didn't know shit from shoe polish."

Michael was there. Bernie was there. Who else? Some of the younger guys, guys who had been to university, guys who had worked in offices all their lives.

"We were out on the moors, and the sarge brings over this trap, and it's got this chicken inside. So he sits us around in a circle, and he starts talking, and he starts to untie the binding on this small little wooden box he's carrying.

"'What d'you think of this little sweetie then,' he says to us, and we watch the thing squawking and flapping inside its cage.

"'Cos you're gonna get to know this birdie, and a few more like her,' he says, and he grabs the bird and pulls it out. 'Cos there's no fucking way that this thing is going back home alive,' he says. And he bends down and he bites the thing on the neck. He bites again, and its fucking head's ripped off, and he throws it at me, this thing flapping, spraying blood all over me. And I push the thing away, and the next bloke gets covered in blood, and then the next bloke."

Michael watched the young guys, drinking their American bottled beer, laughing and yelping, their eyes on Bernie.

"A few months later, we're in the pub. Chucking out time. We're on the way back to barracks, it's dark, and we pass a field. Animals. Farm animals, we can hear 'em. The sarge whips out a knife, and we all slip over the fence. He hands the blade to me, and I can just about make out one of these cows ahead. 'Go on,' he says, 'this one's yours. Make it quiet, make it quick.' I spent the whole night washing the mess off my clothes."

And later.

"'Keep your hand in,' my old sarge used to say. 'Never forget what it feels like. What it smells like. You can't hesitate. Cos next time it'll be some fucking wog shooting at you.'

"He was right, the old man. Keep yourself in practice. Even if it's just with a fucking animal."

Mistakes. Michael had learnt a lot from Bernie, and perhaps some of it he had forgotten. Perhaps he had also forgotten a few of the things his uncle had taught him. His uncle's people never borrowed, that was one of the first rules. Other people did that. And when they got into difficulties and came to his uncle, he lent them cash. It was one of his lines. A tidy business. But not him. And for years Michael had done the same. The nightclubs, the magazines and videos, the hotel deals in Spain, it had always been the firm's own money. Until now. Until this joint venture in Moscow. But these days the banks knew him, they took him for lunch on the thirty-fifth floor and they pointed out the activity and the cranes and the naked capitalism laid out in front of him. And some of this, they said, could be his if he joined up with them, and teams of accountants, some of them blow-dried and smouldering and sexy in their high heels and business suits, made it all sound so mouthwateringly easy and he had fallen in and gone along with their line.

Something had to change. He had to step back. He had forgotten what it smelt like.

After a minute he walked back through the sliding doors and into his office. He walked into his private bathroom, washed his hands, and looked at himself in the mirror. There was a tiny red speck on his white shirt. He frowned. He opened a cabinet door, and then walked back out to the balcony with a bin liner in his hand.

Later he called his secretary.

"Patti, there's some rubbish to be collected. By the sliding doors. Make sure the cleaners get rid of it," he said. "Oh, and Patti, don't look inside. It's a bit messy."

three

Tim and Imogen descended two steps and entered the hat section at the back of the shop, and as they did so, Tim took Imogen's hand. In her surprise, perhaps, she failed to give his the slight squeeze that she might otherwise have done. Tim would not have noticed anyway. As he gazed around the room in its gentle pink lighting he was suddenly standing next to his mother, his head not yet level with her shoulders, and it was her hand that he grasped, her hand in its black glove, his mother's handbag in the crook of the arm that he leant against. As he gazed at the fantastic creations arrayed around him, two dozen veiled and spiky and feathered confections of pink and cream and blue, each one exquisitely mounted and backlit, as if offered for the worship and adoration of a gelded priesthood, a delicate sense of perfumed femininity began to caress and fall over him like a fine rain. He felt a detached calm. And he stood with his mother, the two of them together, a day out, the big city, the trains and taxis, the crowds, and then the lights of the department store and his mother discussing lipsticks and perfumes with painted young ladies, dressed in white coats like the dentist's assistant but wearing those strange pointy shoes that seemed to make their bodies slippery and curved.

He stopped and sighed.

Imogen let his hand go, and began to walk slowly around the room.

They were alone. The room was quiet, their footsteps absorbed and deadened, it seemed, by the density of the scented air they breathed. Tim inhaled deeply and slowly.

"May I help you?"

A woman had silently appeared in front of Imogen.

"I... We're just looking..."

Imogen was unused to shops like these.

"We're going to a wedding," Tim boomed, without looking at them, from across the room. "Not our own, I may add. Imogen needs something to wear."

"Of course," the woman said.

Tim began to examine the hats on his own, one after the other, approaching each with his hands clasped behind his back, stooping slightly, leaning to the left and to the right, and then, as if its ephemeral beauty had been corrupted by the act of looking, moving on to the next, until after ten minutes he stopped and stood back and closed his eyes.

There was a white leather sofa tucked away in a corner, and he walked over to it, turned, and slowly sank onto its cushions. The two women talked softly at the other end of the room.

A man was staring at Tim.

Tim looked away and then glanced back. As he held his stare, the man smiled and began to walk over.

"It's Tim, isn't it?" he said.

"Sanjay."

Tim rose from the sofa. They shook hands.

"What are you doing here?"

Tim pointed across at the two women. "You never met Imogen, did you?"

Sanjay looked across, grinning.

"Vicky," he called out. "Vicky, it's Tim. My old friend. From my university days."

The two women looked at him for a second with curt smiles.

Sanjay turned back towards Tim, still grinning.

"Women." Sanjay's look was conspiratorial.

"Here, sit down," he said, suddenly taking off his jacket and folding it and then laying it on the side of the sofa. He pulled gently at his trouser legs around the thigh and carefully lowered himself onto the couch. "Tim. Sit. Please. Tell me, what are you doing here?"

Momentarily ill at ease, Tim brushed off a few imagined specks of dust from his jacket.

They talked. Tim told Sanjay of his meeting with Pete and Janice. "So it wasn't complete coincidence that we turned up here."

Sanjay's eyes narrowed. "Tell me, what do you do these days?"

"IT."

He continued to appraise.

"My company trades commodities," Tim said. "Oil, metals, grain. That kind of thing."

"Pork bellies? Eh? Men in red coats, funny hand signals..."

Sanjay shook his head, laughing suddenly. He turned back to Tim

"Tim, I can't believe it," he said. "You've joined up. The middle classes. The bourgeoisie. A regular job. You know, I could never quite pin you down at university. That analytical mind, the mathematics degree, yet I remember you at that dive club we used to go to, you know, that dodgy casino, where we used to lose what was left of our student grants."

Tim said something vague about mortgages and commitments.

"Although I remember you used to win from time to time."

Tim said it was all a long time ago.

"Of course it was. A long time ago. And here we are now."

And Tim wondered how much Sanjay remembered, and whether he ever woke up shaking in the middle of the night with those memories. He knew there would be a right time to mention it, to tease the subject out into the open. It was like offering condolences to a friend who had suffered a loss, he had to use his tact and judgement, to watch carefully for that moment. But Sanjay was suddenly on his feet.

"Vicks, I think we need to celebrate. Champagne. I'm sure we've got a bottle kicking about somewhere. And Tim, you haven't introduced me to your lovely friend."

He bounced up the steps into the front of the shop and disappeared behind a door. Tim looked over at Imogen quizzically. Seconds later, Sanjay was back, ice bucket and bottle under one arm, and four fluted glasses expertly held in his free hand. The four of them gathered round as introductions were made and Sanjay popped the cork.

"To us," Sanjay said. They drank. Imogen giggled.

"Tell me, Tim. Do you still gamble?" Sanjay asked.

"When the odds are right. I can be tempted now and then."

Sanjay watched him. They drank some more.

Tim and Imogen were silent as they drove home.

"Why didn't you buy anything?" Tim asked after a while.

Imogen thought for a few moments before replying. "I don't know. Something just didn't seem right."

"What will you do?"

"What do you mean? Oh, the hat? I guess I'll just M&S it."

Later.

"What are *you* going to wear?"

"I've got my suit."

"Please, Tim. It's your brother. We must make an effort."

It was clouding over as they finally turned into their road.

"Are you going to come?" Tim asked. "You heard us talking? We arranged to meet up again some time soon."

"Where are you going to go?"

"He mentioned a casino in the West End. He knows the owner."

Imogen frowned. "You know that's not really my scene."

"Come along. Have a drink. We'll get something to eat."

"Anyway, I thought you were giving up that kind of thing."

"This is special. It's an old friend."

"I'll think about it."

"Well. Let me know soon."

four

Tim paused at a corner on the pavement where an unlit road led off from the high street. He put the A-to-Z back into his shoulder bag, turned away from the streetlights, and peered into the darkness. The twilight had faded over an hour ago, and there was now a slight drizzle. He began to walk down the side road, looking for neon or a sign of some kind. There appeared to be nothing. He came to the end of the road, stopped, and checked his directions again. He began to walk back, and then, on the other side, eyes adjusting, he made out a doorway, imposing, dark and covered, with a canopy in grey stone. Columns, garish, unlikely, stood at either side. There were cars double-parked in front. Two men in overcoats stood outside.

Tim crossed the road, quickening his step as he approached the two men. He avoided their eyes.

"Can I help you, sir?"

Tim slowed. A car door slammed behind him, and a man and a woman, both in evening dress, both silver-haired, drifted past him and entered the building.

"Are you a member, sir?"

Tim cleared his throat. "I'm meeting someone who is."

The two men in overcoats looked at each other. After a moment, the second man stepped back to the door and opened it. No light seemed to emerge from inside. The man looked at Tim without expression as he walked up.

"The receptionist will assist you, sir."

Inside, a woman in a black suit leant over a high desk, one narrow spotlight focussed on a leather-bound book open in front of her. The door behind Tim remained fractionally open for a few moments.

"I'm meeting Sanjay Roy," Tim said.

She wrote something down and then took his coat.

"Go through the double doors," she said. "You can buy refreshments to the left."

Minutes later Tim sat at one end of the bar. A row of vacant stools stretched alongside. He turned and looked out over the heavy brocade furnishing, the subdued lighting, the tables laid out at intervals and, circulating around them, men in dinner jackets. There was a low murmur of bets being placed and cards being turned. In Tim's mind rose a sudden vision, faded, black-and-white, of martinis and bunny girls and sixties swingers. Of blags and old-time villains. A waitress in a short skirt walked by.

He ordered a mineral water.

Tim still wore his suit from work. The flat had been empty when he arrived home earlier in the evening. Imogen was out with friends. He made a sandwich and watched the news. At nine o'clock he wrote a note to say he would be back late. As he wrote, he knew that he hoped Imogen would be asleep by the time he got home. He took a light raincoat from the closet, and then realised he was not sure where the casino was. He walked over to the bookshelf and looked for the streetmaps.

Tim looked at his watch, and paid for his drink. He got up and began to circulate amongst the tables. At one or two, croupiers waited silently on their own. It was early yet.

He hovered in the shadows above a game of blackjack. A man sneezed at the next table. The croupier flinched. Three men seated across from him remained staring at the cards in their hands.

"Are you going to be joining them?" A whisper in his ear.

"Sanjay." Tim turned to his right. "Perhaps later," he said softly.

They watched for a while, and moved over to the bar.

"To be honest," Sanjay said, "playing at the tables no longer interests me so much."

He ordered scotch. Tim stayed with mineral water.

"You don't feel the exhilaration of beating the system?" Tim said.

"Perhaps one's tastes evolve. There are bigger prizes out there. Besides," Sanjay added. "Where's the fun if the system's one's own?"

He looked up as a large crowd of men of Middle Eastern appearance entered the room. The guttural rhythms of their speech cut through the silence.

"What do you mean?" Tim said.

Sanjay looked directly at Tim. "We own this club."

Tim paused for a second as he took this in. "We?"

"My company."

"So that's what you do?" he said. "Casinos? Gambling?"

Sanjay shook his head. "It's... It's a bit wider than that. Property, entertainment, the media."

"And you? You, yourself?"

Sanjay picked at a bowl of olives on the bar. "I control the purse strings. I decide which of our various interests are making money. And I raise hell when they're not."

Tim raised his eyebrows and nodded.

And he found himself superimposing his friend's features on to the face that he held in memory, and was intrigued to find a perfect fit, even if Sanjay had suggested he'd changed. Intrigued, as he had expected a rounding, a greying, a smoothing, which the years and the accumulation of experience might have overlaid on his cheeks and his forehead and his eyes. Tim wondered whether Sanjay had ever experienced the untarnished optimism that Tim and his other friends had briefly felt at university, or whether he had known even then that certainties were there to be ground down, motives to be blurred, and that a life without compromise was for children.

Sanjay laughed.

"I don't want to make it sound too grand," he said. "I have underlings who do the things like adding up the numbers. Mostly I just visit our people, talk to them, make sure everything's running smoothly. Like tonight."

"And your friend's shop?"

"Ah. Vicky. Yes. A small sideline. A favour for a friend."

Tim waited. Sanjay continued to pick at the olives.

Tim changed tack.

"Tell me," he said. "One thing you said the other day. I was amused. You said that you could never imagine what I might become later in life."

Sanjay leant forward and patted Tim lightly across the shoulder.

"Tim, I used to worry about you. I could see you a few years on, burnt out, on skid row. Or worse. Married in Scunthorpe with brats and a civil service pension."

Sanjay wore the lightest of smiles.

"One thing I remember about you, Tim. When we went out, to parties, to clubs, you changed, you seemed to become someone else. Most of us, we have a drink, we become tipsy, a bit chatty. You, it was as if someone had turned off a switch. Or turned it on."

Tim swallowed. He gripped his glass.

"One moment, the studious, cautious type. The next moment, the wild man."

Tim said nothing. It crossed his mind that he had to figure out whether he was being mocked.

"I remember some of those allnighters we had."

Or praised. He had liked to drink, but no more than most other students. Perhaps Sanjay alone never seemed to lose his self-control. And Tim told himself he had been cautious with the other things, the various substances one could buy. At least most of the time. Except that once. Except for that one occasion.

"The wild man," Sanjay repeated. And then he grinned and clasped Tim's shoulder again.

Tim retreated behind his smile. He waited for Sanjay to elaborate, but he didn't. And Tim thought it was if they had both come up to a line, and certain things from their past were off limits for the moment, certain boundaries were now set. They might have to cross that line some time, but not yet. There were things that could for now be left unsaid. Tim began to relax.

"So, Tim, tell me," Sanjay said. "Did you ever wonder what I would become? After we all left."

Tim roused himself off the stool.

"Oh, I don't know. Something like this, I should have thought."

Sanjay chuckled as Tim picked up his drink.

"I'm going to play some cards," Tim said.

Tim walked to a booth at the other side of the room. He extracted his wallet from his pocket and placed two fifty pound notes on the counter, picked up fifty plastic tokens in return, which he placed in a small purse, then walked back into the centre of the room and approached one of the tables. He watched as the four players were dealt their hands, watched them glance at their cards and then bid, and draw or stay, and sometimes bust. He watched and began to recall the language, the rhythm and ritual of the play, its choreography, the slow crescendos and the abrupt climaxes, and the sudden catharsis as the assets were redistributed around the table. He listened. The clink of chips, the thwack of cards being turned. And he tensed his neck and closed his eyes for a second and started counting backwards from fifty-two down to one, and began a mental journey through a house he once knew, a house in which he had spent every summer when he was young, a huge, many-layered building whose rooms and attics and basements he tried at each visit to explore completely and which he visualised now and yet which, every year, had opened out some new surprise, some unexpected treat or hiding place, until one day in his tenth year, his great aunt collapsed and died while serving tea for her guests in the living room and an army of men in black suits descended on the house for a day or two and then they went away, taking her body with them, and his family soon followed, and he never saw the place again, though it remained imprinted on his mind with the immediacy and sharp simplicity of a child's dream.

The croupier gathered the cards, and disposed of them down a chute and then opened four new packs and shuffled them. As one player got up, he glanced at Tim and nodded, and Tim, with a curt smile to the other three players to his right, sat down at the empty place. And in his imagination he placed four large signs at the stairs where they led onto each of four floors, and these he labelled Clubs and Hearts and Spades and Diamonds. Each player was dealt two cards face up, Tim the last of them. He looked at each pair of cards, and the dealer's as well, one of which remained hidden, and he began to think of *Cats* and *Cans* and *Combs* and *Cores*, and for the seven of clubs he placed a *Cock*, spitting and strutting, on the dressing table of the bedroom on the fourth floor; for the ten of diamonds a *Case*, its handle scuffed, its locks fit to burst, in a doorway on the first; and for a Queen and a King of hearts he placed a female and a male doll, garish and sinister, crowns askew, on the bed in a room on the third. Chips were moved, players brushed cards against the table, and Tim watched and waited, betting cautiously, holding his own, winning here, losing there. The dealer dealt, he called the games, he collected chips. The stack of unknown cards remaining began to diminish, and the four floors of his memory began to fill.

But Tim's concentration wavered, and as he was dealt a nine and a six and as the other players considered their positions, he hovered uncertainly between floors, his mind darting up and down. Tens were out, all out, he thought, and jacks and queens were not far behind. And then he paused and the images in his mind blurred. He sighed, recounted, and it seemed that of the lower numbers, fives and sixes had not yet been dealt. He glanced sideways and saw none of these cards lying face up in front of the other players. He stared at his cards, the doubts flickering, and he knew he would just have to trust his instincts. And whereas twenty minutes ago he might have folded, he now increased his bet and lightly scratched his fingernail against the table-top. A four. A total of nineteen. Good. Not that good. For an instant he was on floor two, placing a battered *Comb*, its teeth missing, next to the one already there on the dressing table. He gestured to the croupier that he was going to hold, and he waited. And he guessed and hoped that the croupier had eleven, twelve in his hand, and that he would draw once and hold, a low total. Or draw twice and bust. The croupier turned over his hidden card. Tim stared. He counted. The croupier dealt himself one more card. A six. A spray of burning pinpricks burst across his forehead and cheeks. He wondered whether the others had noticed. Eighteen. He grimaced momentarily. The croupier remained expressionless. A victory, silent, acknowledged only by the movement of chips over to Tim's side of the table.

He won the next hand, and then, after folding early on two occasions, he won the next three in a row. He thought he caught the croupier glancing at him for a fraction of a second, and after two more hands, one of which he lost, the next of which he won after quadrupling his initial stake, the croupier signalled to a man in a tuxedo standing at the side, and new cards were called for. The croupier stepped aside and a woman in a black evening dress took his place. Cards were collected, four new packs were opened. A Japanese man at the table got up, collected his remaining chips and walked away. Another man sat in his place.

Tim took a gulp of water and thought of blue sky, of deep space, of the endless dust plains of the American mid-west. His system, this edifice of cues and images and memory associations that he had once dreamt up and which, he thought, he had long ago mastered. Were his powers now fading? Jesus, had he ever really been any good at it? He tensed and relaxed his shoulder muscles a few times, and then began to concentrate again. New cards. The play started. He was careful, his bets were small. Four floors. Empty. Slowly, as before, he began to populate the rooms on each floor, a raggedy doll, a mangy cat, the maggoty core of an apple, images sharp, absurd, chimerical. He began to spot patterns, to develop a rhythm. He started to bet larger amounts, or to withdraw early where the probabilities ran against him. He won. He lost. He began to win more than he lost. He caught the croupier's eye, and saw that she knew, and then that she knew he knew she knew. And this knowledge of the other's intent echoed back and forth between them, reflections multiplying as in a room full of mirrors. A four. A seven. He doubled his stake. The players around him fidgeted. He looked up at the woman as she prepared to deal cards. She moved around the table slowly, her left to her right. He felt the man beside him twist in his seat. He heard a soft gasp and then a softer curse. The croupier moved on. She faced him. He brushed his hand against the table. A six. Seventeen in his hand. He paused. The worst possible score. He wondered whether he saw the slightest of smiles on her lips. He sighed and looked down, his eyes lost their focus and his vision blurred, and he stood instead in his Aunt's house at the stairs to the first floor. He walked through into a large room. Diamonds. A red room. He looked to right and left. On the bed, on the floor, on the table. He counted. Fast. He drifted up, ghostlike, emerging in the jet black room above. And then, rising again, he now floated in red, and then a moment later, in black once more. Kings gone, queens, jacks. How many tens? Fifteen, sixteen? He had forgotten. Or miscounted. Drop a floor. How many hearts were there? He saw three. One remaining. No. Wrong. The last one, it was there, in his room, mislaid. On a straight backed chair. There, to his right. A row of *Caps*. Nines? A line of *Cuffs*, but the numbers blurred. Eights? One left, or was it two? Sixes. Fives. Fours. Fours and *Cores*. Apple cores, brown, wilting. *Fours. Fours.* And his mind blanked. *I don't know*, he thought. One heart? Two diamonds? No clubs, no spades? He paused again, his eyes lost their glassy stare and he gazed around the table. The other players looked at him, and he knew he had to take a gamble.

He looked up and signalled. A card was flipped over. A diamond card. A four of diamonds. He breathed out and closed his eyes for a moment. He heard a flutter around the table. *The old devil*, he heard someone say.

He swivelled his neck to the left and then to the right. The croupier dealt her own hand, and bust. He loosened his tie and took a sip of water. He stood up.

"That's enough for me," he said, and gathered in his chips. There was a crowd around the table. They caught his eye as he pushed through. He realised he was sweating. *Excuse me*, he mumbled. He needed a drink. *Please, can I get through.*

They sat in armchairs in a corner of another room in the club. The tables had become crowded, the guests more boisterous. Through an open set of double doors, above a constant but subdued hubbub of people moving and chattering, they caught the occasional expletive, the odd whoop of laughter or surprise.

A bottle lay upside down in an ice bucket on a low table between them. Tim watched Sanjay call over a waitress by her first name and point at it.

"How much did you win?" he said as she moved off.

Tim thought for a second. "Hundred and fifty. Plus change."

"Is that all?"

"Why?"

"How long were you there for? An hour?"

"So? It was fun."

Sanjay smiled and shook his head. He pointed back into the gaming area. "I hope our other customers are not so cautious."

Tim shrugged.

The waitress arrived with a new bottle. She opened it and poured two small measures. As Sanjay spoke to her, Tim picked up his glass and took a gulp. He lay back and draped himself across the folds of the leather cushions. He stretched his arms over the edge of the sofa. The waitress walked away. Sanjay remained on the edge of his seat, poised. He sipped his wine.

"You still using your system?" he said.

"I try. I was a bit rusty."

And it had been a bit tiring, Tim thought. He leaned his head back, and loosened his tie.

"You know that we try to spot it when people do that?"

"Of course."

Tim closed his eyes. The conversation skimmed over him

You never thought of trying to make a living out of it?

You're not giving up the day job just yet?

You City people. I guess you just earn too much money.

Tim started. He had a vague sense of being pigeon-holed, and somehow subtly demeaned. He opened his eyes, and remembered from the old days a fine tension, a kind of sparring in their conversation.

"You City people," Sanjay was saying. "Making money out of nothing."

"I..."

"I guess you just need phone lines and PCs these days."

"We..."

"Video conferencing. The internet..."

"Sanjay." Tim was almost shouting.

Sanjay was silent for a few moments. Tim wondered whether he had been over-sensitive.

"We are a bit different," he said. "We're not like all those others. My company is not even based in the City."

"Where are your offices then?"

"Not far from here. In casino land. Actually."

We were once close, Tim thought. Once. Something had bound them together. Those ties had not loosened.

A tension. If he could just talk for a while. Without interruption.

"As I said. We're a bit different. And we don't do much internet stuff."

Tim leaned forward. He finished his drink. Sanjay took a moment before answering. "Why's that?"

"Too public. Too political. It's..."

He poured himself more wine. Sanjay placed a hand over his glass.

Sanjay rubbed his chin and then swore silently. Sometime earlier on in the day he had mislaid his pocket shaver. He listened to Tim talk, he absent-mindedly stroked traces of stubble and wondered how long he would need to stay.

"Yes? It's...?" he said.

"I'll tell you. The oil market. You see, it's a bit ... political. There are always sanctions against someone, embargoes. Special tax regimes. Sometimes we need to be careful how we step round these. The company likes to keep quiet about what it does. Move behind the scenes. Head office's moved out from New York. Zurich's the place now."

It had been interesting to meet Tim again. For a while they had been close. They had shared a few times together. But those times were past, long finished with. Tim seemed edgy. But he, Sanjay, he no longer cared. It seemed to him that they had little now to offer each other. He sat, he nodded, he made conversation, and a part of him began thinking of excuses, something he could come up with to get away without giving offence. There was other business to deal with that night.

"I guess it's all about..." Sanjay massaged his chin, his cheeks. "...it's about margins. A cent here, a cent there. High volumes. Options, derivatives, all that kind of stuff?"

But then something happened to change his mind.

"We do those things," Tim said. "But mostly our guys just trade in the old fashioned way. Trading at its simplest. They buy, they sell. They figure out how to get one of those massive supertankers from one side of the world to the other.

"It's a global business. We have agents. Agents everywhere, all over the place, every capital in every country."

But there was something Tim would say. That same evening.

"It sounds complex," Sanjay said.

"It's not. It's not, really. You need a phone, you need the best possible comms links, you need the right contacts. And also a hundred million dollar line of credit at a Swiss bank."

Sanjay's eyes narrowed. He stared at Tim. Suddenly he suspected he would never make his excuses.

"I remember when I first started working for them. I was put on some of their accounting systems. I couldn't believe what I was seeing. Especially after this bleak old factory where I had been contracting before in North London, where they needed special authorisation to take you out for lunch at McDonalds. Every week their accounts people would produce pages and pages of this drivel, pages of the minutest detail of company expenditure, company trivia, fifty quid here, a few hundred there, every item down to the last penny. Huge payroll runs, thousands of people on minimum wage. Accounts payable, desks, paper, loo rolls for God's sake, each one itemised. Grey old men with cardigans and clipboards quibbling over expense accounts from salesmen in their Mondeos and B&Bs in the north of England. And suddenly there was this new world, where I had a single trade counted in millions. Twenty, thirty, fifty mil. A single contract, one stroke of a pen, one phone call, one shake of the hands. One deal, gobbling up the entire turnover of most ordinary companies."

Sanjay wondered for a second what was up with Tim, this compulsion to talk, he seemed unable to stop, and then the thought disappeared from his mind as he knew he would not leave, nor would he complete his other business. And the evening would begin to take on a surreal quality in Sanjay's mind, whose importance he would struggle to assess the next day.

"I began to see these deals every day. I still do. Annual turnover is in the stratosphere. Costs are low, our offices, London, New York, Zurich, they're comfortable, discreet. There are no prestige tower blocks, no bloated employee rolls. The people who run the company hide behind their billions. And this is a business that never goes away, one that's only marginally affected by recession, by war, by revolution. It's a trade that's somehow strangely democratic, egalitarian. Arab sells to Jew, Chechen to Yank. If the UN steps in and imposes sanctions, well, then, you fly under another flag. We sell to the US and to Cuba, we buy from Iran and Iraq, I'm sure that as we speak there are men quietly signing deals in Zimbabwe and Indonesia, in Basra, Beijing. They do deals with presidents and dictators, with prime ministers and sheikhs. But these despots won't ever dare reveal how it all works. I tell you, their people would rise up and slit their throats.

"The oil majors hate us. Shell, Exxon, BP. They say they do all the work, and we reap the benefits. And yet if there's an oil glut and they can't sell, we take the slack. If they fall short on a deal, we make up the difference. We're like hyenas, scavengers after the big beasts have made the kill. We clean things up, then we pick off the weaklings on the fringes. We keep the system lean and efficient. It works. Because of us."

Tim paused to pick up his glass. He waved to a waiter passing by.

Sanjay spoke to the man as he approached. He watched him walk off before turning back to Tim.

"Buying and selling. That's all it is. The myth of the barrow boy, the kid with the big mouth, the *chutzpah*. The myth's true. But then it's not. There's something else you need. You need the ear of the banks. And I mean the kind of banks that don't have branches in the high street. You need colossal lines of credit, you need to borrow by the bucket load, at an instant's notice. You need them to move this mountain of cash instantly around the world.

"And the banks have made this gargantuan effort to automate the whole process, it works instantly, and we tap in to the whole network."

Tim paused. The waiter approached with another bottle.

Sanjay spoke softly. "I bet there's a ton of security. Your computer systems, the banks'..."

"IT security," Tim said, and he laughed. "People only start asking questions about it when something's gone wrong. When someone's hacked the system."

"And don't things ever go wrong?"

"We've been lucky. But you have to ask, if it all goes bad, who's gonna be behind it? Who has the knowledge to do this kind of stuff? The simple truth is that any time you have codes or passwords or access keys, someone has to program these things into the system, and the programmer is the one who knows it all.

"I guess most IT people are too straight, or too geeky, or too lacking in imagination to think about subverting the system."

"But surely..." Sanjay said, and he paused. He was not quite sure what he was asking. "I mean... Surely the banks wouldn't allow it, surely they would insist on the proper measures to prevent... the hackers..."

"The new systems are tight. You're right. They make sure that no one person knows all the codes. They have encryption technology, digital signatures, password management, dual key systems. But this is the new stuff. The legacy systems are different..."

"... Legacy?"

"The old systems. Old technology. Ones they haven't got round to rewriting yet. There's one of these – I'm now senior programmer on this rickety old piece of code, I know every part of it, every line of every program – it sends instructions to our lead bank in Zurich. Payment instructions. Pay money to somebody. Pay company x some cash. Pay them a fuckuva lot of cash. So there's this set of algorithms to calculate a certain test number. And all that's needed is that this number corresponds to the test code that the bank calculates itself when it receives the instruction. If it does, well then, the deal's done. They'll carry out the instruction. So..."

Sanjay leaned forward. He whispered. "Let me get this straight..." But he didn't need to.

"So, twenty million dollars is going to some New York bank? Fine. Set up the details on screen, put in the amount, the date, the currency. Calculate the code. Send. And that's it. Hours later. Money gone. Deposited with some scumbag corporation on Wall Street. And I know the algorithms. I've seen the documents from the bank. I've coded them into the software. I know it all. I remember thinking, the day before we went live, and we'd sent a dummy transaction for one pound into one of the company accounts, it could have been to me, some Channel Island account that I'd set up. It could have been me. Not one pound. One million perhaps.

"I sometimes wonder. That they allow me to know so much. But that's the way it is whenever you have these huge systems, it's the little guy who writes the code, the guy at the bottom, he's the one who makes the whole thing work. So if you ask why they allow it, I say, well, that's the way it has to be. What do you expect? What do you expect the company to do? If I screw up? You think I might end up face down in the river? These guys, they're mavericks. They duck and dive. They lose money? They'll make it up tenfold with the next big deal. It's not like that trader, what's his name, the Brit, the guy in Singapore, the one who lost all that cash, he was on the run for ages... God, my memory... what's his name?"

Tim shut his eyes and rocked his head backwards and forwards. He tried to lean over to pick up his glass, but the sofa was too deep. He groaned, and then lunged. His glass toppled. Sanjay leapt up, pulled a tissue from his pocket and dabbed at the puddle on the table.

Tim continued to talk. "Whatever... whoever he was... We're not like that, we're already on to the next deal."

Sanjay mopped.

"They pay you off to keep these things quiet. A few people get sacked. The company moves on. No police, no publicity, no... no..."

Abruptly Tim was silent.

After a while he said, "Let me get you another drink."

Sanjay smoothed his trousers. He sat down again. "No. Thanks, I'm fine."

Tim did not move. "I'm sorry." He had run out of steam. "I better call a cab," he said. "Is there a number?" He remained seated. The sofa seemed too comfortable.

Sanjay ordered coffees. He was thinking hard.

Later, just moments later, it seemed, Tim was on the pavement outside scanning traffic for a taxi. He couldn't remember picking up his bag from the cloakroom, but it was there, on his shoulder. Neither could he recall saying goodbye to Sanjay. And yet he must have done. He must have said something. He would ring. The next day.

He was angry with himself. For drinking too much. As if he were still a student. And for talking so recklessly. As if to brag, to compete. To cover up. Perhaps it was just meeting Sanjay again.

He thought of Imogen. He wondered whether she would be awake when he got in. His clothes smelt. Of cigar smoke and drink and late nights. He wondered whether to sleep on the sofa that night.

five

"Sanjay, what's that?... Say it again... I... You're breaking up."

Michael Palmer clenched and unclenched his free hand as he put the receiver down.

He looked at the four men facing him across the conference table, and then at the top sheet of the sheaf of papers in front him. Five similar stacks of documents lay around the table.

"You've all read these, haven't you?" he said to the men. "You've all got your copies?" He looked to his left. "Mick? Bernie? You two as well?"

The two of them nodded, their movements slow, ponderous, as if every communication from brain to limb got lost somewhere in the transmission through their twenty stone bodies.

Michael pressed a button on his phone. "Patti, if Sanjay calls again, put him through."

Then he spoke again.

"No. Forget that. I'll call him myself."

He picked up a small plastic earpiece and strapped it over his ear. He dialled a number on the keyboard, and got up and walked around the room. He looked out the window over the City.

"Sanjay. Me again. Hi... it's..." He paused. "OK. I got that. So see you in fifteen minutes?...What's that?..."

He tensed his fists again for a moment, and sat down.

"He's stuck in traffic," he said to the others as he removed the earpiece. "We'll start without him. Danny, perhaps you can kick things off. You know these guys. You speak their language. What's this all about? What do they want?"

Danny passed a hand through his long, wavy hair. "It's money, is what it is. That's what they want. Money."

Danny wore a hurt expression, as if sulking. He continued to twirl knots of hair between his fingers.

"Danny. We know that. Let's have more. Give us the whys, the hows. Tell me, what's happened?"

"Look, it's simple. They're not finished yet. The hotels, the casinos. Not this year, not the next. Well, possibly next. Look. It's all here. Look. Page six."

Everyone shuffled paper. Danny continued without pause.

"It's all there. Look. You can see it. That section on costs. Labour costs. Look. The strike. When everything just stopped. The go-slow. New overtime rates, new conditions. Those unions, they don't fool around any more. Look. It's there. And then all those men killed. When that crane collapsed..."

"For Christ's sake," Mick's drawl cut through. "Why don't they just bang a few heads together over there? It isn't fucking England."

Danny screeched. "Hey, you can't do those things no more. This is the new Russia. The people, they insist to be treated properly. Don't you watch the news? You don't do things like they used to. It's not like the old days." But his voice suddenly softened. "Look, you guys, compared to here, it's still cheap. Way, way cheaper than England. Or Spain."

"Danny, what I need to know is, will they ever finish?"

"Yeah, Mike, they will. I tell you, it will be great, it'll be fuckin' fantastic. I tell you Mike, workers in Russia today, they're all so smart, so talented. They're all businessmen now. I'm telling you. Look, just trust me. It will be great. It just needs a bit more time, a bit more investment."

Michael frowned. He had stiffened at the kid's familiar tone. But he let it pass. He looked across at the man to Danny's right.

"Alec, the wage bill. This year's. Next. Can we cope?"

Alec spent a few seconds pressing his long, thin fingers together.

"Difficult," Alec said. "A. These figures are well above the inflationary cushion that we built in. B. We really didn't plan on an extra year of expenditure before the returns started flowing through."

"Elaborate."

Michael heard Mick sniff.

"How much will we be over?" Michael said. And at that moment he caught it also, a hint of scent in the air.

Alec paused, and then in his soft voice he presented to them an array of projections and percentages and subtotals. And finally, one single number, a large number with the word *dollars* after it.

Michael frowned again. He turned back to the papers on the desk, and began to re-read them.

"Danny," he said. "This word. Page seven, halfway down. In Russian. What does it mean?"

"Where?"

"In front of you." Michael's voice was sharp. "There. Halfway down. It's got a figure of a million dollars against it. A million. Alec, how much is that?"

Alec shrugged. "Five hundred and fifty. Six hundred grand."

Michael read on for a few paragraphs. The others were silent.

"Yes. So. Danny, what does it mean?"

"It's a kind of... Well, it's difficult to explain... There's no real word like it in English."

"It's fucking bribes, that's what it is."

Michael looked across sternly at Mick.

"Danny, go on," he said.

"It's a tax, some special tax. For foreign investors. The government they say it's to pay for infrastructure and stuff. Make Moscow modern, take it into the twenty-first century."

"Did we know about this before?"

"No. Well. Yeah. Well. The joint-ventureship. I thought our partners would deal with it."

"Alec, what's the story here?"

Alec paused. He carefully unbuttoned the jacket of his suit and leant forward.

"The lawyers have the full details," he said cautiously. "But. It *is* a tax. It's not new. It's for outside investors, a kind of sop to the nationalists, people who think the foreigners are buying up the whole of Mother Russia. You used to get immunity, when the local partners held more than a certain percentage. But the law changed at the last budget. There's now some complex rule based on investment, future earnings, amounts to be repatriated, and so on. So we don't get exemption any more. They've recalculated the formula so that we come out on the other side of the line.

"Now, we might be able to lodge an appeal against this judgement..."

A buzzer sounded. Everyone looked at Michael.

"Yes Patti?" he said.

"It's..."

She said no more. The door opened.

"About fuckin' time," Mick said.

Sanjay charged in, briefcase and coat in hand. "Sorry, chaps. Sorry."

He hung up his coat and walked to the far side of the room. He laid his case on the table and opened it.

"Danny boy," he said. He knew the Irishism annoyed him. "Doesn't it ever warm up in Moscow?"

"How was the flight?" Michael asked.

"Don't ask. I was up at four this morning. Then we had snow at Domododevo. Anyway. I'm here now."

"How are the twins?"

Sanjay paused as he gathered his papers. "In a moment. I need a coffee first."

Michael buzzed his intercom and spoke to his secretary. Bernie began to unwrap a new packet of cigarettes, his fat fingers oddly delicate as he picked off the cellophane. He offered one to Mick, and to no one else.

"Here," Michael said, reaching across. "Let's have one of those. It took me enough trouble to fix things so we could smoke in here."

Patti walked in with a tray. Sanjay handed her a diskette. He asked her to print out the contents. They waited until she had left.

"So," Sanjay breathed out. "I spent a couple of days with the twins. With Borzoi and Chergo. They send their regards. They took me around the complex. I had a look. I met people, saw the site. We spent an afternoon with the accountants."

Sanjay paused to take a sip from his coffee.

"And?"

"Well, it isn't good. They're behind. They're seriously behind."

Sanjay talked, and Michael's mood began to sink further. Sanjay discussed strikes and unions and negotiations, he talked of difficulties with materials, he talked of regulations changing by the day. He discussed taxes, local, regional, national. He talked of miscellaneous expenses, retirement funds, one-off payments, charitable contributions. At one point, Patti came in and handed out carefully stapled folders to everyone around the table.

Later, they drank coffee in silence.

"Mike," Bernie spoke up for the first time. "I don't want to say this. But what about canning the whole thing? It's not our game. Your uncle would never have done it like this. We're not over there. We can't keep tabs on them all. And the twins. These Ivanovs. I don't trust 'em. Never have. Borzoi, what's-his-name, the other. With fucking names like that, they sound like fucking animals."

"Hey, don't say that." Danny's voice was piercing again. "These guys, they're big men. You don't back out of agreements with guys like that. No way."

"Well, why can't they just fix things, then?" Mick said. He passed a huge hand over his bald head. "These unions, these bribes. Christ, it's their job to get these things sorted out. That's their job. Not ours. They're screwing up. They're screwing *us*."

"Hey. Not them. Not guys like that. These guys, you don't piss on them, and they won't piss on you. You can't just fuck with them and walk away."

"OK, OK. Cut it out." Michael got up and stretched. "We discussed all this, a couple of years back. We made our decision then to go in with the twins. We're not going to back out now."

He paced backwards and forwards for a minute.

"Right. Mick, Bernie, why don't you get some lunch. Go to the pub for an hour or so. I want to talk numbers with Alec and Sanjay. Danny, you join them. I'll give you a call when we're ready. I want to get this wrapped up today."

The two big men stared across at Danny. They knew he did not like pubs.

Things you want, and things you need, his uncle had said. *That's the difference between the City gents and us. They supply what people want. We supply what they need.*

Michael smiled as he remembered the conversation. It sounded the wrong way round, but it wasn't. In a way the old man was right. The things that people wanted, the things that British industry was geared up to producing, these things could change. Fashions came and went. The economy went into recession. People stopped wanting, or tightened their belts and did without. Companies went bust. But the things that people needed, for these there was always a market. People would find the money. Somehow, somewhere. *The things that people need are the things that the government won't let them have*, his uncle said. And in his uncle's time, that meant sex, booze, fags. And that's what the old families provided. They ran the brothels, they controlled the after hours drinking dens, they brought in the cheap cigarettes. And then society changed in the sixties and seventies and they began to dip their toes into the drugs markets. The old boys hated it, there were certain lines, they told themselves, that only the real scumbags crossed. But once they had stepped across those lines, and once they had seen it was a commercial enterprise like any other, except that the profits were double, three times, ten times what the old businesses brought in, a frenzy of growth and expansion began to spread through London and the other cities. The cottage industry of hippies and bohemians withered, and Michael and his peers took over, and for a while they surfed on a tide of money and white powder, and the anarchy and brutality of the Colombians remained a distant rumour from across the ocean, to be ignored as long as they got paid, and it seemed that there would be enough for everyone, and the violence of the old turf wars, which had looked for a moment as if it might re-ignite out of the froth of activity and hard selling and money laundering in which they wallowed, was caught early and firmly nailed down by men like Bernie Stubbs. If a few operatives, high and wild and permanently coked up to the eyeballs, if they disappeared and were not heard of again, well then everyone acquiesced and knew that it was an acceptable price to pay for the good life to continue.

The decades turned, and suddenly crack arrived and it all went bad. Michael remembered a copper he sometimes drank with in a bar in Soho, it must have been a year, two years into the nineties.

People won't know what's hit them.

And he described these wild boys from Jamaica, men who did not live by the rules, men whose minds and reason had been eaten away and erased by their short stunted lives of degradation and addiction and casual violence, so that the very concepts of order and rules were things that lay outside their comprehension.

A group of 'em arrives tooled up in Brixton or Harlesden or Toxteth, and they set about kidnapping and torturing the dealers already there, and then, when they have these guys' money and their stash, they kill 'em, and for a while they're king of the hill, until a new gang arrives, and now they're the ones being hunted down and kidnapped and topped.

Some of the families tried to reach a kind of accommodation, but they never got beyond the first step, and some of the big players disappeared for good, they just never had the appetite for that kind of violence.

One day Bernie came to him and told him that they needed to change their tactics, they needed to be subtle where the new guys used brute firepower, and he and a few of the lads could sort it out if Michael wanted, especially as they now had a few boys from Ireland who had once sat at the feet of Gerry Adams but who could see the way the wind was blowing over there with people talking ceasefires, lads who now had families themselves and were seeing for the first time that the king's shilling was not so bad after all. Give him the word and Michael might soon begin to read in the papers of car bombs in South London.

Or better, he said, *rob a few of their bagmen, burn down one or two nightclubs. Stir it up. These guys are so dumb. Let them slug it out amongst themselves and kill each other.*

Michael considered it and he knew Bernie could and would do it, and part of him wanted to fight. But one day, after he had been reading those military histories for the nth time, he had a sudden insight, and he asked himself what those old military supermen would have done, those old Germans, who came within a hair's breadth of snatching the whole of Europe, at least all of it that mattered, away from the bumbling gerontocrats who ran the old order, until they saw that their insane leader had confronted them with a final horizon whose span even they could not encompass; and he had a vision of Wehrmacht generals on the banks of the River Oder in 1945, looking out to the East at the hordes of *untermenschen* about to engulf them. Their men were smarter, better disciplined, they had better equipment, they were better soldiers than their enemy. But they would always lose. For if they killed a million, another two million would emerge from the steppes behind them. What good would it do, Michael suddenly knew, if Bernie's people dealt with one bunch, when another would arrive on the next plane out of Kingston. A never-ending stream of psychopaths. Courtesy of British Airways.

Anyway the economy was coming out of recession and Michael had plans of a different kind, plans involving businesses once on the margins but now mainstream. As he looked on, as British coppers were gunned down in South London, and the police got tooled up themselves and began to form SWAT teams, and the jails were filled to bursting point, he told himself he should be glad he was out of it. Once the decision had been made, the nineties began to click, and then in a kind or irony, he found that the hordes from the East were suddenly offering opportunities of a new kind. With the Berlin Wall down, and capitalism spreading as fast as the Red Army had done in the opposite direction fifty years before, new money was emerging from St Petersburg and Moscow which he and others like him could use and channel and take advantage of. Joint-venture construction projects in Spain had worked well. The Ivanov twins were young, dynamic, they had access to ludicrously large amounts of capital, and they understood the West well. When they said they were looking for London-based partners for a new hotel and gambling complex that they were constructing in Russia itself, Michael saw this as a chance to move up a level. Some people around him cautioned against, they said the market was too far away, there was too much that lay beyond their control, but Michael was looking at the example of Las Vegas, how the city had emerged from nothing, had flourished in the desert itself after the war, and there, in the shining spires of glass and metal, in allnight neon, not in some sordid underground, hidden away – there, there was the gold that a new breed of pioneers was really looking for. He knew it would be long haul, but he coughed up the ante, and he waited, and he endured the delays and the cash calls, until, as he finally crossed the point of no return and the foundation stones were laid, he began to see daylight peeking through the bleak Moscow fog.

Mick and Bernie, their cheeks flushed, their heavy frames surprisingly light on their outsize brogues, loped into the room, sunglasses still on.

"Where's Danilov?" Michael asked.

Mick shrugged.

"We didn't see him in the pub," Bernie said.

Michael paused, as if undecided for a second.

"That's OK. Better that he's not here," he said. "Let's move on. Alec, Sanjay, where were we?"

People took their seats. Michael waited as they settled.

"OK. The bottom line is this. We need ten million. Possibly fifteen. We need cash. And we need it pretty quick. This whole thing is spinning out of control, and we need to get back on top of it. Or we need to back out. Now."

The others looked at him blankly.

"I need some ideas. I need some... some inspiration. Come on, you people. I need something from you."

Four faces stared at him in silence.

"Alec. The banks. What's our position with them?"

Alec slowly shuffled the papers in front of him into a neat pile at a perfect right angle to the table's edge.

"We're stretched," he said. "We're up to our limits. They won't like it if we come calling for more. They won't like it either if we tell them we're writing off our investment so far. It's all on the penultimate page. Here. Let me clarify."

He spoke, and Michael watched his hands, rising, falling, carving imaginary curves out of the air, elegant geometrical shapes whose arc seemed to match the hypnotic cadences of his speech

Later, Michael found himself staring at him, and realised he had hardly heard a word Alec had said. For a while he was silent.

"Sanjay?" he said. And then he paused. "Sorry, Alec." He pulled himself together. "Thanks for that. Let's move on. Sanjay, the other businesses. What have we got there?"

Sanjay shifted his weight in his seat.

"They're looking good, Michael," he said. "But they can't generate that kind of cash. Not overnight. Not out of nothing."

And he discussed the casinos, the hotels, the video businesses, the magazines, the publishing.

"Unless we sold. Unless we sold one of them."

"No," Michael said. "I'm not getting out of things that are known. Things that are proven."

He was silent again.

"What about you boys? You got anything?" He turned to Mick and Bernie.

Bernie took off his dark glasses, rubbed his eyes and yawned.

"Look. Mike. We can always get hold of cash. You know us. Our boys are always on the look out. But not that kind of money. There just aren't jobs like that around these days. You can't just take down the banks and institutions as you could before. They've wised up."

"So what else is there?"

"What do you mean?"

"Look, I need you boys to keep me in touch with that side of things. There must be something going on."

"Like what?"

"Like... like that Rembrandt that I was reading about the other day. Disappeared from some gallery in Holland. Valued at seventeen million..."

"Seven," Alec cut in.

"What?"

"Seven million. Not seventeen."

"Whatever."

The two big men looked on impassively.

"Look, boss," Mick said. "I don't know shit about this bullshit art world. But you say so, you give the word, I'll ask around. We'll plan it, we'll do it. Just say the word."

Bernie got up. "I need the loo," he said.

Mick lit a cigarette. Alec and Sanjay got up and stretched. Michael looked at the three of them in turn. He shook his head.

Ten minutes later, Michael and Sanjay stood at the window. The others had gone.

"Sanjay, I'm staying at Vicky's tonight. Give my wife a ring and make up some excuse, will you. You always seem to be able to say the right thing. Tell her we're working late or something. Tell her it'll be too late to get out to Essex."

They were silent for a while.

"So. How do we get out of this one?" Michael addressed the sky outside the window.

Sanjay walked to the other side of the room. A jug and some glasses had been left on a tray. He poured himself some water. After a while he spoke.

"You know, Michael. I met someone the other night. Someone I knew a long time ago. At university. Bit of a no-hoper. Or that's what I always thought. He was a bright guy, he got a good degree. But... like so many of them, he was just a bit clueless. He hung around on the fringes of one or two of the scenes we had going in those days.

"We met recently. A chance meeting. I invited him to the club, it was last week. He gambled for a while, won something. Not a lot. Then we had a couple of drinks. He had a bit too much. I can't say it surprised me. I assume he got home OK. I haven't spoken to him since. Perhaps I should find out."

Michael began tightening his right fist into a ball.

"Please. Just... just bear with me," Sanjay said. "Let me talk for a moment."

Michael's fingers slowly uncoiled.

"He told me he works in IT. Back-office stuff for one of these commodity traders. Oil. They're major players."

And Sanjay described the conversation they had had that evening and the things Tim had said, about the money, the banks, the lines of credit, the computer systems.

"I've been thinking about it a lot since we met. This business he's in, there are a lot of holes there. It could be just ripe for someone to exploit. Perhaps. Perhaps that someone could be us..."

Michael had continued to stare out the window as Sanjay spoke. A thought had begun to form in his mind. He began to imagine a possibility. *A step back,* he thought. *A step back across a line.*

"How serious was all this? Was he just pissed? Was he just shooting his mouth off?"

"He was, both those things. But there was something, some kernel of plausibility in what he said. I've spoken to Alec since. He agrees, there could be something there we could use."

The room was silent. The atmosphere suddenly seemed dense. After a moment, the air conditioning clicked in.

"This friend of yours," Michael said. "Would he be approachable? Would he work for us?"

"I don't know. It might be hard. We'd have to make it attractive. Somehow. There would have to be some money on the table."

"That's easy, we can do that. But... the other thing. You know what I'm getting at. Would he ever cross that line?"

"Well..."

Michael turned. The two men observed each other for a few moments.

"You think he would?"

"Well, that's it. There's something else. Something that happened when we were at university together. I've hardly thought about it since I left. My bet is that he's never mentioned it to anyone. No one else knows."

"What is it?"

Sanjay was coy.

"Let me think it over," he said instead. "I think I just might be able to swing it. I might be able persuade him to consider it."

Michael turned back to look out the window.

"What would you need? To make this happen?"

"We'd need a team. We'd need to get some of the boys involved. Let me think it through. I'll need to work on Tim. I would have to do it right. Too little, and he would never cut loose. Too much, it might, well, I'm not sure he could handle it."

Michael's face slowly began to relax. He found himself thinking about Mick and Bernie, and for a moment felt a trace of envy, for them, for their lives, circumscribed by their pubs and nightclubs, their girls, their cars. And from time to time a job to keep them amused. He had been right to ensure that Mick's family were looked after during that long stretch inside. And to bring Bernie back into the fold when he returned, subdued, from his time overseas. His uncle would have approved. He had needed them in the past, a long time ago, though for years he had kept them at arm's length. But as Sanjay had talked, he began to contemplate working with them again, and the prospect sent sparks of excitement pulsing through him. He looked out at the City, and then at his faint reflection in the window-pane. He pulled in his waist and brushed the shoulders of his suit jacket with his fingers. After a second he walked over to the phone on the table and dialled a number.

"Vicky? Hi, it's me. How's your day been?" He chatted, smiling as he spoke. "Fine. I'll see you later then. Wear something nice. We'll go eat somewhere."

He put down the phone, walked over to Sanjay, and slapped him on the shoulder.

"Sanjay, I've always trusted you. We work well together. Tell me. Is there really a chance that you can make this work?"

Sanjay said nothing.

"Put a plan together," Michael said. "Work out the details."

Michael breathed in deeply, and walked briskly over to the door.

"Yeah. Sanjay. Ring my wife. Send my love to the kids. Tell her I'll call her tomorrow."

He opened the door of the conference room. He paused.

"You know, Sanjay. I've got a feeling about this. A good feeling. I don't know why. We'll speak. We'll speak tomorrow."

six

Tim and Imogen were late arriving at the reception. The banqueting suite was already filled with guests milling about in tight clusters. Waiters circulated briskly, bottles of champagne in hand. The ferment of the conversation seemed almost intimidating to them as they walked through the large open doors. They stood in the centre of the hall. For a few moments, they clung to each other, alone, looking around, wondering who all these people were, asking themselves what these people were saying to each other, what strange language it was they appeared to be speaking, a language whose construction and formalities seemed temporarily to elude them.

They had driven themselves from the town hall to the hotel. Julian, the best man, had arranged a limousine service to carry everyone between venues, but Imogen had brought her own transport. As the other guests crowded into taxis, stooping and holding on to their hats and their bags, the two of them had skulked off round the corner to find her car, hoping that the meter had not gone into the red.

"Do you know the way?" Tim asked.

"I need to stop somewhere," Imogen said. "I've got a tear in my tights. I must find a shop."

"Imogen." He sighed.

They followed the taxis for a few minutes, and then veered off towards the local mall.

"Why did he have a civil ceremony?" she asked later, after a lightning stop on the high street. "Didn't Brian want a church wedding?"

"My father would never have come," Tim said, and he chuckled. After a few seconds, he added, "Perhaps Brian thought it wasn't quite the right thing for someone his age. He's eight years older than me. Anyway, I thought Sarah looked terrific in that suit. White weddings, all that pomp and stuff, it's for the young. Don't you think?"

"No," Imogen said. "I don't."

Tim was silent.

"Where will you change?" he said after a while.

"I'll need to find a loo at the hotel."

Tim spotted his two brothers across the room, at the centre of a crowd of guests, the bride standing between them. Julian looked up at that moment, and saw Tim. He raised a hand. Tim and Imogen, silent, expressionless, watched him walk over.

"You're here," Julian said. "I think you two need a drink." He tapped a passing waiter on the shoulder.

Julian was carrying a silver tray of carnations. He turned to Imogen.

"Hold this for just a second, will you," he said, and then he paused to look at her. "I must say, I love your hat."

Imogen took the tray. Julian picked up one of the flowers and deftly pinned it into Tim's lapel.

"There," he said. "That's better."

As Julian stooped, Tim noticed his receding hairline. People always said how similar the two of them were. In appearance at least. The same tall lanky body, the same wispy blond hair.

I guess that's what I will look like in ten years time, he thought.

"Have you had a look at the seating arrangements?" Julian asked. "I'm afraid we didn't have room to put you on top table. But we've tried to place you with people that I think you'll like."

"Where's Dad?" Tim said.

"With us."

"No. Now. Where is he now?"

"Somewhere. There. In the corner, at the far end. Sitting with Sarah's parents."

48

"How's he bearing up? I hardly had a chance to talk this morning."

"Go speak to him," Julian said. "Look, I have to mingle. I'll catch up with you."

Tim smiled thinly at Imogen as Julian moved off.

"Don't be difficult," she whispered.

They walked slowly around the reception rooms. They stopped at a notice board at the front where the seating arrangements were pinned up. Imogen got caught up in a group of women who were friends of the bride. They separated. Tim picked up another glass of champagne and moved over to the fringes of the hall where a group of older men and women sat quietly and watched. Special guests, great uncles and aunts. Parents.

"Hi, Dad," Tim said. "How are you coping?"

The old man twisted slowly in his seat to look up at him. He held onto his stick firmly with his right hand. Tim had to admit to himself he looked well. His face, thin, hollow, still had a resolute look about it. His full head of white hair was brushed back, at least partially tamed. An untouched glass of wine stood on the table in front of him

"Tim, my boy."

His father addressed a couple, late fifties perhaps, who sat next to him. The parents of the bride.

"My third son," his father said to them.

Tim shook hands with the couple. He looked at the three of them sitting there, the gaunt old man staring out over the hall, the other two listening to his every word, and it seemed to him that a certain rigidity in his father had never changed. Decades of hectoring undergraduates and directing research projects at the university. Or perhaps the perception was his own, a perception of his father that he would now never escape. He was already middle-aged when Tim was born. Tim remembered friends at school who thought he was Tim's grandfather. And when people saw his mother with him, one or two said she must be the old man's daughter, not his wife.

"You might expect me to ask Tim when he's going to be following his brother Brian's example," his father said. "But I always say, once they reach the age of consent, it's no longer my job to tell them what they should be doing."

Tim winced.

"However, it gives an old man a lot of pleasure to see all these marvellous people here today. Here to celebrate my son's wedding to your wonderful daughter."

The other couple smiled graciously.

"Perhaps I should thank God that I've lived long enough to see this day," his father said. And then, his voice lower. "Not that I've ever believed in the old scoundrel."

Tim began musing about a theory he had long held, that children, upon reaching adulthood, should be required to swap parents, that the things one found so irritating about one's own were precisely the things that others found so charming. His friends always liked and respected his father. He found himself chatting amiably with Sarah's parents.

"What do you do?" Sarah's mother asked Tim.

His father answered for him. "Are you still working for those hucksters?"

Tim nodded with a smile.

"City slickers," his father continued. "Money changers. The kind of people who trade on other people's misery. I remember when I went up to Cambridge after the war. Everything was rationed. Food, petrol. But we knew somehow it was just, it was fair, we knew that compassionate men and women were at the centre of things regulating who got what."

"Dad, I'm just a computer programmer," Tim said. But he let his father talk, he did not bother to argue. He had heard the speech before. And that period of the fifties did seem special, even Tim could see that. As if in counterpoint to the awful violence of the previous decade, there had been a time when it looked as if the disorder and unfairness of life might be bottled up, stoppered, and placed in deepest storage in some remote bunker, rather like those dreadful diseases which, magically, had begun for the first time in history to be contained and then rolled back by the advent of penicillin, and whose only remaining traces existed in test tubes in maximum security research labs. But perhaps to his father the victory was a false one, for the volatility of life, its unpredictability, its easy spread across borders, drawing in its wake a rising tide of trade and globalism, of migration and then anarchy and crime, all these had arisen again like new strains of superbugs resistant to the faltering power of the antibiotics, to threaten the stability and decency, the enduring rightness of the England that common sense men like him had striven to create.

"Well, I'm sure you do your job as well as you can," Sarah's mother said to Tim.

"I try," Tim said, and smiled.

"Are you sitting with us? For the meal?" his father asked.

Ushers were circulating, asking people to take their places.

"No, Dad," Tim said.

"You're not?" the bride's mother again. "I'm sure we could squeeze up..."

"Let's not change things," Tim's father said brusquely. "Julian's got it all worked out. If there isn't room, there isn't room. Tim, we'll talk later."

Tim smiled. "I better find my seat," he said.

Tim and Imogen sat down at a large round table, with eight other people. Eight similar tables lay spread across the room. Imogen began chatting with the other guests.

"Shouldn't you be up there?" someone said to Tim, pointing to the one rectangular table in the room, a table raised slightly, where bride and groom sat, with parents, best man and best woman alongside.

Imogen gracefully deflected the question for him.

The man at Tim's left turned to him. "Hi. I'm Will. William Baker," he said, and suddenly there was a flourish of introductions

51

around the table, and people were apologising in advance for their unreliable memories, and telling each other how hopeless they were with names. And Tim's mind was wandering, once more he was back with his mother, he must have been about twelve, it must have been two years before she disappeared.

There had been a party. It was after the first night of her new play.

How do you remember it all? he had asked her. *All those lines.* And later, when he was introduced to the cast, *How do you remember all those people? All those names and faces?*

And the next day she had told him. *Visual images,* she had said. *Strong visual images. When I hear a name, I think of a visual image. The crazier the better. Then I think of something about them, their bushy eyebrows, or their big nose.*

"I'm Tim," he said to the man, and he began to play a game, a game he had played before, a game which, he knew, had so infuriated Imogen. Baker, he thought. Baker? Maker, Laker, Taker. And then, Faker. He imagined a man, brown, naked save for a loin cloth, suspended at the top of a vertical rope. Faker? *Faqir.* And he looked at William Baker and he looked at the scar the man had on his left cheek, and he imprinted on his mind the image of a faqir, tiny, bizarre, emerging from that scar and floating up his cheek.

And then I put those two things together, his mother had said. *It's fun. You do it. Don't worry if it's mad or illogical. Just try it on a group of people you don't know. People at school. You'll be amazed.*

"So, Will, tell me. What do you do?" Tim said.

Waiters began to serve the soup. As Tim talked, he looked up to the dais, and wondered how his brothers had taken it that day, just two years later. A day of small announcements and mortal consequences. He realised he couldn't remember how they had been told. But his brothers would have been adults by then, it would have been different for them. All he could recall was coming home from school one day and his father taking him aside and telling him his mother would not be with them for a while, he didn't know how long for. She was staying in America. And he wondered why they couldn't go over there if she wasn't coming back here, but his father never considered it.

"Tim." Imogen was talking to him. "Angela here was asking where the couple are going for their honeymoon."

"Hi." The woman next to Imogen reached across and extended a hand. "I'm Angela Darling. Pleased to meet you."

Tim thought of *starling*, and imagined birds nesting in her thick hair.

Had they been an unlikely pair? Tim wondered. The physicist building a reputation for himself, already being marked out for high office on the faculty, and the drama student looking towards the London stage. Yet a year after they met at the festival in Edinburgh they were married, and within three years there were two sons. Somehow she managed to get her career going again in her twenties, and Tim knew there must have been periods of separation as she followed repertory companies around the country. He suspected it was a different woman who got pregnant for the third time when she was thirty, or perhaps it was someone who now had the self-confidence to treat child-rearing as something she would do on her own, rather than her husband's and society's terms. And the balance of his relationship with his two parents, the close affection from his mother, the more distanced warmth of his father, was, he knew, different from the care that his brothers enjoyed. He could see that now, as he watched his father beaming at Brian and Julian seated on the podium beside him.

"Tim," Imogen said. "That's Pat and Jane Gunderson. Opposite us." *Blunderson?* No, not good enough. Tim imagined instead a *blunderbuss* firing off smoke and grapeshot from the man's wide nostrils.

Tim had moved on to secondary school, his brothers had followed his father to Cambridge, and his mother began to get parts on television. The feisty barrister, the attractive doctor, the concerned magistrate. *I really fancy your Mum* – who was the snotty fourth former who had told him that? And he covered up his pride in a show of anger that got him a black eye and a detention. But those twin punishments represented perhaps a kind of high point, for a week after his fourteenth birthday she flew to Hollywood for a film part that she had been offered, and she never came back. It killed him now that in his despair he had destroyed the letter she had sent him a month after she left. *My dearest Tim, Please forgive me for what I am doing...* He could remember only the first line.

He never saw her again. As the years passed she was mentioned less and less in the household, his father never remarrying, his father's manner hardening, becoming dry, pedantic, intense as the years passed. But Tim wrote a few times, months later, after his frustration and anger had begun to wane. He waited and waited, but no response ever came, until after a while he stopped and tried never to think of her again. He had often wondered, since, whether his father intercepted replies she may have sent.

One day they found out she was dead. They were informed by the American authorities that she had had a sudden and massive heart attack, and Tim's brothers went out to California to sort out her affairs. His father stayed home, and decided that Tim, studying for his 'A' levels, should stay with him. His brothers returned and said little. She had been living in some sort of commune in San Francisco, a commune just for women, it emerged, and Tim, taking a lead from his brothers, did not enquire much further. But six months later Tim received a parcel, perhaps his father had softened, a parcel from an American woman called Grace.

Your mother was a special woman, she wrote in an accompanying note, *and we all miss her terribly. She asked me before she died to send you these things if anything happened to her, she thought you would be old enough by now to understand.*

There were photos, some notes on plays and films that she

had done. There were a few essays, on general subjects. And there was a brief letter.

It was so hard at the beginning, and I wished so much that you, and Brian and Julian as well, could come and join me. But you must understand what was going through my mind at the time. For a woman like me, living my life in the shadow of a personality like your father, someone so sure of himself and everything, I suddenly found that when my chance came, I had to take it. So I took a gamble.

I've changed, Tim. I've discovered things about myself that I could never have suspected, here in my new home with Grace and the others.

Perhaps Tim was not yet old enough after all. The next few months, under the watchful and less than sympathetic eye of his father, he kept the parcel hidden away and only slowly began to go through its contents.

I work, a few minor parts in Hollywood and the soaps each year. In the summer we run a theatre workshop, and we get people from all over, people of all ages, of all types and sizes. Many stay with us, they come with just a sleeping bag, a few t-shirts, and loads of books. For a few months it is absolute chaos. But it is so beautiful in our big house here, and we're just a short distance from the beach.

Perhaps if it had been a few years later, he might have been on the first plane out. Perhaps. If it had been after he had left home. When he had moved away.

Grace is a very talented painter, and meeting her and working with her has been one of the most rewarding experiences of my life. She has done a few portraits of me, and I hope that one day you might get to see them. There is something of you in her, I always think to myself. I'm sure you two would get on so well.

There was a card, with a picture of a woman sketched in black crayon, a woman looking away from the artist into the distance, and it was the sense of quiet satisfaction that Tim discerned in that look, a sense of serene accomplishment in a new and previously unimagined life, that began to form a kind of template for Tim's emerging sense of independence, especially when it became apparent that his grades would not effortlessly guarantee him the place at the Cambridge college his father and then his brothers had taken before him.

His father urged him to work harder, but when he examined prospectuses for universities in other parts of the country, he knew that there was another world out there, one different from the somewhat cloistered existence his brothers described to him in fond reminiscences of their undergraduate days. It was this other world that began to tug at him. It was this world, he would later say, that had moulded him into the adult he became. As he would one day insist to his father and brothers. And to Imogen.

"Sorry, Tim," Imogen said as she leaned into him, trying to catch a conversation on his side of the table.

"As I was saying, this is already the fourth wedding I've been to this summer."

Waiters cleared plates and glasses.

"This is Will Faker." Tim made introductions. "And this is Imogen Carroll."

"Baker."

"What?"

"Baker. You said 'Faker'."

"Did I? Baker. Of course. Will Baker."

Imogen gave Tim a sharp look.

The conversation in the room was beginning to subside, and Tim saw his brother Julian standing at his place at the table, his gaze raking up and down the hall, a glass and teaspoon in his hands.

"Let's hope the speeches are short." A tactless whisper at Imogen's side.

And Julian's speech was at least brisk. Brief acknowledgements to organisers, ushers and bridesmaids, a few witty anecdotes smoothly delivered. But then extended thanks to special guests, dear friends, to people who had come from far and wide.

"Tom Dixon. Tom? Where are you? Where are you, man? Come on, stand up."

Eyes were turning, a man stood at a table on the other side of the room. He bowed twice.

Brisk. Smooth. And Tim saw the effortless passage of time and experience that had led his brothers here, as if the wedding itself were just another pre-arranged step in their progress through life. Brian and Julian had distinguished themselves at university, they had soon eased themselves into graduate fast tracks in industry and government, and their careers now seemed entwined in some kind of self-feeding double helix, Brian's successful electronics firm on a Cambridge industrial park the perfect complement for Julian's increasingly influential role in the Department of Enterprise or whatever they styled it these days.

"Frank? Frank Murray? Or should I say *Sir* Frank Murray? Soon-to-be. You gave Brian – and me – such a wonderful start in our careers..."

Tim tried to remember whether his brothers had ever offered him any help with his own career when he emerged after three years with a solid but unremarkable mathematics degree from Bath University. He suspected that they were astute enough to realise they could save embarrassment on both sides, and the question remained unasked.

"Tim? Tim?" A voice boomed.

Imogen was nudging him.

"Stand up, Tim. Come on. Julian's calling your name."

"And Imogen," Julian called out. "You as well..."

The two of them stood, and they looked out over a sea of faces, smiling, replete, a world at ease with itself.

"And Dad of course." Julian turned to the old man at his side. "Dad, without whom none of this could ever have been possible."

There was applause, and Tim's father gripped his stick and

struggled to stand, and it seemed as if it took both Julian and Brian, both of them quick on their feet, their arms on his shoulders, to persuade him to relax, to remain seated, he, the guest of honour today.

No mention of their mother, Tim thought he heard, it could have been the table behind him.

He strained to listen.

I gather she left them. A long time ago, someone replied.

The speeches were over. Tim poured himself another drink. He was beginning to relax and enjoy himself. The band started to play, and, after a brief turn from Brian and Sarah on the floor, tables emptied and other couples followed. Tim found himself admiring the women in the hall. Friends of his two brothers, or the wives or girlfriends of their colleagues, they seemed, each one of them, so smart, self-assured, so flawlessly groomed. And when Imogen left the table for a few minutes, some of them sat down to talk to him.

"So, you're the youngest," they said. "I can see the resemblance." Tim was flattered, for once glad of the family connection.

Imogen hovered at the edge of the table as the ladies fussed. Tim made introductions, and then, slightly embarrassed, asked her if she wanted to dance.

"Not quite my type of music," she said. But when Brian joined them at their table later, and the bandleader had slowed the tempo down, she joined Tim's brother on the floor for a few of the ballads.

Afterwards the three of them talked. Tim opened a new bottle of wine, but Brian said he and Sarah were leaving early the next day, and he did not want to start his honeymoon with a thick head.

"You know, Tim," Brian said, "everyone was asking about you. They never knew Julian and I had a younger brother."

And later, he asked Tim about his own future.

"How long have you been in your job now?"

Tim thought for a second, wondering what was coming.

Brian looked at him. "A good few years?" He began to talk about the opportunities in his own company.

"You can't stay in London all your life," he said. Tim asked him why not.

"My firm is always on the hunt for good people. Good IT people."

Tim and Imogen glanced at each other.

"Look, I'm not suggesting anything. But perhaps in a year or two you might be thinking of... well... you can't raise kids here. It's not right."

Sarah joined them. She listened to her husband as he tried to persuade his younger brother. Later Tim noticed her chatting alone with Imogen at another table.

They were amongst the last to leave.

"We better get a cab. I've had too much wine," Imogen said. "I'll pick up the car tomorrow."

She took Tim's arm.

"I could have killed you when you introduced your brother to the Blundersons," she said, and the two of them began to giggle.

They wove an unsteady path down the pavement.

"You know," she said. "I just thought. Throughout the whole evening, I never once saw Brian and Sarah kiss. Did you?"

*

At the same time as Tim and Imogen stumbled into their flat, two large men stared down at a third man who lay in front of them on the floor of a damp basement room. He was naked. His dull white skin hung in folds over thin ribs. There was a bulbous purple swelling over his right eye. He was handcuffed to one of the legs of a metal bed.

He had lain there for the last forty-eight hours.

One of the men spoke.

"Do you want some of this before I get it down his neck?"

He twisted the cap off a bottle of vodka and took a swig. The other man shook his head.

"I've had enough."

The first man drank some more, and then knelt by the man on the floor.

"Here, Danny. Open your mouth."

The man on the floor gazed into space. Saliva dripped from his mouth.

"Danny."

There was no reaction.

"DANNY!"

The big man grabbed his long greasy hair and yanked his head back. He put a hand on his chin, and forced his mouth open. He raised the bottle to the man's mouth and poured. The man swallowed reflexively, and then began to cough.

"Here, I hope you're using the cheap stuff."

The big man slapped the naked man hard, on one cheek and then the other. He then looked him in the eyes.

"He's out of it."

He stood up and put the bottle on a plastic table. The only other furniture in the room.

The other man began to unbuckle the belt on his trousers.

"Hey, what the fuck..." the first man said. "Why do you bother? You know they have some new girls at the club. Colombian. I've seen them."

The second man paused with his belt. He walked over to the table and picked up some keys. Then he walked towards the man on the floor and grabbed his arm. After he had taken off the handcuffs, he picked the man up and pitched him on to the bed. He turned his body over. The naked man thrashed about for a second, moaned softly, and then lay still. The big man sat at the side of the bed and began to untie his shoelaces.

He looked up.

"You going to watch?"

The first man passed a hand over his bald head.

"I'll be upstairs. In the bar."

*

Imogen sat in the café at the end of the road, waiting. From time to time she thought about scales and arpeggios. She had been sitting alone for an hour, and was wondering whether to have a second cup of coffee. The radio was playing, a hit from her youth. She had danced to this song with Brian the previous Saturday. She had once danced to the same song with Tim. Someone's party, a long, long time before. She could not remember what it was called. The music irritated her for a moment. Then she felt the prick of tears.

She stared at her hands, and began to flex her fingers repeatedly, until a churning rose up inside her, and she stopped, counted to five, and took half a dozen deep breaths. A piece of cutlery crashed to the floor, and as the waitress stooped to pick it up, she had it in mind to ask her to change the station they were playing. But the thought got muddled up as the chorus line began to blare out again, soppy, sickly sweet, the doo-wop high, controlled, immaculate. Cheap music, cheap sentiment. Irritatingly potent. Even her sister's children no longer listened to stuff like this.

She waited. It was another four hours before she stepped out onto the stage, four hours before the little curtain closed behind her and she walked those five yards over to the piano stool. A quick glance out to the audience, her hands stretching and tensing at her sides. Fifteen feet. Her steps slow, measured. This was the worst moment, before she had played a note, a moment when everything was still in her head, everything was hypothetical, yet to be transformed through the agency of her fingers into the unalterable clarity of the action of hammer on coiled wire. Was it a plot, she thought, a male plot, that she, nine inches shorter than the other two pianists, must walk this five yards more slowly and so endure this moment for a second or two longer, seconds where her mind might suddenly open, her head split, and those notes, those tunes and harmonies, might flutter off into the ceiling high above, like a release of caged birds, suddenly free, a flickering rainbow of plumage, a clamour of cooing and shrieking, and then a beating of wings and a release of tension, leaving her empty and alone at the piano stool, with nothing to say, no music to perform for the judges and orchestra directors sitting in semi-darkness a few rows back.

She had not told Tim about the audition. She had been on the point of doing so at the wedding. After the speeches were over, before the band had started playing, while the table was breaking up. They were talking. And then the opportunity passed somehow. Later Brian came to join them, and he and Tim talked about the future.

A move up to Cambridge. Perhaps it would be right for Tim. But she sensed a certain defensiveness in him when he was around his brothers, and sometimes a wilfulness that put her on edge. And on their part, a condescension.

"You've been together quite a while now," Brian had said to her when they were dancing. *Eight years*, Imogen thought to herself. She thought of Tim the first time she met him, backpacking in Thailand, blond, tanned, gaunt on his rice-and-chicken diet. She was there for two weeks with some girl friends, he was starting a gap year trawl through Asia. They swapped home phone numbers, and he said he would call her. Nine months later he did, and they met again in London. Things started slowly, but when he began to earn money, and her career was still very much at the stage of scratching around for grants for courses at the music colleges, she was happy to rely on him to pay the bills and they moved in together. It was only now, with both their careers stabilising, each of them with their own friends, professional acquaintances, and schedules, that she found it sometimes wearing that they seemed to have no communication with each other beyond the bedroom.

She should have told him.

She had felt so flattered and excited when the orchestra contacted her and invited her to apply for a specialist position as an accompanist. Especially when the approach was made by her ex-professor, now working with them as an advisor.

"Come on, Imogen, it will be great," Anton had said. "They have a three-month tour in America coming up. You'll accompany the orchestra for the Mahler and Stravinsky, and then you'll do the piano quintets for the chamber concerts."

Three months. It could destroy them.

She knew she would never reach the top of the tree in her profession, she just wasn't good enough to win the big prizes, to get the top solo spots. She did not have the temperament. The role of the accompanist seemed to suit her better. As Anton had delicately suggested.

She remembered Anton from a few years before, when she was still at music college. He had once invited her to join him at a modern music festival in Strasbourg. She remembered him playing Bartok to her, she remembered him at the piano, his chin jutting, his eyes darting from left to right, as he followed the angular tread of the music, its dissonances pushed to both high and low extremes of the keyboard.

"None of this Mozart and Beethoven," he had said. "It's become so tiresome."

And she had loved the music, its rawness and power. And perhaps also she had loved that he loved the music, its modernity, its political statement. She had been a bit overawed in Strasbourg by his clout, his connections. Eurocrats applauded when he deconstructed the sterile art of the old Europe, when he discussed Freud and Hitler and the break-down of romanticism. Imogen found herself accompanied to concerts by commissioners and politicians, though she felt repelled by their manners when they answered their mobile phones while the applause was still ringing. They pestered her in the bars afterwards, but, as the days went by, they began to ignore her. And then, Anton as well. Perhaps she had been too young, too impressionable. Eventually she had flown back on her own.

But last month she'd felt a quiet thrill as she heard Anton's voice again.

She listened to the radio. She remembered how embarrassed she had once been when she used to tell him some of the music she liked. *Aretha. Joni. Kylie.* Not now. Perhaps Tim had done that for her. Anton had offered to coach her, but she had gently refused. Tonight she would play Schubert. Tonight she wanted some warmth. She knew she had a good chance of beating the other two pianists auditioning for the job. So long as she kept her nerve on stage.

She thought of Tim. Three months. Perhaps a break would be good for them.

The waitress walked by again.

"Excuse me," Imogen said to her. "What was that song called? The one on the radio just now. I can't get it out of my mind."

seven

Tim, Sanjay thought to himself.

He adjusted one hand behind his head as he lay back on the pillow. He let the fingers of his other hand trail gently down the back of the girl who knelt at his side. He brushed the ridges of her spine, the curved flesh beneath her shoulder blades. The smoothness of her skin was an exquisite delight to him.

She was talking about herself. About a time she had spent travelling the previous year. In Australia.

Tim, Tim, Tim, Sanjay thought. He sighed, and looked up.

"Are you seeing anyone else tonight?" he said, interrupting.

"No," the girl said. "You're the last."

He slowly laid his head down again.

"You can take your time," she said. "Have a shower later if you want."

She rubbed a hand in an absent-minded circular motion over his stomach.

"Here, let me get rid of that," she said abruptly, and prised up the limp piece of rubber. Sanjay winced as it caught for a second.

"Sorry."

She flicked it into the bin. She went back to her travels. The sun, the beaches. The men.

"It's all regulated over there," she said. "The girls have to pay income tax on each punt."

He had almost phoned Tim a couple of times earlier on in the day, and both times he had hesitated and put the receiver down. He could not decide on a suitable place to meet. He wanted him to come by himself, and, thinking it over, figured that perhaps that would not be too difficult to arrange. Tim's girlfriend had seemed cool and slightly distant when they met at Vicky's shop.

He wanted Alec to meet him. Alec knew the banks, how they worked, what their computer systems were like. He was much better at the technical details than Sanjay. Alec would have to be sure, he would have to approve if they were going to persuade Michael to go ahead with this project.

And Michael himself. He had begun to take an interest. He wanted to know how Sanjay planned to get Tim on board. Mick's views had been predictable and blunt.

Carrot and stick, he had said. *But the stick's the most important part. When you've got someone on the inside, you make it clear to them that you know everything about them. You know where they live, where the wife works, where the kids go to school.*

Michael had laughed. He had described those old IRA operations, where they kidnapped someone at random and told them to drive to an army checkpoint with a boot load of explosives, or else they would shoot up the man's family. *Suicide bombing*, he had said, *only it's someone else's suicide.*

But Sanjay had been uneasy. The operation would need some subtlety, the planning and execution would need precision and finesse. You could not expect people to operate under those conditions out of compulsion alone.

Oh, Tim, Tim, Tim.

"Do you like that?" the girl said. She let a drop of lubricant fall onto Sanjay's navel.

She chattered as she spread the lotion. She described a deep sea fishing expedition she had been on. She and her friends had flown up to the northern territories for a few days.

"The sea was so blue, the sky so perfect. We motored out for a few hours, not another soul visible. The guys set the bait and showed us how to use the fishing rods. Then we waited. And waited. We began to get a few nibbles. The whole thing took ages."

They would need specialist input from Tim, Sanjay had told the others. They would need his expertise. And stuff like that would have to come willingly, he had said, it couldn't be forced. Eventually Michael had agreed, though he told Sanjay that time was pressing. They could not wait forever.

"It's all psychology."

"What's that?" Sanjay said.

"It's in the mind," the girl said. "That's what the guys on the boat told us. Think like the fish, they said. Give it a bit of what it wants, and then when it's interested you begin to reel it in. But just a fraction. Too much and you lose it. It's a dance. You have to learn the steps."

Sanjay raised his head and kissed her gently under her right breast.

"Sounds fantastic," he said.

"You know what it reminded me of," she said. "It made me think of when I used to hang out in hotels. You'd size up a guy, and you'd let him catch your eye. You would show him just enough to get him interested. He'd buy you the drink, you'd chat. Gradually he would begin to figure out what was on offer, and after a while he'd talk money and the deal was done. It was just like that. On that fishing yacht. You wait for your catch to take a small bite, you play hard to get, then you tease a bit more. It's all the same. Move slowly, bit by bit. And then, finally, boom. You've got this huge silver monster thrashing about on the deck of the boat."

Sanjay began to stir.

He was about to say something, and then she burst out laughing.

Tim dreamt.

He dreamt of a party. They were late arriving, the streets outside the college were dark and empty, and when they entered the huge, ornately decorated hall, everything seemed to freeze. A line of young men and women of almost ethereal beauty stood silent along the wall, men, in black tie, staring straight at them, women, elegant in their long dresses, lingering as if caught forever on the opening steps of some minuet or ancient court protocol. Tim looked down at his jeans and the bottle of gutrot he clutched in his right hand. He grinned vacantly. Sanjay tried to make conversation with their spectral hosts.

Later. Through high windows Tim saw stars turning and then a faint blue light. He sniffed, his jaws felt numb. He had some of the white powder left. Somewhere. In one of his pockets.

Later. They were driving. The town's spires lay behind them, black outlines, sharp, jagged, etched against a cold dawn. Three hours from Oxford to Bath. Sanjay slept in the passenger seat, but the cocktail of chemicals in Tim's blood burned inside him.

Gusts of rain on the outskirts of a city. Black clouds, mist, and a figure caught in the glare of the faltering headlights. Tim turned the wheel, but felt instead a terrible lightness. A face fixed in their sights, dead ahead, bearing down on them. A vain foot on the brake. Time slowing, shrinking, subdividing endlessly, the face growing ever closer by corresponding degrees. Tim, eyes wide, gripping the wheel, Sanjay shouting.

There was a bump as Sanjay eased his chair back against the wall to let the waitress through. She placed the bottle of wine on the table and poured into two of the three glasses. She picked up Sanjay's credit card and walked off.

Sanjay looked around the wine bar and hoped it would not become too crowded. He had chosen the place because its prices usually discouraged the brasher elements of the West End's after work drinkers. He shifted his seat again as Alec rejoined him at the table.

"I said eight o'clock," Sanjay said in answer to an unspoken question. "He should be here soon."

He looked at Alec, and suddenly realised that he still did not know whether the story of his first meeting with Michael was true, or simply part of company mythology. One day, he would ask him about his past. His time on Wall Street a decade, almost two decades before. But the company was what it was in large part due to Alec and the team he had assembled. The property portfolio, the publishing empire. These had grown to the point where they began to need people who understood financial planning strategies, IT systems, who could negotiate with the banks and the Inland Revenue. Sanjay knew that Alec had been jobless, drowning in a sea of cash from golden parachutes after the shake-out at the end of the eighties. Then the fabled meeting, at a Mercedes show room where Alec was negotiating to buy the thirties *décapotable* that had just come in. He had been haggling for a month, and he watched amazed as another man walked in with a suitcase full of cash and drove out half an hour afterwards in the latest S Class. It sounded like Michael, Sanjay thought. An improbable alliance was formed, and for a while Michael had tried to gloss over his past and to keep details of some of his longer running enterprises out of the picture, but Alec took to it all, with an enthusiasm which, he told Sanjay one time, he could never muster for the bloodless world of the banks and the finance houses he had left behind.

There had been an important incident soon after, when Alec had been carjacked in the same Mercedes. He had been hurt badly, but a week later, coming out of hospital, he was personally presented with a get-well gift by Mick and Bernie. His car, intact, with one or two scratches but driveable and ready to go. And the quiet promise from the two of them that the people who had done this would never, ever, try a stunt like it on anyone again. It amused Sanjay that they liked and admired him. Alec bet their spare cash on the markets, he told them when to bail out as the internet boom faltered. They got rich. Money for nothing, they said, they could not believe it.

"Is that him?"

Sanjay looked up. A man stood at the bar on his own. He was peering round, into the corners and alcoves.

At least he's wearing a suit, Sanjay thought.

He rose from his seat and beckoned. Tim raised a hand in acknowledgement. He threaded his way around tables and chairs.

"Tim. So glad you could come."

They shook hands.

"I was surprised you rang," Tim said.

Sanjay eyed him carefully. "Why's that?"

"I'm glad you did. It's just that... Last time, I think I had too much to drink."

Sanjay smiled to himself.

"I hope I behaved."

He patted Tim on the arm. "Don't worry about it," he said. Alec was standing.

"Let me make introductions," Sanjay said.

They shook hands. Alec asked if he had had trouble finding the place. They made small talk.

"Alec tells me you work together," Tim said.

"How many years is it?" Sanjay turned to Alec.

"And you, Tim?" Alec said. "What do you do?"

Tim mentioned the name of his company, and he began to talk about where they were based and what they did. But Alec stopped him.

"I know about them," he said. "A lot about them. They have a reputation. On Wall Street."

Tim looked surprised. "I usually get blank stares."

"I'm sure that's the way your company wants it. I'm sure they do not want to make waves."

Tim shrugged. "Perhaps," he said.

Sanjay excused himself. At the bar, speaking to the waitress, he gazed discreetly at the two of them talking, and he thought of his first arrival at university, his first introduction to the sons and daughters of the English middle classes, all of them so fair, innocent somehow, their accents soft and inoffensive, their manner so sweet, charming. For a week, he had felt as if he was drowning, as if he would never cope. Although he was unable to admit it at the time, he knew now that it was the horror of a

70

return to the drab suburb of Leeds he had just left that kept him there those first few days. He walked back slowly, watching them. Tim had an almost puppyish quality when he became animated, his mouth pursed as he smiled, he waved his arms. He, Sanjay, had once been so intimidated. By this.

He rejoined them. They were talking computers. He heard Standards, Interfaces, Protocols. Firewalls, Encryption, Intrusion Detection. The ugly jargon of IT. He was happy to leave them to it, Alec, he noticed, as involved as Tim. He sat back, drinking slowly, cautiously, until Alec glanced for a moment in his direction.

"Gentlemen," Sanjay broke in. "We're here to have fun. Alec, give him a break."

Tim was still talking. Alec pressed his hands together and looked over at Sanjay. "Tim, I think we're boring him." He chuckled and held Sanjay's gaze. "Force of habit, I guess," he said, still smiling. "Perhaps we could do with another bottle."

Sanjay looked around for the waitress.

"Tim," he said. "There's something we'd like to show you. Some place we'd like to take you."

Tim glanced across at the two of them.

"I can't stay late," he said warily.

"Trust me. One more drink. Then we'll go."

"It'll be a surprise," Alec said. "It'll be fun."

Forty-five minutes later, the three of them were sitting in the back of a taxi crossing the river from north to south. Sanjay looked to left and right at lines of stone buildings, grey, severe, massive. Nineteenth century monuments to the great departments of state that ran the business and the lives of the populations of half the countries in the world. Then beyond them, to the east, a brash strip of skyscrapers, permanently illuminated, row upon chequered row of offices, self-deceiving symbols of Britain's new but lesser role in the world, a mere cog in the wheels of the modern imperial powers. As they reached the other bank, they left this behind to enter another world, its buildings older, its brickwork darker, decaying, its inhabitants secretive and somehow vulnerable. They passed under dank bridges, railway lines funnelling the city's workers over the top of this world out towards the suburbs. They saw a pub with blackened windows, outside whose doors lines of men in leather and chains waited in silence. They saw a sprawling hotel under an unlit nameplate, boarded up and empty. Broken down terraces, dismal pubs. Metallic police notices on the pavement, yellow and garish. A violent assault, a robbery, a murder, *did you see?* Futile requests for witnesses.

They stopped under broken streetlights on a cobbled alley.

"Sure you know where you're going?" the taxi driver said. Sanjay handed him a generous tip.

He led the others across the road to a windowless building. He stood at a large semi-circular door, and knocked. A small slat was withdrawn, halfway down. A soft light from inside. A terrace stretched away in the shadow. After a moment, the door opened slightly and they walked in.

They saw a half-lit hallway. Cold, grey plaster walls. At the end was another set of doors where two men stood, in black suits and light rollneck sweaters. They greeted Sanjay. One of them reached down, turned a doorknob, and waved for them to go through. As they walked across the threshold, darkness became light. Brilliant. White. They were hit by a wave of sound. A warehouse, high ceilings. Hundreds of people, some seated, some standing, all of them shouting and screaming, all of them huddled around the edges of an area twenty foot square cordoned off by ropes. Above were two spotlights. Within the perimeter of the ropes, two men circled each other cautiously, torsos naked, hairless, dripping, their gloved fists raised. A third man, in black trousers and shirtsleeves, stepped nimbly around them. Tim had stopped and was staring. Sanjay took him by the arm, and the three of them moved closer to the ring at the centre of the hall. They looked at the crowd. Clumps of men in suits, their ties loose. Others in jeans, t-shirts. A few women, as vocal as the men. They found three seats a couple of rows back, and they slid in. People at their sides stared straight ahead, oblivious to them. Then a bell, a roar. The umpire raised his hands, the two fighters withdrew.

Alec shouted something in Tim's ear.

Tim shook his head.

Waves of movement, the tension suddenly sagging, the audience collapsing into its seats, men and women relaxing, each of them turning towards a neighbour, a hundred necks twisting. Trainers scurrying at the corners of the ring, grey haired men in white t-shirts, with towels and quiet frowns, speaking through the ropes to their boys. The two fighters, sphinx-like on their stools. Breathing steadily and deeply, their gloved hands on their knees.

Sanjay leaned across and shook hands with someone sitting beyond Tim. They cupped palms to ears and shouted at each other over the noise. The umpire began to pace around the ring. One of the fighters got off his stool, and ran lightly on the spot. The other remained seated as his coach grabbed his shoulder in his left hand, and screamed into his right ear. A call and a gesture from the umpire, and the other fighter was on his feet. Both men advanced slowly upon one another, the crowd faced forward again. A bell. A sudden flurry of punches, and the stench of sweat wafted over. Sanjay glanced to his side and saw Tim wince and close his eyes for a second. He looked back. One of the fighters sank to his knees, and the umpire rushed between him and his opponent, but he was up again in a moment. They circled around each other again, necks bobbing, their punches probing, quick, ineffective. Then, a burst of accelerated movement, a crouch, a feint, blows to the body, fists raised. The umpire separating the two men. Stand-off.

They watched round after round, the boxers matching each other punch for punch, fall for fall. Then suddenly it was over, and Sanjay knew he had missed the decisive moment, as he always did. A blow to the chin, it had seemed light, innocuous, but one of the men was down. The umpire crouched and counted. The man struggled to his knees on seven and then collapsed.

Shouting, screaming, a rush of flunkies into the ring. The umpire stood up and grabbed the left hand of the victor. He raised it into the air, and the two men rotated slowly. Cheers. Oaths. An amplified announcement for the next fight.

Tim was drenched in sweat. He took off his jacket. His shirt clung to his back. But he could not take his eyes off the man with blood dripping from his left eye.

The third fight, perhaps the sixth round. He had lost count. The contest was one-sided. One of the men, English, a kid with a name that Tim might have read on those rolls of the Great War dead that one saw in northern towns, he had already been knocked down twice within the first few minutes. And yet each time he rose to confront his attacker, his expression grim, unchanging. His opponent danced a samba in front of him, his head bobbing, a slight smile on his lips, a kind of contempt, it seemed to Tim, perhaps for four hundred years of empire and his foe's imagined racial superiority. The left eyebrow opened in the third, and still the Englishman came. *Shouldn't it be stopped*? Tim thought, watching the umpire pace around the two fighters. He tried to remember bouts he had seen on television.

The white man's face spun ninety degrees to the right, blood sprayed over the first two rows of the audience. The Latino pressed in closer, both fists jabbing. But he withdrew for a moment, as if to examine his work, and the other man turned to face him again, his steps now slow, his arms raised in dogged protection of his disintegrating face. And Tim detected a kind of hopelessness and wondered whether he might therefore win, whether a quality of sullen pig-headedness would somehow see him through, and he caught himself willing the man forward, at first silently, and then quite openly and loudly.

Perhaps it was the wine he had drunk earlier, or the surreal intensity of the lights above. He cheered.

Sanjay tapped Tim on the shoulder, and the three of them got up. They moved down the row of seats. Sanjay pointed to a bar, with some tables, a few chairs. They headed towards it. They sat and drank bottles of beer.

"Enjoy that?" Sanjay asked Tim.

Tim shook his head. He pressed his fingers against his ears and let them pop, as if just now getting his hearing back.

"Is this place legal?" Tim said.

Sanjay laughed. "Why do you ask?"

"I don't know," Tim said. "It's not your lot running it, is it?"

Sanjay, still laughing, looked at Alec. Their eyes met.

They chatted about the fights. Sanjay let Alec explain the finer details. He himself could never appreciate aspects of technique, he could never understand which boxer had the greater natural talent, why fights sometimes ended so suddenly, why some were decided on points.

After a couple of minutes, he left them talking, and went to circulate. There was a door in the far corner, scarcely visible from the main arena. He approached and knocked. A man poked his face round, and then let him in. Sanjay stepped into a smaller room, more darkly lit. There was another fight going on inside. Again, two men facing each other. But this time, they wore jeans and trainers. Nothing else. Twenty men stood around them, baying, spitting. There were piles of cash on the floor. The two men circled each other. They raised their bare fists. One of them struck.

Sanjay returned to find Tim and Alec talking still. Alec sounding out, testing. Sanjay unwrapped a cigar, he watched, he waited.

Silence for a moment as Tim sipped at his drink. "Do you know," Alec said, "I once met the founder of your company? In New York. Nineteen eighty..." And he counted. "Six. Eighty seven."

75

"You did?"

"He lives in Switzerland now. That's true, isn't it?"

Tim nodded.

"He won't go back," Alec said.

"What was he like?"

"Bright. Charismatic. Ruthless. I say 'won't go back'. Perhaps I should say, 'can't go back'."

"I hear things."

"They say in the City that there are extradition warrants."

"Could be."

"The Americans want him back."

"Perhaps."

"Do you know what he did?"

"What do you mean?"

"What they say he did? Why they want him?"

"Tax evasion?"

"You don't know? I'm surprised. You do work for him."

"Well, so what? What do I need to know? Here in London we're perfectly kosher. The police are not knocking on our doors."

"It doesn't bother you? That your founder's a fugitive?"

"It's the Americans who want him, not us. They'll sue anybody."

"It's not the same."

"He never hurt anyone. Apart from the IRS."

"It's a tough business, isn't it?"

"What? What we do?"

"Oil trading."

"Is it worse than any other?"

"Well." Alec spread his hands. "Corrupt regimes, bribery. Offshore accounts. Half the countries you do business with are war zones."

"I don't see it's different for any other commercial enterprise."

"With respect... you know that's absurd."

"Why?"

Slow down, Sanjay thought. Alec seemed to catch his eye for a second.

"Why?"

"They've got quite a contentious past, your company, haven't they?"

Sanjay was suddenly alert.

"How so?" Tim said.

"Well…" Alec seemed to reflect for a second. "Allegations of sanctions busting. Against Iran. I hear they do a lot of business with Cuba. Uncle Sam wouldn't be too pleased with that now, would he?"

Tim smirked. "*Viva* Castro."

"A liberal conscience. Isn't that just the tiniest bit naïve?"

"It's one in the eye for a redneck President."

"But… international law, playing by the rules, isn't all that kind of thing important?"

Sanjay saw Tim stirring in his seat. "Well, perhaps in a strange kind of way, I admire them, I admire their freedom to move so fast, their freedom to act as they will."

"So you don't believe in the constraints of the law? You don't believe that there are certain limitations on the exercise of power?"

A smile. A pause. Tim swallowed.

"Just tell me this. Who gets hurt?" he said. "Who loses out in all this? We're not talking murderers and torturers here, we're not talking Hitler and Stalin. It's money. Oil. Money and oil. That's the difference."

"Fine. Good point." Alec leant back. He leant forward again. "So take me back. You've just joined the company. You're speaking to people, you begin to see how they operate. You must be thinking, there's something not quite right about these guys. I can choose to stay. Or not. Perhaps you were headhunted. Perhaps you had two or three offers at the time. There may have been a moment when you chose, them over the others. A moment when you decided to cross a line."

"For God's sake. I'm a programmer." Tim sighed, and then he began to laugh. "That's all." His voice lower. "I go for an interview, and we talk about hardware and operating systems, about databases and systems analysis. Then we haggle over salaries and working conditions. They don't ask me whether I go to church every Sunday. And I don't check them out with Amnesty International."

There was a pause.

"So you would work for Big Tobacco? For pornographers? Gun-runners?"

"Or the gambling industry?" Tim said. His eyes narrowed, alert once more. "People like you, you run casinos."

"People like you, you bet in them," Alec said.

Tim was laughing again. They drank.

Later, Sanjay pointed to a corner where there was a toilet. As Tim walked off, Sanjay drew his chair closer.

"You never told me, he's quite good looking," Alec said.

"About the other thing," Sanjay said. "What do you think?"

Alec picked up his beer. He was nodding.

At midnight, Sanjay and Tim took a taxi up to Soho. Alec had left already. The two of them sat in a restaurant. They ate prawn toast, seaweed, noodles, crispy duck. They drank a vile white wine. The restaurant was full. There were the remnants of the theatre crowd, a few City people. Actors and musicians shouted across tables the details of the shows they had just done. A large crowd of Chinese men sat in a corner drinking beer and arguing incomprehensibly.

They talked about the fights.

"It was like a pit in that place, a cauldron," Tim said. "Tell me, just what were we doing there?"

Sanjay asked him what he was getting at, but Tim could not quite find the words. Instead he asked about Alec.

"He seemed so precise at first, so fastidious," Tim said.

"So?"

"I guess it's just a bit of rough for him."

Sanjay looked up from his food. He had a sudden image of Tim, in khaki and pith-helmet, surrounded by arguing villagers in rags, a district collector in some dusty outpost of the Raj. How did they do it? he thought to himself, two hundred years ago. Men like him. But at least their forebears had the vision to go out there and look. They were so parochial now, these young professionals, with their mortgages and four-wheel drives and their narrow aspirations. So true to their class, to their Englishness.

"Don't underestimate Alec," Sanjay said.

"Tell me," Tim said after a while. "What kind of company is it you two really work for?"

"What do you mean?"

"Well..." There was silence for a few seconds. "The casinos. The publishing. I checked out some of the titles after we met last time."

"And?"

But Tim was again struggling for words.

"And then, tonight," he said, after a minute.

"What about tonight?"

Sanjay waited.

"Tim, London's a bigger city than you could ever imagine," he said. "There's a whole world bubbling under the surface that people pretend isn't there. Perhaps you got a glimpse of it tonight. It's not going to go away, whatever we do."

Later. The waiters collected plates.

"You know, Sanjay," Tim said. "I never expected to see you again after I left university. After what happened to us. Somehow, when we left, I thought it was like a slate wiped clean. Yet here we are, living and working almost on top of each other. How is it we've ended up this way? Doing what we're doing?"

And Sanjay thought he detected a chink opening up in Tim's guard.

"Let me say something, Tim," he said. "We're not quite what

you think we are. My company. It's not just magazines and nightclubs. We're changing, we're growing. You should come see us. Meet my boss."

They walked out into the night air.

"You know, Sanjay, I really…" Tim said. "It was…" The words eluded him one more time. "Thanks for everything. We must do it again."

"Absolutely," Sanjay said. "We will. Soon."

Sanjay watched him walk off in search of a taxi. He tried to work out how soon it would be.

eight

Beethoven, Berg, Berio, Bernstein.

Who were these people? Tim thought to himself. And what kind of people collected their music, who was it who loved it, practised it and played it, who was it who scoured the libraries and archives for these forgotten scores?

Bloch, Blow, Boccherini, Boellman.

I was once good myself, he thought. He had learnt the piano as a child. *And I let it slip away.*

It was only when he met Imogen that he began to rediscover his interest in the classical repertoire, and for a while they had trawled the concert halls, and he had followed her backstage for signed programmes from conductors and soloists. But time passed, and Imogen began to go on her own, or with colleagues and teachers from the music school.

Clementi, Corelli, Couperin, Cramer.

He fingered the spines of the manuscript books on the high, dusty shelves. He looked across the bookstore, this scruffy, chaotic backroom, stuffed with papers, old editions, and a few solitary customers in unseasonable coats and scarves.

Imogen stood in a corner reading. He came up behind her.

"Have you got what you wanted?" He placed a hand on her shoulder. She did not look up. He sniffed the stale air and looked at the other people around them, and for a moment was touched by the love and the dedication he saw in them. He felt a prick of embarrassment that he was there, intruding.

"I'll be another few minutes." Her voice languorous, distant. "Why don't you get a coffee."

He was halfway through his second espresso when she arrived. He ordered a third for himself and a tea for her.

She looked at the trail of cups.

"What time did you get back last night?"

"Two. Two-thirty. I can't remember."

He examined the sheet music she had bought.

"You didn't sleep well last night," she said after a while.

"I didn't?"

"I thought you were having a nightmare."

Tim looked up at her.

"Why didn't you rouse me?"

He knew he had slept badly, but he recalled only fragments of his dreams. *Would it have done any good*, he thought, *if she had woken me*? This was something that would not go away quickly, this hideous fascination, this tight ball of terror that lay concealed in the cratered no-man's-land between his waking and his sleeping life. Like a craving for tobacco, or illicit sex, it would return. *This has happened before*, he had thought as he showered and got dressed. Once before, for three months in his final year before graduation. *How did I forget about it? How could I have erased it from my mind?* Each night, the same images, a cold dawn, a frenzied cross-country drive, a figure in the headlights. Each morning, sheets tight to the skin with cold sweat. Then one day, for no reason, they had stopped. The dreams, and all memory of the dreams, just sank, without a ripple, out of sight and out of mind. Until now.

"What were you dreaming about?" Imogen said.

"Oh, nothing. It was..." Tim paused.

"Can't you remember any of it?" Imogen persisted. "Not even a bit?"

She leant across and closed the score that Tim was leafing through. He sighed.

"I'm back there. Back at university. With Sanjay. We're driving, the conditions are bad. There's an accident."

"Tim."

"Don't worry, nothing happens."

She looked at him.

"Is this real?" Then. "Why haven't you ever told me about this?"

"It's not important. The mind exaggerates things."

Imogen frowned into her mug of tea.

"You know I don't like him."

"Who?"

Imogen collected together the music she had bought. She looked at a list of items she had written on a piece of paper. Half the list was ticked off.

"You know who I mean. How was last night?"

"It was strange..."

"Where did you go?"

"South London."

"Where in south London?"

"I don't really know. I don't think I could find my way back there. It was... we went to see a boxing match."

"A what?"

Imogen stared. Tim smiled and looked into the distance.

"Did you actually enjoy it?" Imogen said.

"It was..."

He thought of the spotlights above the ring, the ring drenched in light, so bright it seemed to have sucked all colour from the ordeal going on beneath them. Even the blood. Where had they been? It could have been five miles underground, or the surface of the moon. It could have been hell. He remembered a moment in the fight, the final round before the knockout. One of the fighters on his knees, arms at his sides, mouth wide, eyes gaping upwards. The umpire counting. The man's white skin, his black gloves, his white shorts, his black boots. His opponent, bouncing on his toes, his fists raised. The whiteness around his eyes, the dark stuff oozing down his victim's cheek. A kind of compulsive quality in that moment, in the image that stuck in Tim's mind, in the power and the submission, the violence, its threat, its actuality.

He looked down again at her purchases.

"Do you still need to buy some more music?".

"There's another shop down the road that I want to try." Imogen finished her tea. "Tim. Listen. We have to talk."

He shrugged. "Let's talk."

She took a deep breath. "I've been offered a job. I have to decide what to do about it."

"Well, that's great, isn't it?"

Imogen frowned again. "Let's try this other shop. I'll tell you about it later."

Perhaps if he had not been sleeping so deeply just minutes earlier. Perhaps if he had not been back there in his imagination, until he felt her hot breath against his ear.

An image wormed its way back into his mind, a face, blurred, distorted, and instantly his passion began to puncture, to decouple itself from hers. He held her more tightly, her face pressed close to his neck, but he knew she had felt the hesitation as well. After a moment, his grip began to loosen.

"It's all right," Imogen whispered, and she kissed him on the cheek, and then, slithering from his grasp, she kissed his shoulder, his left nipple, his stomach. Tim rolled onto his back as her tongue darted, but his breathing remained steady.

After a couple of minutes he said, "I'm sorry."

Imogen shuffled up the length of his torso and nestled her head in his shoulder. She sniffed twice.

He raised his arm, sniffed as well. "Sorry," he said again. "It's hot in here." He made out the ghost of a smile on her lips.

"What time is it?" she said.

"It'll be light soon."

Imogen adjusted her position.

"You were dreaming again."

"Yes."

"Same thing?"

"Yes."

"Aren't you going to tell me?"

He clenched his eyes shut. It was still dark.

"There's nothing to tell," he said. *It always ends in the same way*, he thought.

She frowned and looked across at the luminous glare of the alarm clock.

"I had a call from Anton," she said after a while.

"Who?"

"My old professor."

"What did he want?"

She said nothing for a minute.

"You remember when I went to Brussels with him? Ages ago."

"Vaguely."

"You were jealous. A free holiday."

"Did I ever meet him?"

"You know he tried to..." Imogen chuckled. "You know ... he tried to get me into bed with him. When we were out there."

Tim breathed out slowly. He felt Imogen's hands, her breasts, her cheek, a million sensors waiting for every minute reaction of his to her news. Waiting for a reaction that should have been instinctive and immediate. And that to flinch two, five seconds, after she said it would be to expose a brittleness in his feelings for her as much as to remain cool and detached.

"So what did this chap – Anton – what did he have to say this time?"

"Nothing much."

He tautened, and then he felt he had blown it, that by measuring his response to this, the admission of an indiscretion, he had signalled that his feelings for her were layered, artificial. Somehow dishonest.

"Why are you telling me this?" he said. "Why are you telling me now?"

"Because..." Imogen yanked at the hairs on his stomach with her fingers. She whispered. "Because I said no."

She waited a while and then got up. Tim saw a sliver of light underneath the door. He heard the fridge opening and closing. He sensed he had been outmanoeuvred. After a minute Imogen walked back in. She sat at the side of the bed.

"Why don't you like my friends?" she said.

He guessed what she was referring to. He had arrived back from work a few days earlier to find her seated on the floor in the living room surrounded by three other women, in jeans and Camden market cardigans, giggling over their glasses of wine, all within easy cushion throwing distance of her. They had frozen in mid-sentence as he walked into the room. He had loosened his tie, said hello, and then went to get a beer. He wondered as he left the room whether he had simply imagined the whispered gibe, *Does he vote Tory yet?*

Later, as they cleared up, he had asked her whether any of them actually had jobs. She was silent in her fury, but he knew as well that he wanted to characterise their opinions as immature and therefore partial and probably wrong. To deflect what they had said, for it had hurt. Not the gibe itself, but more its easy assumption of the political opposite, and his feeling these days that that constituted a labelling, a voluntary ring-fencing of what it was one could think about the world, and the ways in which it might be ordered by its people and its politicians.

"I do like your friends," he said. "I just... don't know them that well, I guess."

"So why do you say those things about them?"

She did not look at him. "*It's all wrong, but it's all so right.*" She sighed. "Do you remember that? Those words?" And chuckled. "That evening, my friends and me, when we were talking repertoire, and *Ravel* came up. His piano concerto, the slow movement. Someone mentioned that phrase. Does it ring a bell?"

And Tim struggled to recall the piece. Early twentieth century, impressionism, a new tonality.

"Do you remember we once went to see it at the Festival Hall. You, me. My girlfriends. Years ago. That's what you said about it afterwards. That phrase, it was you. They all remembered it, the other night."

But he did not.

"They all remembered it. They all remembered you, Tim."

Later, too late, it came back to him, its dreamy melancholy, with - to his ears - its arbitrary introduction of a flattened sixth here or an augmented third there, its songline a precise waltz around the very rim of the conventionally tuneful, this piece which, within its eight or so minutes, had somehow sliced open his heart, and then put it back together again.

She drank from the glass she held in her hands.

"What do you two do?" she said. "When you go out?"

"Us two?"

"You and... him."

"I told you."

"Boxing. Gambling. Yes, you said. Are there girls there?"

Tim laughed. "What on earth...?"

"You know what I mean."

Tim laughed again.

"Is he married? Sanjay."

"No."

"Gay?"

It always ends in the same way.

"What is this?"

"Why do you like him?"

Sanjay was there, Tim thought. *He saw it all.*

"Look, Imogen, he's an old friend." *But he never says. He never says a thing.*

"This morning. One thing I didn't tell you..." Imogen turned away. "Tim, if I went away for a while..."

He never says a thing.

87

"Tim, are you listening?"

"Your sister? Is she pregnant again?"

"Tim!" she shouted.

The train began to slow. After a few minutes it stopped. Sanjay looked out the window. Empty countryside. He stared. He would be late. His meeting would be delayed. Perhaps he could leave it until the next day. He thought some more. No, he would finish it today, no matter how late he arrived. He frowned, and cursed silently that he had broken one of his rules. Fly, drive, do anything but take the train. But Cardiff was a difficult distance from London, too short to make the flying any quicker, too long for the driving to be comfortable.

There was a hum, then a second or two of white noise, and after that the sound of a throat being cleared on the intercom. An announcement, an apology. Engineering works, delays. Sanjay shook his head. There was a saying of Gandhi, the only one that he now remembered, *I would rather have the trains run badly by Indians, than run well by the British.* What amazed him was not the unbending statement of intent from the country's future leader, but rather the hidden context, that the British were once the type of people who could actually run a railway. As a ticket inspector walked down the gangway and caught Sanjay's eye, he shook his head again and laughed. These people, he thought to himself, these pathetic people, how did they ever do it? He experienced a sudden mental displacement, the pull of a distant memory, and as his mind raced he remembered himself as a child at the deathbed of a great uncle, a man who in his younger days, with his fundamentalism and psychotic temper, had terrorised his wife, her family, his four daughters. Seeing the man, frail, now silent, his power extinguished, Sanjay had looked at those vacant eyes and asked himself, how did he do it? Recalling that old man now, the same question came back to him, but also, how did they allow it, why didn't someone just say no?

Why don't people say no? It was the same with those men and women of the Raj, about whom he had read as a boy in schoolbooks which, he was sure, no longer existed in the enlightened syllabuses promulgated by the functionaries who ran the education system today. The people of India had allowed them to get away with it, those men and women whose behaviour seemed to enthral and insult his boyish intelligence in a kind of crazy equal measure he could not understand, and yet which he knew, even at a young age, was somehow related to the insufferable condescension of the housewives who visited his father's small shop, and his father's fawning unctuousness as they opened their tight purses.

"Do you know how long it will be?" Sanjay asked as the man punched his ticket.

"I'm sorry, sir, I don't," he said. "There will be an announcement."

How did they do it?

How?

A young boy plays with model airplanes in the streets of a northern town, he shoots down the hun. He reads comics, tales of derring-do, where men with fair skin, blond hair, and a resolute look, pacify wild bands of dark-skinned tribesmen on the North-West frontier. His parents indulge him. But one day a group of older boys steal his books from him and beat him up and tell him that reading all those lies is bad and wrong and insulting to his parents and to his gods. He recognises the boys, their parents go to the new temple his parents also attend. He follows them around and in time comes to think like them. In secondary school a few years later, where he is increasingly surrounded by similar gangs of youths and also by tough teenagers who go to the local mosque, the formal curriculum that has been taught for generations, a curriculum of Greek declensions and Caesar's Gallic wars, becomes ever less relevant. A teacher, one of the few remaining from that brief post-war era where the maps of the world still contained huge swathes of imperial red, tries vainly

89

to impart her long and fond fascination for the ambiguous history of her own island nation. But her classes are becoming unmanageable, and there is chaos one day after she expels a boy from her class, as she is presenting a lesson on the great Indian Mutiny, on Cawnpore, Lucknow, the Black Hole.

"But this is England," she cries, in tears as the headmaster, a progressive, leads her away.

Her replacement also teaches about empire, but he stresses the duplicity and the lying, the terror and the subjugation that underpinned the Raj. How otherwise could so small a number have achieved so much? The children are all encouraged to despise them, those old despots and murderers.

How did they achieve so much? The boy wrestles with the question and then finds that he cannot come up with a satisfactory answer. Despite the best efforts of a new, more balanced, multicultural interpretation of history, he finds he cannot quite shake off a sense of the spirit of audacity and *élan* that hangs over names like Clive and Curzon, or the stories of the surveyors and engineers and adventurers who had roamed this huge undiscovered territory and tried to make it their own.

It tires him, trying to reconcile the differing views that he has of his own people's troubled relationship with the country in which he lives, and he finds himself leaning towards areas of study less open to controversy. Maths, the sciences, economics. It confuses him again when, with 'A' levels approaching, some of the boys begin to whisper about radical colleges of further education dotted around the north of England, or even elsewhere, even back East. Some of his parents' friends seem to encourage this stark vision of his future. But his grandparents flap, his mother wails.

"Your grades are good," they say. "You can go wherever you want, you can become whatever you want." They outline their expectations. Medicine, the law. They hail the success of the local MP.

"Make us proud," they tell him. They talk of Manchester

and London, or, closer to home, Leeds and Bradford, he wouldn't even have to leave home or learn how to cook. But the idea sounds so constrictive, and when one day he sees a prospectus for a course in the southwest of England, amidst rolling hills, majestic curved terraces, country pubs, the kind of places those explorers and adventurers had no doubt yearned for as they battled across deserts and jungles, a hidden part of him sees a route out, a way of escape. When he tells them of his decision the flapping increases, the wailing intensifies, until one day his father senses a strength of purpose that his own father may once have felt when he left a village in Maharashtra for the last time a generation ago, and, in an act of generosity he fears his son may never understand, he gives him his blessing and lets him go on his way.

Sanjay hated Cardiff.

He was there to sack a man. The man did not know it yet, but the evidence against him was there in Sanjay's briefcase, the inflated expenses, the forged cheques, the fake accounts.

"Do you want someone to go with you?" Michael had asked.

"What do you take me for?" Sanjay had said with a smile. Anyway, the man knew that if he made trouble, a couple of Mick or Bernie's men would be heading out his way soon enough.

As the train finally pulled into the station, Sanjay wondered to himself whether to go straight to the casino, or to check into his hotel first. He decided on the hotel. Both were in the centre of town, he could walk from one to the other.

He could walk. But somehow of course he wouldn't. As he looked for his limousine, as he tipped the porter who carried his bags, he knew he would never walk. He hated this town, the only city in Britain where he felt so ill at ease. It had been a visit he had made with some student friends from Bath, years back. They had gone drinking on the town's main street, and suddenly he had felt uneasy, he, the only brown face within the febrile crowds of pasty white.

"You're over-reacting," his friends said. "They despise us all... It's a town vs. gown thing."

But it was more than that. His white friends would never understand.

He stood at the taxi rank and tried to imagine the city through the eyes of the uncertain teenager who had come here so many years before. It was impossible. That person had disappeared.

That person. That boy.

The lad from Yorkshire, his first week at university, his accent, a strange mixture of northern and immigrant, his garish clothes, his food parcels from back home. Surrounded by wispy boys and girls, barely out of childhood, the great great grandchildren, he thought, the descendants of those who had trod countless lonely paths out east, with their trade and their bibles and their guns. And he felt so wrong, in the way he looked, the way he spoke, in the way he was. But despite this they talked to him, they asked him about his subjects. They seemed to choke him with their kindness, and he could not answer back.

He nearly died in that first week, but the threat of a return to what he had escaped roused in him a desire to change. He began to throw away the food that arrived every week from Leeds, he forced himself to master his vowels, he used his first grant cheque to scour the clothes shops. His accent seemed to bend to his will, though one day it all seemed undone when he was on the phone to his parents from the communal kiosk down the hall, and one of the girls, laughing, told him how different he sounded, she had come out her room to see who it was. He never called home from a public phone again.

Things changed. He changed. Gradually he began to feel an excitement burning inside him, a sense that, by some piece of quixotic fate, he had somehow stepped into a magic circle of the chosen. These people, his new people. He got to know them, he went out with them, he began to behave like them. But as the months passed, his elation began to subside, and a suspicion grew in him that he would look in vain for the charismatic and exotic supermen he had once read about. Who amongst those of his new friends was planning to subdue a continent, to claw his way up a mountain to the roof of the world, to cross an uncharted desert? Their horizons extended no further than the students union bar. They spent their evenings in an alcoholic stupor or a haze of cannabis smoke. This was what made them content, fulfilled.

"Why didn't you tell me, Tim?"

They were all out one night.

"What's that?"

"Your Dad's pretty well known, isn't he?"

"I guess."

And Sanjay thought, *Why is he here? At a provincial university like this? Couldn't his father pull a few strings?*

"Are you going to follow him?"

"Where?"

"Into academia?"

But last orders was ringing. "Sorry, Sanjay." Tim was out of his seat.

He began to despise the way they thought and the way they acted. And above all, the way they looked. The chic poverty that they affected appalled him. He felt he had to escape from this, he needed to look and dress as he pleased. Once more he felt constricted, and he felt the suffocating closeness of a small town bounded by its own self-image. He bought his first car and began to spend his evenings and weekends in nearby Bristol, at first just checking the place out, but soon working in bars and in nightclubs. His friends sneered at him, then they began to depend on him when he drove them to the pub and had the cash to buy everyone a last round just before closing time.

In his second year he was already well known on campus, aloof, better dressed, better connected than most other students, and he found himself being noticed by a small crowd of people who for the first time seemed to be the real thing. Young men with names like Jasper and Hugo, who had girlfriends at Oxford and who drove in their sports cars by moonlight to meet them. He watched them, and began to discern the quality that marked them out from the hundreds of other undergraduates with whom he had already had some contact. The quality of arrogance. It was their arrogant disdain of everyone and everything about them that astounded, their easy assumption that they were always right, they would always get their way. Their arrogance was never cruel, it was never hostile. It simply side-stepped, or elegantly skipped over, the doubts, the difficulties, the indecisions that the rest of the population took as its inevitable destiny in the world. He saw it in the way these people tipped their waiters in restaurants, the way they dealt with the mechanics who fixed their cars, the way they charmed the secretaries who ran the vice chancellor's department. These were the heirs of the soldiers and merchants, the great viceroys, the pillagers and plunderers, who had opened up and then ruled over his country. They were the people he wanted to get to know.

These people were always destitute, they were always rich. They broke the law, they seemed above the law. Sanjay was talking with them once.

"What would you do if you killed someone?"

"Woman trouble?"

"Just hypothetical."

"All's fair in love and war."

"No. It's not that."

"What then?"

"Tell me, what would you do? If it happened to you."

"Just remember this. Some people deserve to die. Some don't deserve to live."

Years afterwards, in London, he would run into the Jaspers and Hugos again. He would discover that they were not quite what they seemed. One had been the son of refugees from the Nazi camps, and not the last of a long and distinguished line of Scottish landowners. Another the son of a serial fraudster, a man who had been in and out of prison all his life. He would discover that they were all misfits, to one degree or another.

At first he had been surprised. Later he thought how naïve he had been.

Sanjay found a flight back to London the next day.

He had been impressed by the man he had just fired.

Their meeting had been short, Sanjay had laid it on the line. He would pay back everything he had stolen, and more, and quickly. He would leave town.

"If you ever breathe a word of this to anyone, I'll let the dogs loose on you."

Sanjay then called in two security officers, and the man was given five minutes to collect his things. After that he was led out the front door and onto the street.

As Sanjay had talked, the man had smiled. As if to say, he had no intention of remaining in this dump anyway. The scam had been a good one. He knew it. Sanjay knew it. There would be a next time.

He made a mental note to discuss the whole business with Michael. They would keep an eye on this young man. He had a good CV. Probably phoney, Sanjay thought. But faked with some style. They might want to make an arrangement with him in the future.

nine

Sunday was warm and bright.

Tim had arranged to meet Sanjay at a café on the South Bank overlooking the river, and around midday he and Imogen arrived at Charing Cross station. They walked out onto a sprawling concourse, and then down a small side street that skirted the old station building and took them to a main road running along the north side of the Thames. They joined a mass of tourists clambering up a stairway onto a footbridge crossing the river. The pathway led alongside a rail line bringing trains into the city from the south of England. A web of heavy plating and steel barriers separated pedestrians from the punctuated shrieks and roars of trains approaching and slowing, jockeying for their places on platforms a hundred yards up.

Tim and Imogen moved along slowly with the crowd. They stopped partway along the bridge and leant against the barrier. They looked at the river following its stately curve away from them into the far distance.

Tim spoke softly. "This view."

"What's that?"

Layer upon layer of history pushing forward against both banks. Nineteenth century mock-gothic, post-war concrete and high-rise, the glass and steel of the Big Bang. A sprinkling of ancient church spires, all of them arrayed in a kind of circular homage to the extravagant vision of St Paul's at their centre.

"It makes it almost bearable," he said.

A blast of released steam exploded behind them.

This city, he thought. With its squalor and overcrowding, its hidden pain, its sordid pleasures. It seemed momentarily redeemed.

Later, over on the other side, they walked along the promenade for a few minutes. Imogen bought the papers. At the café they ordered coffee and cakes, and found a table outside in the sun. Imogen scanned the headlines. The minutes passed. She made as if to speak. Tim watched as her eyes narrowed. He waited for her to say something.

"Where's Blackfriars Bridge?"

"Along a bit. You can just see it."

"It says here a body was found underneath."

She was silent as she read on.

"It's horrible," she said. Tim saw her frowning. "Where did you say it was?"

Tim pointed.

"He was found naked, badly bruised. He had been dead for days."

"Was it murder?" Tim said.

"They can't tell. He could have jumped. The bruises could have been caused by the fall."

"Who was it?"

"They don't know."

"Illegal immigrant?"

"It doesn't say."

"Is there a description?"

"Slim, late twenties. White. Long hair. It says there was alcohol in his blood when he died. A lot."

Tim could see Imogen scanning the article one more time.

"For your life to end like that. No Missing Person. No one's even claimed the body."

A few minutes later she spoke again. "Tim, we have to get out of here."

"What do you mean?"

"It's no good here any more."

"So what would we do instead?"

"Have you spoken to your brother?"

Tim grimaced and shook his head.

He was not surprised at her question. It seemed part of a pattern that was developing between them. The details of the opportunity that had come her way had emerged slowly. The audition, her old professor, the tour. The three months away. She said she was undecided, and yet it seemed to him that the pieces were slowly lining up in a particular way.

He had encouraged her. She would regret it, he said when she told him for the first time, she would regret it if she let the chance go. But somehow it all got confused with other issues between them. "Why do you say that?" she had flared. "Are you trying to get rid of me?" Tim had felt trapped. He could not think what to say. It came to him that a part of her was probing for a way out. Later she apologised, she said she did not know why she had said what she did.

A man stood gazing down at them. They looked up, their hands protecting their eyes from the mid-summer glare.

"Well, you two seem comfortable."

Tim got up. He and Sanjay shook hands. "I didn't see you."

Imogen extended a hand from her seat. Sanjay took off his dark glasses.

"Imogen. A pleasure. How are you?"

They sat down, feeling the sun on their faces. Someone came over to take Sanjay's order.

"So." Sanjay broke the silence. "What could be more pleasant than this?" He leaned back in his chair. "Sorry I'm late. It took ages to find a space."

"We walked," Tim said. "Over the bridge."

"You're not driving these days?"

"Parking's too expensive around here."

"Tim. You're not earning enough."

Sanjay put on his sunglasses and surveyed the crowds walking up and down.

"Tim, you need money to survive in this town," he said. And then. "You should come and work for us."

Tim laughed. "That's the second offer I've had recently." Imogen turned to look at him.

Sanjay shrugged. "I'm serious. This IT stuff. We need good people who understand it."

A waiter laid a cup in front of Sanjay.

"Imogen," he said. "Encourage him. Tim needs a change of scenery."

"Tell me, Sanjay," she said. "What is it exactly that you do?"

Sanjay smiled at her. He looked up and then stood and waved an arm. Tim and Imogen twisted round. They watched a woman walking towards them. Tim stared, he could not quite believe she was coming their way. He sighed. He sighed at the clinging swirl of the polka dot dress around her knees, the pinching of her slim waist behind a tight leather belt, a cut-glass delicacy in the clip-clop of her ankles. *Oh Imogen*, he thought. It was the absence of passion in his life, he knew suddenly, which made his senses so finely tuned to the brittle surfaces of the woman's sensuality. The way she carried a thin black clutch bag in one hand, her sunglasses in the other. Her light make-up, the tight wave of her black hair pulled back under a scarf. She arrived at their table, and Sanjay kissed her on both cheeks. He turned to Tim and Imogen.

"This is Lily," he said to them. They all shook hands. She sat.

"I was telling Tim," Sanjay said to her. "He should come and work for me."

She turned to Tim.

"Tim's a computer whiz. But, who knows, perhaps there are other skills he could offer."

"Well?" she said. She smiled. "Are you persuaded?" Lip gloss, perfect teeth.

Tim was silent. He realised he was staring. He turned away.

"But Sanjay," Imogen broke in. "You run a casino, don't you? It's casinos, entertainment, that's what you do." She paused and put a hand on her coffee cup, as if to take a sip, as if to give herself a second to think. "Tim's with a world class company. He's got ambitions of his own. He can't just give all that up. He can't walk away from that at the drop of a hat."

Tim said nothing. It irked him sometimes when she spoke of him in the third person.

He remembered himself and Imogen eight, nine years before, without regular incomes, their lives a daily re-invention, their horizons circumscribed by the concerts or the gigs they were seeing that day, the bars and the parties they would be crashing that night. Bed-sits, basement flats, each month a struggle to collect their remaining cash and loose change so that they could guarantee, for the next few nights at least, a roof over their heads, and a narrow bed in which to explore the curves of each other's bodies.

"Tim's a mathematician," Imogen said to her friends, and they, musicians, artists, actors, took him in as one of their own, and asked him to explain to them what Einstein had really meant, what it all signified, this magic of curved space and parallel universes. But as Tim's father and brothers caught up with him, as they started suggesting that he should really begin to look to his future, and as he began to fall ever more deeply into debt, the attraction of the straight world existing alongside, the world of commuting and career paths and pension plans, this other world began to tug at him. One day he joined eighty other young hopefuls in the training department of a huge banking and insurance conglomerate, and soon he and Imogen had put down a payment on a comfortable two-bedroom apartment, and Imogen was telling him he looked really sharp in his suit as she kissed him goodbye at eight o'clock every morning. She still told her artistic friends that he was a mathematician and not a company drone, and Tim knew that she was grateful she could pursue her musical ambitions now without the fear that she would be forced out onto the streets at any moment. But the illusion began to puncture at the first Christmas party, a company bash at a London hotel, where she was finally introduced to the reality of the corporate dream.

"The wives of your friends," she said in the taxi on the way home. "They were ghastly. Talking all evening about extensions to their houses in the suburbs, the private schools they would send their kids to."

Later, in bed. "We're not going to end up like that, are we?"

"Of course not," Tim said.

He had lasted two years, and then he had contracted for a while, until the travelling began to get wearing. One day an agency contacted him with a lucrative offer from a trading firm in the west end of London. He was enticed at first by the money, and then later, once he began to understand how they worked – though he would admit this to no-one – by the almost anarchistic opportunism he observed in the way the company did business. Untrammelled capitalism. For a while he felt that Imogen was glad that his suits were no longer dull and pinstriped but more Armani, but later it was as if she began to smell something she did not like, and she cheered when the plate glass of the office entrance got trashed during an anti-globalism riot. She no longer came to the company's Christmas functions. He no longer came to her concerts.

Sanjay and Lily were staring at him.

"You should come and see us," Sanjay said. "Meet Michael. My boss. Come have a chat."

Lily was nodding.

Tim excused himself to find the gents. When he returned, Imogen seemed flustered, defensive.

"We couldn't possibly," she was saying. "At such short notice."

Tim asked her what was up, and Sanjay raised his two hands, palms out.

Imogen looked down. "Lily was making a suggestion."

"An invitation," Sanjay said gently to Tim. And he explained that his company was running a project down in the south of

Spain that was nearing completion, blocks of luxury flats, holiday homes. He was going down there to help wrap things up. His boss would be there. Lily also.

"Join us for a few days. A long weekend."

Tim caught Imogen's eye.

"You won't have to pay for a thing. We can provide you with a car at the airport. You'll stay in one of the apartments."

There was a pause.

"Tim, we can't," Imogen said. "We have commitments."

Later the four of them walked along the promenade amongst the crowds and the tourists. The two women lingered at a bookfair.

"Are you serious?" Tim whispered to Sanjay. The two men strode ahead.

"Come out to Spain. Meet Michael. We can talk."

They looked out over the river.

"I might have to persuade Imogen."

They argued at home that evening.

"What do you want me to do?" Tim said.

"Why did you agree so quickly?" Imogen said.

"To what?"

"You seem to trust him more than your brother."

"That's not true."

"You can't just give up everything you've worked for."

"Let's at least meet them, let's see what they have to say."

"That bunch of crooks? With their bimbos?"

Tim groaned.

"Listen, I'm going anyway. It's just one weekend. I'm booking a flight tomorrow."

Later. In bed.

"Have you thought any more about the tour? With the orchestra?"

Imogen put down her book.

"You're right. I must decide soon," she said. "They won't wait for ever."

"Come out to Spain next weekend. Sunbathe, take it easy. It'll focus your thoughts."

"Perhaps, Tim. Perhaps I will."

The following Friday, after an early start and then three hours crammed into economy seats amongst fractious families and bands of pasty-faced young men shouting across the aisles for more beer, they disembarked from their plane into the brilliance of a midday Mediterranean sun. Collecting bags and presenting passports to uninterested security staff, they took a few minutes to compose themselves in the cool marble of the arrivals area. They picked up the hatchback that Sanjay had arranged for them at one of the rentals agencies, eased it out of the car park, and headed eastwards.

For half an hour the coastal road wound past hotels and sprawling construction sites. Out of town they stopped at a lay-by. Imogen changed shoes for sandals, Tim finally figured out how to work the air-conditioner. Countryside. Tim glanced at Imogen and began to relax. Old villages. Dark stone churches in sharp outline on the slopes overlooking. He marvelled at the intensity of the blues where the sea met the sky, the dusty yellows and the greens in the distant hills around them. He marvelled that a generation of mass tourism by his countrymen had not yet corrupted the essence of this land.

After a couple of hours, the road began to head inland.

"I've been here before," Imogen said dreamily. "Years ago. When I was a child. I came here with my parents."

Tim waited for her to say more.

They passed through villages, knew they were getting close. Imogen searched for a sheet of instructions that Sanjay had faxed over to them.

"Tim, let's forget them," she said. "Let's forget them all. Let's drive on, find a hotel on our own. Let's spend the weekend eating seafood. Drinking chilled rosé. Making love."

Tim laughed. He said nothing. He drove.

A beeping sound came through on Tim's phone.

"That'll be Sanjay," he said.

Imogen picked it up. There was a text.

"He says he'll see us this evening," she said to Tim.

There was a town ahead. They took a turning off the main road, and began to wind their way around streets leading through clumps of holiday homes, with a smattering of shops and bars, all closed and shuttered up in the afternoon heat. The road came to a dead end.

"Here, let me see that," Tim said, leaning over and looking at the directions. After a few moments he turned the car round and headed back. They came to a complex with a high white wall and a set of steel gates. They stopped the car and walked up to the entrance. There was a bank of electric buzzers enclosed in a steel case at the side. Tim examined it. Sanjay's fax had mentioned a concierge. He pressed the bottom button a couple of times and waited. He pressed again. After five minutes, an old man appeared from inside and walked up to the gates. He stood and looked at Tim and Imogen.

"Hello. I'm Tim Scott." The man waited expressionlessly. "*Mi nombre es* Tim Scott." Imogen began to giggle.

After a moment he produced a set of keys and unlocked the gates. He raised an arm and pointed. There was a curved drive that led past half a dozen apartments. In the centre was an elaborate construction of flowers and grass. A sprinkler system sputtered into frantic and periodic activity.

"*Número cinco*," the man said. He pulled the gates open. Tim and Imogen got back into the car and drove in. They parked outside their flat. Theirs was the only car in the drive.

The front door was unlocked. They walked through, into the hall, and from there into a large living room, spacious, bright, the decoration modern. It looked out onto a courtyard with a swimming pool. On a table in the middle of the room were a vase of flowers and a set of keys.

Imogen explored. A huge kitchen. A wooden staircase leading up to three bedrooms.

"What's the idea?" Imogen said. "Is this all to ourselves? Or is Sanjay staying here as well?"

They dumped the bags down on the floor.

"I don't know," Tim said. "I just don't know."

They got back into the car and drove out the estate. Getting back onto the main road and proceeding on into town, they could see that on the drive over they had cut across a headland jutting out into the sea, but they were once more just a short distance away from the coast. To the west, inland, there were plains, and then the faded contours of hills. The apartment complex was on the outskirts of town. The road narrowed and sloped gently down to the seafront. They passed a promenade of shops and cafés, and then caught a glint of deep blue.

They slowed. There was a stretch of beach to their right, and, beyond, a stone promontory that enclosed a marina. A profusion of masts and flags, yachts, cruisers. Wealth on display.

Imogen wanted to explore on foot. Despite the lingering heat, the beachside roads and promenades were packed. A middle-aged, even elderly crowd, white shorts and polo shirts, socks and deck shoes. A few younger families. They walked hand in hand around the marina, then sat at a café and had coffees.

"Where do you think all this money comes from?" Imogen said.

They looked at the names and the pennants on the sterns of the boats. They listened for accents.

Tim fired off a text to Sanjay. They had a glass of wine.

Fifteen minutes later, Tim received a reply.

"He wants to know where we are."

Imogen pointed out a sign. He texted in the name of the café.

The sun was low in the sky, it was cooler. They observed an

acceleration of activity in the waterfront bars. The crowds changing, fewer children, more couples.

"Glad you came?" Tim said. He began to brush his fingertips up and down her forearm. He looked at her.

"That dress..." he said. Splashes of yellow and orange.

"Cancun. Last year."

She held his eyes.

"Sanjay?" Her voice a low murmur. "How long?"

"An hour. Perhaps more."

"Do we have time?"

They drove back fast. He was already grappling with the zip at her back as they stumbled through the door.

Later, she lay with her right cheek against his chest.

"We need to get back," he said.

"Please." She tightened her arms around him. "Just another five minutes."

The same café. They had another glass of wine, and then walked, but not far, keeping an eye on the crowds around the bar and the pavement outside.

Tim saw him as it was beginning to get dark, walking alone along the promenade. With hardly a word, the three fell into step. Sanjay patted Tim lightly on the shoulder. They strolled, propelled forward gently by the early evening crowd, Imogen for once happy to see him. Wisps of conversation swirling around them, the light tang of sea salt in the air. Slowly the seafront lit up, coloured lights in bars and restaurants, a dull gleam from the cabins of the yachts where some chose to entertain.

They found a place to eat, and sat at a table just feet away from a bank of stone steps that led down to the water. They had crab soup, and fish and rice, and then cake, and fruit which was served with a hard, bitter cheese. Viscous red wine, sparkling water, and later strong coffee and brandy. Tiny sweets to suck as they left.

Sanjay took them to a night club, where they saw two tribes observing each other across a symbiotic divide: an older crowd, at tables with their wallets and their German beers, faces red and blotchy under thinning white hair; and bands of Spanish teenagers, behind the bar, or on the floor, lithe and strutting, trays of drinks held high above their shoulders. Later, Tim wanted to feel the night breeze against his face, and he picked a way around the marina under the glimmer of the stars. They stopped at a stone outcrop at the most distant point from the beach, and watched the lights out to sea, fishing boats, preparing for the catch at first light. Imogen shivered at his side. They turned back, and found a quiet tavern hidden in a back street where the lights were dark. Wooden benches. A few locals whispered and smoked in a corner. An old woman served them hot chocolate. They lost track of the hours. There were streaks of blue in the sky when they drove back through the gates into the complex. Sanjay parked by the flat next to theirs. The three of them stared at each other for a minute as they stood outside. They said nothing. A bird flapped its wings. Sanjay glanced up, and then opened the door of his flat. Tim leaned forward and kissed Imogen's hair.

At eleven the next morning Sanjay knocked on the door of Tim and Imogen's apartment and walked in. Tim was preparing coffee in the kitchen. He wore a pair of shorts. Nothing else. There was the sound of someone showering upstairs.

"Hi. Want some coffee?"

Sanjay was looking crisp, in cream slacks and an open-necked shirt.

"No. Well, perhaps a quick one." He took a chair at the kitchen table. "How are you two this morning?"

Tim grunted. "So where is everyone else?" he said.

"On their way. They're on their way."

Tim placed a cup in front of Sanjay.

"You're looking fit," Tim said.

Sanjay dropped a thick bunch of keys on the table.

"Look, I've got to head over to Malaga to pick up Lily. Her flight's due this afternoon. I'm going to be away for the next few hours. I've just spoken to Michael, he's in town, just tidying up some business. He says he's coming over this morning, he should be here soon."

Tim glanced at Sanjay as he heard Lily's name. "The mysterious Michael," he said. He sat down at the table, a mug in his hand.

"What I suggest is that you wait here, relax. Use the pool. He'll be turning up soon, he can show you around."

They drank their coffee. Imogen was still not downstairs when Sanjay snatched up his keys.

The water in the pool was cold. They swam, and then pulled a shade over two sunbeds. Tim rubbed suncream into Imogen's shoulders. They lay back and read their books.

They heard voices inside the house. Arguing. Growing louder. One voice raised.

"... we can't let them..."

Tim and Imogen looked up.

"... let 'em fuck us over like that..."

Tim stood. He put his book down.

"Calm down..." The second voice.

Two men stood at the sliding doors to the living room. The smaller of the two stepped forward. He was dressed in white. White leather shoes, white trousers, a white shirt. His black hair was combed back. There was silence for a moment. He took off his sunglasses.

"I'm Michael."

Tim approached warily.

"Hello. I... We're..." Tim felt as if he had been caught trespassing.

"It's Tim, isn't it?" The man said. "And Imogen. Sanjay said you'd be here."

Imogen had put on a bathrobe. She walked over. She looked at Michael, and then over his shoulder at the man who stood behind him.

She extended a hand.

"And this is Bernie," Michael said. He turned to introduce his companion.

"Pleasure." The first voice. The one doing the swearing. His arms remained at his side.

The four of them watched each other for a few moments. Then Michael spoke.

"Look. You two relax. Enjoy the pool. We're going to grab a bite to eat soon. Why don't you join us? There's a good place next door. We can go for a quick tour afterwards."

Tim looked at Imogen.

"Sounds good," he said. "What, half an hour?"

"We're a few doors down. Number one."

Michael smiled. The two men left.

Tim and Imogen remained absolutely still until they heard the front door slam.

The four of them piled into Michael's BMW. Bernie drove. There was a hotel with a dining room close by. The drive took all of two minutes.

Michael seemed to know the manager. They were led to a table. There were no other guests.

"Beers all round?" Michael said. "No? Too early? Perhaps you're right. Just you then, Bernie?"

Tim and Imogen picked at the tapas. Michael talked. About property development, Spain, the expanding economy. Imogen seemed preoccupied with her asparagus.

"How long have you been doing business here?" Tim tried to make conversation.

"Ten years now. Right, Bernie?"

The waiter brought salads and steaks.

"Must be difficult. Language, local customs, that type of thing?"

There was a grunt from Bernie. Michael laughed.

"No," he said. He took a mouthful of meat. "Well, maybe. But I like to think there's always common ground. Bernie doesn't always agree. The local agents, well, some of them have their own ideas. We have ours. We try to meet somewhere in the middle."

Tim looked at Imogen and Bernie sitting opposite each other, heads down, eating silently. He turned back to listen to Michael.

"These apartments, what's the story with them?"

"They go on sale next month. So don't break anything," Michael said, and he laughed again. "I'm joking. Relax. Enjoy the place. Everything's insured."

After the meal, Michael and Bernie stayed behind for a moment to talk to the manager. Tim and Imogen waited outside.

"What do you think?" he said.

"That Bernie. He's..."

"He's huge."

"That as well."

It was still hot, but Michael wanted to show Tim and Imogen the estate. He picked up a set of keys from the concierge, and they walked around slowly. Past swimming pools, reception areas, through stone courtyards, balconies. He described his battles with architects, regulators and tradesmen. They walked up to the gates. He pointed to the hills and the views in the distance, and then the high wall. "Security is important here," he said. He stood by the central fountains and did a slow twirl.

Later he invited them over for drinks. His was the largest of the apartments.

There were some personal touches. Magazines, a shelf of books, some photographs. There was a picture of a fortyish woman with her arms round the shoulders of two girls. Ten, eleven years old, perhaps. And some, black and white, of a younger man, various poses. Smartly dressed, with an older person at his side. Then, more casual, with friends. On another shelf the same man, in shorts and gloves, arms raised.

"Is this you? You used to box?" Tim said.

Michael looked up. "A long time ago," he said.

Imogen sat. Tim remained at the bookshelf.

"Bernie," Michael shouted. "Find us something to drink, will you? The fridge should have been refilled." He turned to Tim and then Imogen. "Too early for booze still?" He shouted again. "Water for our guests. Bernie? I might try a glass of wine."

Tim saw thrillers, travel guides. A Spanish dictionary. And then some hardbacks. He pulled one of them down and looked at the first few pages. A history of the Eastern Front. Pictures of German troops in the snow. Panzer tanks in the Ukrainian countryside. Then a page of portraits, *Wehrmacht* generals staring out. Handsome men, austere, resolute. He put the book back. There were others, the desert campaigns, the battle of the Atlantic, the fall of Berlin.

Tim carried one over to the sofa.

"Interesting collection," he said as he sat next to Imogen.

"Borrow one if you want."

"A hobby?"

"I like to see it from the other point of view."

"The Germans'?"

"Or as the exercise of power. How much they achieved, from a standing start. The re-building of the army in the thirties. The weapons programmes. How they overran Europe in a matter of months, fought two superpowers to a standstill. In the east and the west. How they were finally betrayed by the politicians."

Bernie walked in with a tray. Tim looked at Imogen. She was staring at her hands. He reached forward and picked up two glasses. He handed one to her. She looked up.

"Imogen, what do you think?" Michael said.

Tim saw a frown on her face.

"I was just thinking," she said after a few moments. "They lost."

Bernie sniggered.

"The limits of power, perhaps," Michael said. He sipped his wine. Bernie twisted the cap off a bottle of beer. A fly had found its way into the living room. It buzzed around the ceiling, and then flew into the sliding doors at the back.

"Perhaps you're right," he said. He got up and walked over to the other side of the room. He opened a window.

A phone rang. Bernie pulled out a mobile and muttered into it. After a few moments he folded it shut and put it down on the table.

"That was Sanjay," he said. "He's got Lily with him. Vicky as well. They're on their way."

Michael walked slowly back.

"Imogen. I apologise. It's just a hobby of mine. Let's forget it. Let's think about tonight. It looks like we've got a little party." He counted. "Five, six, seven of us. We must think of somewhere to go."

"Do we have to?"

"We're their guests. We've got to go."

"I can't... I can't spend all evening with people discussing the rights and wrongs of the Third Reich."

"But Imogen, it won't just be them. Sanjay will be there."

Imogen searched through her bags for something to wear.

"You've met Lily," Tim said. "She seemed very nice." He immediately regretted mentioning her name.

At eight o'clock, Tim and Imogen knocked on the door of apartment number one. Bernie grunted as he let them in. They heard voices, laughter. They saw Lily and another woman sitting on the sofa. Sanjay and Michael stood around the coffee table in front of them. Michael had a bottle of red wine in his hand. The four stopped and looked up as Tim and Imogen walked in to the living room. Michael put down the bottle and approached. He introduced the new arrivals.

"We've met, haven't we?" Imogen said to Vicky. "It was your shop, all that time ago, wasn't it?"

Michael poured the wine.

Fifteen minutes later, a convoy of three cars left the estate and headed into town. They passed the marina, and then headed away from the beach a couple of blocks. Inside the restaurant, they were given a corner, and Michael immediately ordered champagne. Sanjay tried to arrange the seating, a balance of the sexes, but no-one seemed to be listening. When Lily sat at one end of the table, Imogen joined her.

Sanjay joked to Imogen about the delays at the airport, the laconic Spanish officials, the crowds of flustered northern Europeans arriving, sweating and irritable. Michael spoke quietly with Vicky. Occasionally he shot out a question to Bernie. Tim, seated midway along the table, glanced for a second at Lily as she unfolded her napkin, and then caught Bernie's eye. He leaned back, and followed the shifting patterns of conversation around the table.

The waiters brought starters.

"You ever boxed?" Michael was looking at Tim.

Tim laughed. "No."

"Never? Even as a kid?"

"My dad wouldn't have allowed it."

"Really?" Michael looked at his plate of whitebait. "My uncle encouraged me."

"Your parents didn't object?"

"Died young. I never knew them."

"I'm sorry."

"Don't be. You don't miss what you don't know."

Tim was silent for a few seconds. He remembered the evening with Sanjay and Alec. He tried to recall what he knew about the sport.

"What weight did you fight?"

"Welter," Michael said. Tim shrugged. "Between light and middle."

They ate.

"I was good," Michael said. "I lost my first two fights, then something clicked. I won ten in a row."

"Why did you stop?"

Michael said nothing. He spoke to the waiter and ordered more wine. He picked at his food.

"Have you ever had nightmares?" Michael again addressed Tim. "Recurring dreams, bad dreams, that kind of thing?"

"I... well..." Tim saw Imogen glance his way. "What do you mean?"

"I do. Often. I'm in the ring. It's a guy I've fought before. I've beaten him before. I know the face, I know his name. I'm sizing him up, and I'm thinking, can I do it a second time? Can I beat this guy again?"

Tim was silent.

"Do you know what I mean? You've done it before. You've been the full twelve rounds with him. Now, in your head, you're having to go out and do it again."

"So do you? Do you win?"

"I never find out. I wake up."

Waiters poured wine.

"Do you like to analyse dreams?" Michael said.

Tim did not know how to reply for a moment.

"No?"

"It's a bit of a cliché, isn't it?"

"Ever dream about exams you've taken?"

"No."

"Not that I took any," Michael said. "Left school too early. I guess you did."

"A few."

"You know what they say? That you have nightmares about the ones you passed. Not the ones you failed."

Tim stared open-mouthed.

"That's right, isn't it?" Michael said. "That's what I'm dreaming about. The fights I won. Could I do it again? Do I have the guts, the bottle? Or have I lost it?"

Michael returned to his food.

I do dream, Tim thought, half-mouthing the words. But no one was paying attention

Michael finished his plate.

"So I stopped when I got injured. Someone bust up my shoulder. I had to retire."

"I'm sorry."

"Don't be. It was time to move on. I had a business to think about."

Tim leant back as waiters picked up plates. *I dream most nights*, he thought. *Does Imogen still notice?* Sanjay would understand. Or perhaps not. Tim looked at him whispering into Lily's ear. Did he dream also? Or had he simply erased the incident from his mind? He felt suddenly exposed, stripped bare. This person Michael seemed to have done it unwittingly. But had Sanjay ever spoken about the incident with him? Tim looked round the table. At that moment, he felt a craving for someone in whom he could confide. Right there and then.

They started on their main courses. Tim pulled himself together.

"I was a bit like you," he said. "When I was a kid. I used to collect all that stuff about the war. My books, my model airplanes, my comics..."

"I never read a single book when I was a kid," Michael said.

"I'm sorry, I..." Tim felt he had been caught out again. "Those books in your flat. I thought you said, a hobby."

Michael laughed. He put down his fork.

"I wasn't a kid. I was in jail. That's when I read all that stuff."

Tim had stopped eating as well. Michael picked up his fork again.

"I was young. Twenty-four. I was involved with some bad guys. I did six months inside. It's in the past. I paid my debt to society."

He looked at his food for a moment.

"That's when I started to read."

Michael ate. After a while he carried on.

"Once you've got over the initial shock, you realise the biggest problem you have is time. It stretches away from you, seemingly forever. So you think. About the future, what you'll do when you get out. And I started reading. Anything and everything. There was a room full of old books there, stuff even the libraries wouldn't bother with, stuff that people had donated when they cleared out dead relatives' houses. So one day I read this old book about these guys who ran the German army in the nineteen thirties. Don't know why. Something about them. All aristocrats, university educated. More like you, or Sanjay, than a kid like me. They and a few others figured out a new type of warfare, which exploded onto the face of Europe a few years later. They swung into France, swatted aside the British, pushed west, north, south, hundreds of miles a day. And then, east. They finally ground to a halt twenty miles outside Moscow. Just half an hour's drive away. Just think, if they'd pushed on that last bit. What would the world be like today?"

He poured himself, and then Tim and Vicky, another glass of wine.

"I was hooked. I read as much as I could. I asked my friends to buy me everything they could lay their hands on. They thought I'd gone nuts. But when you're in that situation, when you're stuck inside, you can't act, you can't do anything, so you want to know about people who can. People who strut the grand stage. You know what I'm getting at?

"It's the sheer scale of what they did. The application of this iron will. I know there was a lot of bad stuff as well. But these men weren't involved in that. They were too busy fighting a war. Most of them fell out with Hitler towards the end. They tried to assassinate him. For once, they screwed up. The best ones were hanged. Some committed suicide. But tell me, honestly, what's the difference between them and Alexander? Or Caesar? A thousand years from now, they'll talk about them in the same way. Guys with this immense vision. And the balls to make it a reality."

Tim ate slowly.

"You're not convinced," Michael said. "I can tell."

"How can I admire them? They would have destroyed us," Tim said.

"In fact, you've got it wrong. They respected us."

Tim shuddered. He imagined how his father would have reacted to this conversation.

"No," Tim said. "No. For once, there was a choice. It was clear. They were wrong. We were right."

"You think we were on opposite sides of a divide? Were we that different? They just wanted some of what we already had. When we carved up Asia, America, Australia two centuries before."

"But we didn't raze cities, we didn't eradicate populations. And there were good men, like the guys who stopped the slave trade. And when the empire collapsed, we walked away from it. Voluntarily."

"Voluntarily? Or because the Yanks told us to? We lost our nerve. We knew our time at the top of the tree was up."

Tim dared not turn to find out whether Imogen was listening.

"I would say, Tim, that you have a pretty sunny picture of human nature. What do you think really drives people? Tell me, what do you think it is? Money? Sex? Power?"

"I don't know. Many things. It's..."

"Or opportunism?"

Michael paused.

"People do what they do, because they can. They stop when they can't. When someone, or something, prevents them."

Michael pushed his plate forward. He put his napkin down.

"Have you ever felt it, Tim? The exhilaration of being able to act, the power of being able to do something outrageous? Something that changes the state of things? That changes people's lives?"

Tim had lost interest in the remaining flesh of the grilled fish in front of him.

"You know, Tim, I worry about the kind of people who've never experienced that thrill. They've lost their nerve. I don't know that I trust them. Perhaps I even despise them a little. You're not someone like that, are you, Tim?"

He picked up the menu.

"You should come and work for me. Rediscover your sense of fun," he said. "Think about it. Come and work for me."

The following morning was cloudy. Imogen was already at the poolside reading when Tim came downstairs and made coffee. Half an hour later Sanjay called round. He suggested a drive into the hills. The cooler weather would be good for walking, he said.

"I'm not moving," Imogen said without looking up. "I'm staying by the pool. I might go into town in the afternoon."

An hour later they left in a four-wheel drive. There were only three takers, Sanjay, Tim and Michael. Sanjay drove. They had maps but no destination. They followed a main road that headed away from the coast.

The Sunday traffic was light, and mostly in the opposite direction. Families heading towards the beach. Michael played a CD. Vintage Stones.

For an hour the road stayed straight and level. The countryside was drab, the thin vegetation a pale yellow. Later the road began to rise, and to curve round the side of the first hills. They passed through small villages, each deserted except for occasional knots of people standing, clothed in black, in the squares where they could find shade or on the steps in front of the churches. The road descended again and then levelled, and the scrubland around them became denser, wilder. Sanjay and Michael talked quietly above the music. Tim dozed in the back.

After a while Sanjay turned off. The side road twisted away. It narrowed, the surface was bumpier. After an hour it became an uneven dust path, and Sanjay slowed. They continued for another fifteen minutes and then he pulled up. Someone switched off the music. Michael and Sanjay got out and stretched. They were in a clearing, a rough circle, of perhaps a hundred yards' radius. At the circle's edge were clumps of bushes, knee-high, and Tim, sitting on the back seat of the car, his legs dangling out the open door, could see the scrubland stretching beyond. They were alone.

"Are we walking?" he said.

Sanjay and Michael moved about silently. Michael went to the back of the car and opened up the boot. He took out an old wooden tea chest and then a metal suitcase. He laid both on the ground.

Sanjay picked up the tea chest. There was a sound of glass clinking. He began walking. At the edge of the clearing, he upended the chest. A stack of empty beer bottles fell into the dust. He placed the chest upside down on the ground, and then positioned six of the bottles on top. He began to walk back to the car.

Michael bent, and opened up the suitcase. There were padded sections inside. He picked up a number of metal clips from one of them, looked at them briefly and then put them back. He picked up something else. It rested gently in his hand. He bounced his arm lightly up and down, as if admiring the object's weight and balance, he rubbed a finger along its slim neck. He stared at the pistol for a few seconds, gripped it, pointed the barrel away from him into the ground, and then, satisfied, rotated it in his hands and studied it from all angles. After a minute, he picked up one of the metal clips and inserted it into the gun.

Sanjay came and stood by him. The two of them turned towards the tea chest. Michael stepped forward two paces and raised the gun. He placed two hands high on the gun's grip, stretched his arms, and pointed. Tim sat up in the car seat. He waited. He watched through the car window. There was a stillness. Grey rock. Granite hills in the distance. A pale sky, thick clouds pressing. All life at rest. Movement, growth, decay, for now suspended. A dryness. In the dead scrub, in the dust beneath his feet. In his throat. Time measured. By what has yet to happen, by each remaining instant of silence.

There was a crack. Tim was blinking rapidly. Wings fluttering. Somewhere. Michael's arms rose slightly, and then settled back to their pointing position. Tim opened his mouth and gulped in air.

A sense of batteries recharging.

Or of pressure rising.

Or cord stretching.

A crack. A crack, glass shattering. Tim's neck shot round. He saw broken glass flying in the distance. Crack. Crack. Crack.

Tim stared at the remaining bottles, but Michael and Sanjay were suddenly laughing and whooping and whispering to each other. As he turned back, they were faced away from the tea chest, and Michael examined the gun again. Sanjay pulled out a flask from his pocket. He opened it, and took a swig. He handed it to Michael. Michael raised it and swallowed. He lowered the flask, and then started whispering again. It seemed as if he was telling a joke. Sanjay listened, and then threw his head back. Tim wondered what it was he had said that could be so funny. He looked at them through the window of the car door angled away from the chassis by his legs. He stared through the glass. His window into their world.

They turned to him and spoke. He could not hear a single word they were saying. He began to shrink back inside the car. He pulled in his legs. Sanjay walked up. Tim could see his lips moving. Slowly he began to make out words, as if the source of the sound was approaching at great speed from distance.

"Ever tried this before?"

Tim stared at him.

Michael had wandered off. A flock of doves had landed at the edge of the clearing. He stood ten feet away observing them. They were tame. He began to move forward slowly. He came up close, stood over them, and pointed. Somehow, at a distance, the report seemed to echo more loudly. There was a puff of dust. A feather, floating upwards. The birds rose a few feet into the air. He waited till they settled and fired a second time. Squawking. A flurry of wings. He fired once more. He stood watching the remaining birds, and then squatted and picked up a carcass by the tail. He got up and began to walk back.

"Want to give it a go? Tim?"

Tim clambered out the car. Slowly. He needed a few seconds. *You could bury a man here*, he thought. *No one would ever know*. He walked over slowly as Michael neared, and a fear began to grow inside him, it started as the tiniest pinprick in the bottom of his stomach. A thought, a possibility, a terror. It grew, and as it grew, suddenly he wanted his phone, he wanted it in his hand. But it was in the car, and he couldn't go back, it would give the game away, he simply couldn't go back there. But he wanted to hear Imogen's voice. He thought, if he might never see her again, then he wanted to hear her, just once more, her voice, modulated, dispersed through the ether and reconstructed, a fake, a simulacrum, perhaps, but a counterfeit nevertheless derived from the real thing, conveying ideas which she thought, emotions which she felt, secrets to which the two of the them had given birth a thousand times when they retreated from the world and their bodies had fused in their own private hideaway. The fear expanded and thrashed about inside him, its malignancy embodied in the hidden intention of the two men who joked and fooled around in front of him. For a second he imagined the fear externalised, animate and raging, its gaze raking the ground at his feet. If he just remained still, if he just kept out of its line of sight, if it just ignored him.

"Well, Tim?" Michael said.

Tim still said nothing. Sanjay took the gun from Michael. He took one step forward, and placed his feet apart. He raised his arms. Tim watched him squinting. Seconds passed. There were four explosions. Quick, fierce.

"Sanjay," Michael was laughing again. "You're useless. You didn't get one."

Tim heard Sanjay cursing softly. He watched him stiffen his

legs, and then his grip. He fired. Again. Four more times. The bottles remained undamaged in the distance.

Michael slapped his thighs. He crumpled, laughing.

"Sanjay, Sanjay." He couldn't speak for a few moments. There were tears in his eyes. "Vicky's a better shot than you are."

Sanjay walked back, a smirk on his face. "Here. Gimme," he said.

Michael handed him the hip flask. He took back the gun, steadied himself a second time and shot four rounds. Two bottles, smashed to pieces. He walked back to the suitcase and adjusted catches on the handle. He removed the clip.

Tim inhaled deeply.

"Tim." He heard Sanjay talking. "You're next."

He felt the panic attack returning, and tried to concentrate on his breathing. He found it difficult to exhale.

Michael knelt in the dust. He took a rag and began to clean the gun. He flipped it open. He gaped carefully down the barrel. Sanjay picked up a bottle of water from the car, poured a few mouthfuls down his throat, then handed it to Tim. When Tim did not take it, he poured some over his head and drank some more. Sanjay handed the bottle to Michael, but he pushed it away. Instead he fastened another clip into the gun, and stood up. He walked forward a few paces, the gun in his hand, and looked into Tim's eyes. He pointed the gun, and then reversed it in his hand and presented the grip to Tim. Tim breathed out. For a second he was overcome by the exhaustion he felt after making love, the sudden lethargy that he always felt after a burst of intense emotion. But then there was a kind of tingling, an expectation, and instantly his terror seemed to belong to another lifetime.

Michael shrugged. He positioned himself and began the target practice again. Tim watched. He slowly began to smile, and then to applaud, as Michael hit two bottles in a row. After a while Michael walked over to the tea chest. With a piece of scrap wood he cleared away the broken glass, then placed six more bottles on top. He walked back. Tim found that he could talk.

"Yes. I'd love to give it a go."

Without a word, Michael handed him the gun. Tim grabbed hold of it delicately. Michael walked around the back of him and placed a hand over his shoulder. He turned him towards the tea chest. He showed him where the safety catch was, showed him how to grip the gun, both hands straight out, in line with the ground, to minimise recoil. How to place his legs. How to lean a fraction to keep his body taut. He told him to keep his fingers out of the trigger guard until he was told.

He reached forward and released the catch. "When you're ready," he said.

Tim stared ahead and placed a finger inside the guard. He felt the gentle pressure of the warm metal of the trigger. For a second he thought about the difference between a squeeze and a pull, whether to clench his fist or merely the finger by itself, whether to rub his finger, to stroke the trigger, or press suddenly, whether...

A shot rang out. His arm bounced upwards.

"Whooaaaaaa."

He felt Michael's hand on his arm again.

"Let's try once more. Prepare for the recoil. Balance your shoulders against it. Now. Relax. Grip, both hands. Aim. Fire."

Seconds passed. Another shot. Another. Another. Another. A bottle blew apart, its neck rising and twisting as the body disintegrated.

Tim bent his head back and shrieked up at the sky. He raised both hands and shook his fists.

"Hey. Hey. Careful with that right hand. Whoa."

He pointed the gun down at the ground and apologised. He was still laughing.

He fired six more shots. He destroyed two bottles.

"Pretty impressive." Sanjay was watching at his side. "You're a natural."

He fired two more shots. And then he had had enough. He stood with both hands stretched rigid, the gun pointing into the far distance.

Michael came up behind him again. "Right. Take your finger out the guard. Safety catch? You saw me doing it." He spoke gently in Tim's ear. He disabled the weapon.

Michael reached for the gun. For a moment, Tim held on to it. Then he let it go.

They sat in a triangle in the dust, talking as they drank. Michael reminisced.

The afternoon began to cool. They left the broken beer bottles on the ground where they lay. Michael packed his gear carefully back into the suitcase, closed it and put it into the boot of the car. He climbed into the passenger seat beside Sanjay. The doors were open. He unwrapped a pack of cigars, offered one to Sanjay and to Tim, and then took one for himself. He lit all three from a gold lighter. They smoked in silence.

After ten minutes Sanjay got out and ground the butt of his cigar under his boot. He stretched. He got back in to the driver's seat. The others chucked their smokes out the window. All three of them slammed their doors shut. Sanjay started the engine. He did a wide circle in the dust and eased the vehicle back on to the road.

ten

Tim sat in a conference room with his boss and three other colleagues. They had been in there for an hour, discussing strategies for replacing ageing legacy systems with newer technology. Newer systems, faster, more secure, more closely integrated with other key applications. They had an agenda, carefully typed up on a sheet of paper. They were a quarter of the way through. At the top of the sheet was a title. *Critical Paths for the Evolving Corporate Enterprise.*

"Tim," his boss said. "Your little baby, the Foreign Banks Payment System. You've had a chance to look at some of the off-the-shelf software out there. What do you think?"

Tim started. His thoughts shunted back into engagement with the present. For the last five minutes he had been somewhere else, somewhere deep and primitive. He had been thinking about the feel of warm metal against the palms of his hands, the shock and the blast as the muscles of his fingers flexed, the choking exhilaration he felt when a target fifty yards away exploded and dissolved in front of his eyes. He looked around him, at people he had worked with for years, people he thought he knew. They had asked him about his weekend. What might he tell them? He showed off his suntan, he said they had found some great restaurants. They asked if Imogen had enjoyed herself. They all liked her. He said she had. But he didn't really know.

She had been out when he had arrived back at the apartment late Sunday afternoon. She got back at nine, she said she had been in town with Lily. He asked her whether she had eaten but she did not reply. She made herself a cup of tea and went straight to bed. Tim fretted for a while, and then called Sanjay. They drove down to the waterfront and found a bar. At some point the evening got lost. He couldn't remember what time he had arrived back. Or how.

Imogen had driven the two of them to the airport the next day. She hardly spoke in the car. She put on a CD and concentrated on the road. Mozart sonatas. It suited Tim. He had a headache. Fragments of the previous evening began to return to him as they drove. He remembered that at some point Sanjay had starting asking questions about his job and about his company.

"Tim, do you remember all that stuff you once told me at the casino?"

And later.

"Doesn't it ever tempt you?" he had asked. "The idea of writing yourself a virtual cheque for a million quid. Five million. Ten. Then getting your company to pay."

On the plane Tim pretended to doze. He closed his eyes. But he found his thoughts running repeatedly over that conversation. More and more came back to him. *I could never do it*, he had said. And Sanjay had said, *Why not? Explain to me why not?* Tim had come up with all the technical reasons, and then he began to dismantle his own arguments, one by one. He laughed, he said he had amazed himself with the breadth of his own expertise. But then he was silent and had shaken his head. *It's just not me*, he said softly.

And Sanjay's reply, a few minutes later. Did Sanjay really say all that? They had drunk so much, Tim's judgement was so skewed.

"Tim, what do you think?" his boss said.

"I'm sorry." Tim rubbed his forehead. "My mind was drifting."

"Let's take five. Let's get some coffee."

Sanjay had gone for more drinks. He returned with two bottles of beer.

"You say it's not you. Explain to me, why?"

Tim snorted.

"Have you ever thought it through?" Sanjay said.

"No."

"But that's wrong. You just have. Just now."

"Even if I did it, they'd catch up with me in the end."

"How? Tell me how, Tim."

Tim was silent.

"You know, we could help you."

"Help me with what?"

"You say you would never be able to cover your tracks. But perhaps you could. We know people, Michael and I. People who might be able to tell you how."

They drank.

"You know, Tim – perhaps you've guessed already – the company – us – we're not whiter than white." And Tim felt aghast at his words. But Sanjay had laughed.

Tim had not replied. Sanjay let the subject drop for a while. They talked of other things, they talked about guns, they talked about Michael. About Lily.

"She's gorgeous," Tim said. "Where did you meet her?"

And Sanjay asked about Imogen. Tim drank more beer.

They moved to another bar. Something was eating away at Tim.

"What did you mean back there? You said you could help."

Sanjay shrugged. For a while he evaded the question. But later he said something else.

"We broke the law once before. You and I. And we came through it."

Tim felt a subtle shiver resonating through him. He excused himself. At a sink in the washroom, he ran a cold tap and splashed his head and face and neck. He stared at himself in the mirror. But when he got back to the table, Sanjay picked up where he had left off.

"Of course, I hardly saw any of what happened. You were

the one driving, you had the amphetamines kicking around in your blood stream. I was asleep most of the time."

For a moment Tim thought he was going to have a repeat of the panic attack that had almost overwhelmed him earlier on in the afternoon.

"I was going to bring it up the other night," Sanjay said. "When we were with Imogen..."

"Don't."

"... And then I thought, perhaps not."

"Please, Sanjay. Don't. Ever."

"Anyway," Sanjay said. "He was a tramp."

What difference does that make? Tim thought. But those words seemed to offer a way out. Emotions gliding and slithering. The alcoholic euphoria, the memories of the day, the intoxication he had felt when he had the gun in his hand, the multiplying possibilities that seemed to be opening out in his mind as Sanjay talked. Tim's paranoia became transmuted into a smouldering excitement.

"That figure in the headlights," Sanjay said. "Who cared about him? At the end of the day. Who gave a damn?"

"Five minutes then?" The others shuffled out.

"Tim, Do you have a few moments?" his boss said as Tim stood up. "How long have you been with us now, Tim? Four, five years?"

His boss walked around his desk and sat on the edge of the table. He looked down at Tim.

"Have you got any thoughts about your future here? You need to consider it. You're one of the team now. There are opportunities. Here. Or in Zurich perhaps. Have you ever thought about where you want to be in another five years' time?"

A phone rang. His boss frowned. His secretary was waving an arm outside.

"I must take this. Think about it. Think about what I've just said."

Tim was thinking about something else. *Sanjay's right. We did come through it.*

*

Sanjay and Michael arrived back in London on separate flights a day after Tim. They met in Michael's office later in the afternoon.

"Where's Bernie?" Sanjay asked.

"I told him to stay on for a few days."

"Any problems?"

"Nothing he can't handle."

"It's gone well, hasn't it."

They sat at the table in the meeting room.

"I'm flying to Zurich," Michael said. "Monday morning. I'm meeting the Ivanovs."

"Why Zurich?"

"The twins wanted a neutral venue."

Michael began to discuss the weather in Switzerland. He paused.

"You know, I once took a holiday there with Angie and the kids."

Sanjay listened. It was unusual for Michael to speak of his wife these days.

He talked for a minute, then suddenly paused mid-sentence. "Have we got Tim on board yet?" he said.

Sanjay breathed in deeply.

"He's coming round. Slowly."

Michael doodled on a pad in front of him. "You two, how did you meet?"

"At university."

"Yeah, but... you know what I'm getting at. You became mates?"

Sanjay reflected. "I once thought he... people like him, they were important to know."

"What do you mean?"

129

"His father's part of the establishment. Old England. You know the kind of thing."

"So? So what?"

Sanjay laughed. "I was young. I once thought you needed to surround yourself by people like that." He shrugged. "So what? You're right, so what. Perhaps I just needed someone to go gambling with."

Michael began talking about the Alps again.

"About Tim," he said later. "We haven't got forever, you know."

Sanjay had missed his graduation ceremony. He had already found a job in Bristol managing the late night bar of a city-centre hotel. His parents had written one last imploring letter, asking if they could attend. They begged him for a picture, of him in university gown and mortarboard. But the thought of his parents, his grandparents, a ludicrous army of uncles and aunts and their families taking up a whole corner of the university reception hall, it was all laughable. He had not bothered to reply.

There were no formal goodbyes at the end of the last term when the results came through. Somehow the students he had come to know to a greater or lesser degree over the last three years assumed that they would all be meeting again, somehow, somewhere. Perhaps in a backpackers' hostel in Bangkok, or riding the surf on Bondi Beach. Or perhaps on the road in a motel outside Tucson when their newly formed band got its first break. Sanjay suspected otherwise. When they met again, if they met again, his colleagues would be discussing their fledgling careers as solicitors or TV executives in fashionable bars in Covent Garden and Soho. But whatever might have been, he found that he himself was not really that interested. He was good at his new job. He liked it. He was earning money, good money, some from his respectable position on the hotel's payroll, some from a range of other discretionary activities that he began to feel it was almost his duty to provide for his guests. A Korean businessman needing a girl for an evening, he knew whom to call. An Australian rock band, on tour in the area. He, Sanjay, knew where to find the fine-ground powder they needed for the next gig. He knew the people in town who could fix things. Yet few knew him. He moved, chameleon-like, within his own twilight world. He rose at eleven, went to bed at four. But it was a small world, one that suffocated, and on a weekend, eighteen months after he had started, he packed everything he owned, his suits, his papers, his address book, into the boot of the sports car he had just bought, and he moved to London.

Soon after, on the late shift at a casino where he worked as under-manager, he was called at one in the morning to deal with a disturbance. Two men, their ties undone, their balance unsteady, belching and shouting at the croupiers and the barman. A waitress stood nearby in tears.

"What's the problem here?" Sanjay said.

The two men didn't look at him.

"Who's the Paki?" one said.

"There's no need for that," the barman said, and the two men lunged. Everyone backed away.

Three men appeared at the other end of the bar. One man of medium height was flanked by two rather larger characters at his side. They walked up and then stood still, waiting. Sanjay could not recall afterwards whether anything else was said, or even needed saying. Within twenty seconds, the punks were sprawled out in the street. Later the three men had accompanied Sanjay to his office. The big guys stood silently by the door.

"I'm Michael Palmer," the other one said. "I guess I'm your boss."

They watched each other. Sanjay grappled with the moment, he tried to define it and its opportunity. The men at the door were still. He caught a whiff of violent history oozing from them.

"I'm getting good reports about you," Michael said. "I like the way you run this place."

Michael contacted him soon after and said he wanted to close the casino for an evening.

"Give the staff the day off. Be there yourself at midday," he said.

Sanjay asked him what it was all about.

"And don't bring your girlfriend."

That Sunday, Sanjay watched camera crews and lighting engineers organising themselves around the gaming tables.

"Do you know the difference between American and British porn?" Michael said to Sanjay.

Sanjay laughed.

"The American stuff's so slick. Ours is, well, *cosy* is the best word you could use. Women with bad teeth, men with drooping guts. We're going to change that."

He went off to speak to a man with a megaphone and a baseball cap.

"This location's perfect," he said to Sanjay as the action started. Two naked girls with all-over tans lay draped across a card table. A beautiful man in black tie and dinner jacket stood over them. He was wearing no trousers.

"If you want to make this stuff glossy and smart, you need location, you need storyline," he explained. "You need actors. With big pricks of course."

Michael told him how the business worked. A cottage industry, lots of small players, no resources to look for the prettiest girls, the best writers, the best equipment.

"We're going to change all that. We're taking over. All these small guys, they won't be able to compete. We'll play them off against each other. Divide and rule."

Divide and rule. Sanjay remembered the phrase in another context. In history lessons at school, the secret weapon of every empire builder. How successful the formula had been.

"But is it legal? Filming scenes like that here?" Sanjay had asked.

Michael looked at him for a moment.

"We'll do it first. We'll think of the consequences later."

And Sanjay had burst out laughing. Michael asked him what he thought was so funny. Sanjay said nothing, he did not want to seem to grovel. But what he had just heard seemed so right.

Sanjay had few friends. He floated between two worlds, the world of his boyhood, the world he had left behind and to which he could never return. And the other world, the *English* world, as he thought of it, the dry, gutless world he had seen at university, a world of gentle decline towards an insipid future, a job in the City and a cottage in Provence, a plump wife and two graceless children. His brother came to see him one day. He had become a dentist in Nottingham. He had seamlessly ascended from that first to the second world.

Sanjay knew his brother must have done a bit of detective work to track him down. He took him to a restaurant off Sloane Square. They talked about their respective careers, and then about their parents.

"They're not getting any younger, you know."

Sanjay had not meant to yawn at this point. It had been a long day. But he knew he would probably have to abandon his plan to take his brother to the casino for a nightcap.

His brother left early the next morning.

Soon he had forgotten about it. He concentrated on his job. He watched Michael, he watched as he reshaped the adult film industry, as he opened up his clubs across the country. He watched him carve out a future.

One evening, Michael told him to go back to school.

"Get yourself a masters. Business studies. Company'll pay. I read somewhere, this is what all the smartarses do in America. We need a few people with initials on the company notepaper."

They were with Mick, in the basement of a pub in East London. There were stacks of unmarked crates littered around the floor. Mick prised one open. Boxes inside, upmarket packaging, Swiss goods. Mick tossed a couple over to Sanjay. A watch. Some jewellery.

133

"Things are changing. We've got to move on from the old ways."

"What ways were they?"

Michael rooted around amongst the other boxes.

Sanjay did go back to school. He took an MBA. And as time went on he also found out about the old ways. About Michael's uncle, the old guard, the old personalities. Mick and the others began to open up. They told him about the things they had done in their youth. The scraps they had been in. And their stories had the siren appeal of all history, its ability to distil the pain of the past into a kind of footnote to its pleasures, to hint at an intensity of experience that was just gone from the present. To define an almost unbearable sense of loss, that when it all happened, he just wasn't there.

He told himself that he was sorry to see the passing of this old world, and one evening over a drink he said so to Michael.

"Don't be," Michael said. He talked about Spain, Europe. The East. "We're going to be pushing hard out there. New frontiers," he said. Sanjay thought about it and he realised that Michael would never quite lose his own way of doing things, his ability to work out the rules as he went along, his ability to invent the rules.

"There are going to be people out there who don't like us," Michael said. "People back here who want to shut us up. It may get rough."

People back here. Sanjay asked himself who these people were and he realised it was just about everyone he had ever known. The people back here, the ordinary and the good. The placid, the spent. Out there in the distance, something wild and unconstrained, the thrill of an unknown frontier. Something big, theirs to take on, to overcome. It would never be dull. He was looking forward to it.

eleven

She realised her phone had been stolen a hundred yards before their house. She stopped, felt her pockets, and opened up her bag to check again, but even as she fumbled amongst her things, a sense of contamination began to grow and fester inside her, and then she felt it over her clothes, her skin, her hair, the touch of fingers, the afterglow of a brush with something clinging and malignant, its intent so casually achieved. She closed her bag, strode forward two paces and began to run.

She pounded on the door.

"Imogen," Two faces. A smile, a proffered cheek. "How are you?"

"Juliet, I'm sorry." She pushed past her friend, her friend's boyfriend. "I need to call the police. Close the door, please, quick."

Three couples listened from the living room.

"I don't know. In the street perhaps. Or on the train."

Someone gently rubbed her shoulder.

"What colour was he? I resent that question... Anyway I never saw him... Of course my bag was zipped up... No. It's not at home or in my drawer... No... No... no, no. I said, no."

A long, unvarnished table, couscous, falafel, feta salad, bottles of Chilean wine scattered around. Prints of pre-Colombian ruins on the wall.

"Tim's busy tonight?"

She paused momentarily and moved the conversation along, her response deft, the act of lying so well rehearsed. She had said the same so often over the last few days. Perhaps he *was* busy, after all. She neither knew, nor had she even tested the possibility by inviting him that evening.

A call came through from Imogen's service provider to say that her mobile number had been cancelled. The guests talked burglaries, car theft, muggings.

"You just can't escape it."

"Let's change the subject."

"It's become so blatant."

"Imogen. Your new job. Are you taking it?"

"Tim must be so jealous. Is he going to join you?"

She sat in the loo. After a while she wondered whether the others might begin to notice. She waited one more minute, then got up, washed her hands, and stared at her face in the mirror. She frowned at what she saw and then thought of Lily. She opened her bag and looked inside. Her mascara. Lip colour. She looked at the array of cosmetics on the shelf beneath the mirror, and suppressed an urge to wipe the shelf clean, one sweep of her hand, everything in the bin, flushed away. *Was that what Tim secretly desired?* she thought. *The artifice, the surfaces.* She looked at herself again. Her face, her features, rounded, comforting. Bland. Too well known.

That disastrous weekend. She had not asked him about his trip inland on the Sunday. In part because of what he might tell her, in part because she feared what the act of telling might itself reveal. His reaction to those awful people. Or his lack of reaction. And Lily. Every man's eyes turning. The things Lily had confided, the things Imogen later found out. She had a sense of an acceleration of events around her, the kind of events from which she had been shielded all her life, or which she had read about and ignored, the kind of events which, by simple probability, would catch up with her one day. She felt that the theft of her phone was therefore entirely to be expected. And that the only way she could escape drowning in this tide that was swirling around her was to step right out of its path.

She opened her bag again. Her address book, it was still there. Old fashioned, hand written. She looked for Anton's number. It had to be somewhere.

*

Tim had been given the name of a restaurant. It took him a few minutes to find the place on the high street after he had parked his car. He was uneasy when he saw balloons and streamers pasted to the window, more so when he entered to find knots of weekend shoppers, families with children, a corner where a clown goofed around and half a dozen youngsters sat dreamily around him. He saw Pete sitting in a corner with his older daughter. Pete raised an arm.

Why here? Tim thought as he approached. Flowing blond hair, a toothy grin. *And why did he bring her?* She looked at him, and flashed a smile of such naked joy that he paused. For a moment he felt an impulse to walk straight out.

"You remember Jessica," Pete said as he sat down.

Tim smiled at her. She bounced up and down in her chair.

"We're about to order. It's pizzas and burgers, I'm afraid."

"Where's Janice?"

"At her mother's. With the other two."

Tim picked up a menu. *Just what is she doing here?* he thought.

"You OK?"

Tim looked up quickly. "Yeah. Sure."

"How's Imogen?"

She's preparing to leave. She's preparing to leave me.

"She's preparing to... she's going to be in the States for three months. She's on tour there."

"That's fantastic."

"Yeah."

"You're going to be on your own for a while?"

"Yep."

"Well, call me when she's away. We'll have to meet for a beer."

The waitress came over.

"Look, I'm not hungry," Tim said. "You go ahead. I'll just have coffee."

The menu had gaudy pictures of flame grills and whoppers and ice cream sundaes. The child's eyes widened. She pointed.

Pete ordered for her.

"Daddy, can I go see the clown?"

Her father hugged her. "Just stay where I can see you."

Her father stared after her as she rushed off.

"It's so hard these days," he said. "You have to be so careful."

There was a mirror on the wall behind Pete. As he talked, Tim began to scan the reflections of the people entering and leaving the restaurant, the people standing outside. He had started doing this a few days ago. The absurd notion had come to him that he was being followed. He had no evidence that he was. Another kind of logic told him he had no evidence that he was not.

"Pete, there's something I want to ask you," he said.

Pete caught the attention of a passing waiter. He asked for a beer.

"You want one?" he said. Tim shook his head.

"Pete, did you..."

But Pete looked away. "Sorry, Tim." He scanned the kids' play area. "Sorry."

Tim waited. And then Pete asked a question.

"Did you ever get to meet Sanjay?"

"I did."

"How was it?"

Tim sighed.

"Shouldn't I ask?"

Tim looked down.

"You were close at university, weren't you?" Pete said.

"Well, not at first."

"I thought..."

"I met lots of people."

Too many, perhaps. Tim looked at Pete and could not help but re-imagine the past. He remembered how he had found the freedom and chaos of student life so difficult to assimilate after the closeted, rule-bound world of his sixth form.

"We shared a few classes," Tim said.

"But you went out a lot together?"

"That was later."

In his second year. Tim still unsettled. One day his brother Julian had come to see him. He had taken one look at Tim's basement flat and its tiny kitchen, and then suggested they go out for dinner. They drove to Bristol, and sat in semi-darkness in an up-town restaurant with pretty waitresses and leather bound menus. As they had cocktails, Tim saw someone he recognised at the bar, an Indian guy, he occasionally attended the same stats tutorial. He looked at ease in well-cut navy jacket and white shirt. With a slight swagger for his brother, Tim excused himself to say hello. His friend asked him whether the two of them wished to join him at the casino next door.

"Are you kidding?" Julian had said when Tim returned and suggested it, and since Julian was paying for the meal and driving him back, he let it pass. But when he met Sanjay at lectures soon after he said he would like to try it out one day, and, a week later, after he had cashed in a dangerously large portion of his grant, they drove out to Bristol a second time in Sanjay's car.

Tim learnt quickly, he turned out to have a knack at the tables, and after a few early losses, he came out ahead. Sanjay appeared impressed, and Tim felt a kind of elation, especially when Sanjay began to ask him to join him whenever he went gambling in the months ahead. Sanjay, who seemed to float in different circles from those of most other students. Sanjay, who seemed partially disengaged from the academic world of the university.

"But we drifted apart," Tim said.

"Why was that?"

"I don't know," he said. But he did know, and he clenched and unclenched his fists under the table as he said it. Sanjay began to invite him to his parties, and he would drink, he would try the occasional coke or speed. He remembered the brief sense that he could hold his own with the brightest and the best.

The wispy euphoria. And that time, once, when they had done something bad.

"Are you going to keep in touch now?" Pete said.

"What?"

"With Sanjay."

And Tim realised, almost with a sense of yearning, that he needed to believe that Sanjay recognised the importance of what had happened to them both, and that he ascribed a value, of some kind, to their shared experience. He seemed instead to dismiss it. Tim could not understand how someone could do that.

"Perhaps. Perhaps we will."

He paused as cutlery and plates were laid out on the table.

"I'm sorry," Pete said. "I interrupted. There was something you were going to say.".

The food arrived. Pete called out and Jessica ran over.

"Daddy, I want to play with the other children."

"In a moment."

Father and daughter began to eat.

"We must meet up," Pete said. "Sanjay. You, me. The three of us."

Tim ordered another coffee. As the others ate, he talked about Imogen, her tour. He watched the child clear half her plate. She began to fret.

"Please, Daddy."

A kiss. "But be careful."

Gawky legs flying. Waiters twisting in their tracks. Her father watching.

Tim spoke. "Do you know someone called Michael Palmer?"

"No," Pete looked down at his french fries. "Was he at university with us?"

"But I thought..." Tim played with a sachet of sugar. "Are you still working on the crime desk?"

"Sure am."

Pete looked up. "*That* Michael Palmer?" He had a knife in his hand. "What do you want with him?"

"Just... just tell me what you know."

Pete thought for a while. He cut off a segment of his cheeseburger and considered it as it lay in front of him on his plate.

"He's not been much in the news recently. Though someone on the business desk was telling me he's up to his eyeballs in debt. Some foreign venture that's gone wrong."

He ate as he talked.

"I once had to dig up the dirt on him. It was one of the first big cases I covered when I joined the paper. Major fraud case. He was being sued by customs over unpaid VAT bills. But he got off, the whole things collapsed. He had a smart lawyer.

"You know he's Maltese? At least he was born there. I think he came to England when he was very young. *Palmier*. That's the family name. He anglicised it years later. He lived with his uncle. The old man had been in the merchant navy. Full British passport. Settled here after the war, was soon running small time stuff in London. Prostitution, protection. This was Britain in the fifties. It seems innocent and parochial today. Almost laughably so.

"His uncle did some time. Not much. The Soho Met were so corrupt you could get away with just about anything so long as it remained out of the public eye. But he moved up a gear in the sixties when the cops finally moved against some of his bigger rivals. A few years after that junior began to attract attention."

Pete's voice lowered. He looked across at the children playing. He took a sip of his beer.

"Car theft, joyriding. Later, armed robbery. The old pattern. The worst ones, it's the violence they become addicted to. The kid boxed when he was young. Apparently he was good. One day he got into a fight away from the ring. The story goes they broke both his arms. Career over."

Tim listened. He said nothing. In a way he had not heard anything that at some level he did not already know. He had a growing sense inside him that he understood the facts of

Michael's life with an immediacy that Pete could never appreciate. Like the difference between a soldier who has trained for action and one who has been under fire.

"The eighties were about drugs. Palmer was no exception. He got caught once. A tip-off, a major bust. But most of the charges got dropped, and he ended up doing just six months. That was the only time he ever went to jail. You know..."

A dry chuckle.

"I hear people talk about him now and they talk about the success of rehabilitation, the ones they turn round, the ones who go straight. This is bollocks. He just got smarter.

"After his uncle retired it looked as if he was going kosher. But it was the drugs money that funded the property deals and the media acquisitions. He's got a good head for business. He married shrewdly as well. Some dopey Surrey girl, the daughter of some old gent in the City. I gather there are a couple of kids. But he's been lucky in other things. Scotland Yard haven't got time for people like him these days, what with the Yardies, Al Qaeda, and the rest."

Children running all over the restaurant floor. The clown was packing away his things. Pete raised a finger and placed it against his lips.

Jessica deposited herself on the seat next to her father. She put her arms around his shoulders. Tim gazed at her. He frowned and checked his watch.

"He's done well for himself." Pete's voice was normal. "A pillar of society."

The waiter brought ice cream. Tim ordered the bill.

"Yes, he's a character, our Michael," Pete said. "You can tell me next time. What your interest in him is all about."

Sanjay had phoned Tim just about every day since they arrived back from Spain. They met after work for drinks. Their first meeting, Tim apologised for the things he may have said during that last night in the bars by the marina. But Sanjay, whose memory of it all seemed faultless and clear, brushed aside his concerns. He filled in the gaps in Tim's hungover recall of the evening. And Tim had the feeling that an idea, which had emerged out of a few chance conversations, was suddenly spinning right out of his imagination and his control, was acquiring a substance and a kind of inevitability he could no longer reverse. A tangibility, which, under Sanjay's relentless probing, began to take on a sharp focus.

Probing. *How? Why? When?*

"I can't tell you these things," Tim protested. "I could lose my job."

"They're just *what ifs*," Sanjay said. "I'm just intrigued." His tone mock-naïve. "I'm just letting my imagination run."

They drank beer. Sanjay talked.

"To write oneself a cheque for a few million dollars. How would one do it? How would you hide it?"

"Hide it? From whom?"

"You tell me. From your systems, your databases, your auditors."

And then.

"Which bank would you use? And where? Switzerland? South America?"

A pause. Later.

"Which one? And why? And how long before you could gain access to the cash?"

Tim had looked around nervously at the other drinkers. "You seem to have it all worked out," he said.

"No I don't. But I think you have."

He sensed that Imogen was ignoring him more and more. She was out when he was in, in when he was out. She said she had not yet made up her mind about the tour, but she began to practise incessantly, she spent evenings with colleagues going over repertoire. Some nights she rang late to say she would be staying over and not coming home, and then she stopped bothering to do even that.

One afternoon, as he came home early from work, he found her in the bedroom packing bags. In the living room there was a man whom she introduced as Anton. She asked the man to wait outside.

"You've decided, haven't you?" Tim said. "You're going."

She was silent. She continued collecting her things.

"Imogen, we have to talk. Perhaps not tonight, if you're going out. Tomorrow..."

She turned on him. "Why not tonight? Why not now?"

"What about...?" Tim pointed a thumb towards the door.

"He can leave."

"I can't do it. Not tonight."

"Why not."

"I'm..."

"Sanjay. You're meeting Sanjay. Tim, what's got into you? What is it with him? Are you blind? How have you let things come to this?"

He lost his temper. He swore, he told her she was selfish, she did not make an effort with his friends. He told her she could not bear people who were different. People from other backgrounds, people with other types of goals. He shouted, and then something flipped inside him, and a need to defend, to evade, to stall, became washed away in a sudden and luscious *why-not?* that began to work its way into his mind, the possibility that distance, separation, might enable him to live without this constant call on his motives. To live, at ease, with his new inner life, his own secret past. He was quiet.

Imogen had turned away. She was fidgeting with her bags. She reached for a box of tissues.

"Tim, you're living in a dream world," she said softly. She zipped up her bag. "That afternoon, when you drove into the hills. I went out with Lily. She talked. She talked and talked. About her acting, her modelling, about her plans, how Sanjay had promised her this and that, how..."

She sat down on the bed, wiped her eyes. Then she spoke quietly.

"She has a website. It's all fantasy. Tim, she's a prostitute. That's the reality. That's Sanjay's world. You could have her if you wanted. Perhaps you have. For three hundred pounds an hour."

Imogen left fifteen minutes later. The next day she phoned him to say that she would be spending the remaining few weeks before the tour with a friend. A violinist. It would be better, she needed to focus on her music. She would stop by some time to collect the last of her things.

Tim drifted. In the evenings he went to restaurants on his own with a book. He spoke to Sanjay on his mobile phone. They discussed theoreticals, possibilities. There were no names, neither of companies nor people. They spoke of As or Bs or Cs, Xs and Ys. Once, nine o'clock at night, as he sat in a corner, the only customer in a local Indian restaurant, he was hooked into a conference call with Alec. For ninety minutes they went through scenarios, Tim sensed him diagramming his questions, constructing hypothetical boxes and arrows and walkthroughs. He started at the end and worked back; he started at the beginning and they went forward. At each fork in the flow he paused and waited for Tim to fill in the gaps. *You say this will happen, why? And after that? What next? Why? How?* Tim told himself the things they were discussing were just speculation. Of only academic interest. *I have done nothing*, he told himself. *I have thought things, I have imagined things, but I have done nothing.*

It is no crime to think.

One evening Bernie arrived at his flat unannounced, and took him for a drive. After an hour they stopped at a pub on a side road somewhere on the way to Greenwich. It was dingy and badly lit. They sat at the bar where an elderly couple served drinks with excruciating slowness. Bernie called them Ma and Pa.

"Your parents?" Tim said.

"Nah. Everyone calls them that."

Bernie made introductions. They fussed and flapped. *Such a nice looking young man,* the old lady muttered.

The bar-room was quiet except for crackly hits from the fifties which belted out when the juke-box kicked into sporadic motion. Tim and Bernie sat silently on stools, drinking pints of light and bitter.

There were pictures on the wall, black and white, men with slicked back hair and sharp looking suits. Thin lapels, thinner ties.

"That's Michael's uncle," Bernie said, pointing.

"That's me," he said, pointing again, and this time, Tim got down to take a closer look. He saw a young man, a taut body, big-boned, athletic. In army fatigues. Another. Fleshy, uncomfortable in too-tight jeans and leather jacket.

Tim said later, "I killed a man once. I ran him down. I didn't mean to. But I did. I killed him."

And Bernie ordered crisps and peanuts with the next round.

He drank quickly, two pints for each one of Tim's. He had a scotch just before they said goodbye and piled back into his monster four-wheel drive. They drove fast, through shortcuts and side roads that Tim did not know, yet suddenly they would emerge, from some unpredicted angle, into the lights and the bustle of a square or a roundabout that Tim recognised. Elephant and Castle, Waterloo. Then off again, a murky trawl through one-way streets, tiny mews, dead-ends that miraculously and despite the road signs opened out onto busy streets. They were south of the river. No. North. Parliament Square, The Mall. Tim could not recall when or where they had crossed. Or how. Bernie pressed down on the accelerator. They passed over the water again. Vauxhall, Battersea. There were flashing lights behind them. Bernie slowed, the police van overtook and disappeared off down a junction to the left. But Tim was lost again. He looked at the streets, the shops, the houses, the parks around them, and said to himself, *Where am I?* As if plunged into a new place, a different city, built from the template of the

London that appeared on the maps he owned, but bearing only a faint and fading resemblance to the town that he knew and had lived in. Chelsea Harbour, King's Road. This new world, this new London, this would be his home from now on, this strange netherworld, with trapdoors and gateways into the regular city in which he used to spend all his hours, but from which he now withdrew to discover his real life, his real friends, his real motivation, his true desires. They stopped at a bar where Africans drank beer from bottles whose labels he could not decipher and where plants with strange leaves were traded and then chewed by men who became still and glassy-eyed. They bought pastries of intoxicating sweetness at a brightly lit café where men smoked long pipes and argued and gestured and where women were absent. They saw ladies under broken streetlamps, costumed and plumed, teetering on high heels, and Bernie slowed and told Tim to stop him if he saw something he liked. And Tim said to Bernie, *Where am I?* and Bernie turned a corner and Tim recognised his street, he saw his flat at the end of the terrace.

"You're home," Bernie said. "We're back."

He walked with Sanjay. He had just finished work. They were looking for a bar.

"Sanjay, you said something to me once."

"What's that?"

"About telling Imogen."

"Telling her what?"

"About what happened to us. At university."

The after-work crowds on the streets gave them anonymity. They walked slowly.

"Did I?"

"She's left."

"Perhaps that's for the best."

Tim was silent for a few seconds. "I wonder."

"Tim. You're with us now. It's between just you and me."

twelve

Tim sat on his bed with old letters and photographs scattered around him. Mementoes of his mother.

He had arranged to meet his brother the following evening. He flipped through pictures and postcards and wondered what he would ask him.

Brian had rung Tim at work. He was coming down from Cambridge the next day, and suggested they catch up. Tim told him he already had another engagement, but his brother was insistent.

"I have to be back the following morning," he said. "What's there so important in your diary?"

That's my business, Tim thought.

"It's tomorrow or not at all," Brian said. "Can't you re-schedule?"

But Tim was glad now that he had made time. There were some things he wanted to discuss.

He picked up the sketch of his mother, the drawing the American had sent him after she died, and placed it next to an old photograph. His mother, a young woman, before he was born. She looked good. As a young woman. In her maturity as well. An idealised view? He could never know, he could not see through the eyes of the artist. The view was not his own. It was that of a friend. Or perhaps a lover.

What would you do? he thought as he looked at the pictures. *If you were in my position.*

He looked at her.

Why do we act? Why do we do the things that we do?

He thought.

Why do I act? Why do I behave as I do?

I act, because.

I act, because of a sense of morality.

What morality? He read the question in the face looking out at him. *And even if you do have a sense of morality, how many actions in your day are dictated by it?* He smiled to himself. *Name one thing, a single thing you have done today, yesterday, the day before, where you made one choice over another, because you knew it was the right thing to do.*

I act, out of habit.

I act, to be the same.

I act, to be different.

Once I did something bad. I don't know why.

I act out of confusion.

I act out of fear.

I do not lie or cheat or harm.

I act, because there are rules.

I do not steal.

I act, because I am afraid to break the rules.

For a woman like me, he read from her last letter once more, *living in the shadow of a personality like your father... I suddenly found that when my chance came, I had to take it.*

I act, because I don't know how to break the rules.

So I took a gamble.

But suddenly you found out.

Tim waited in the lounge of the hotel where Brian was staying. Groups of businessmen and a few business-women sat at the tables. They were tooled up with laptops and mobiles, they doodled on PDAs, they were wireless, they were bluetooth enabled. They downloaded, they emailed, they networked. They talked jargon. They talked gibberish.

Brian appeared in his suit.

"Let's not stay," Tim said. "I have my car."

Fifteen minutes later they sat in a pub with pints of beer in front of them. They talked. About Brian's new life as a married man, about Cambridge.

"How's the job?" Brian asked.

"It's fine."

Brian asked about Imogen. Tim explained she was going away for a while.

"You're both well?"

"Of course."

Brian fidgeted. "Have you had any more thoughts? About what I said?"

"What was that?"

Brian scratched his head. "Your future. Perhaps a future out of London."

Tim looked away for a few moments.

"Are you going to stay here all your life?" Brian said.

"Why are you asking me all this? Now?"

"We're... You. Me. Julian. Dad. We're family."

"Suppose I want to stay?"

"For what?"

"Perhaps something's come my way."

"Really?" Brian raised his glass. "That's great news. Something good I hope." He reached across and patted Tim on the shoulder. "So. Tell me."

"Not just yet."

"Not even a hint?"

Tim smiled.

"Nothing dodgy, I hope," Brian joked.

"Here. Let me get some more beers." Tim got up to go to the bar. As he waited for the drinks to be served, he thought about the letter his mother had written him. *For a woman like me, living my life in the shadow of a personality like your father, someone so sure of himself and everything.* He wondered whether Brian had ever read those words.

He set the drinks down on the table. "Brian, can I ask you something?"

His brother sipped his beer. "Fire away."

"When Mum died. When you went to the States to sort out her affairs. What was it like?"

Brian was silent for a few moments. "Why are you asking this?"

"Because I never have."

"Why now?" And then, more quietly. "It wasn't easy."

"What wasn't?"

"It was all very strange."

"You were her son .How could it be strange?"

"Julian and I weren't really very welcome there."

"Where?"

"This place where she had been staying."

"What was it like?"

"I don't know. A huge house. All women. A few kids. It was weird."

"Did you meet Grace?"

"Who? Yeah. Yes, we did. It's such a long time ago."

"She was a painter?"

"I don't know. She may have been. They all pretended they were artistic. New age nonsense."

"How do you know it was nonsense? She may have been good."

"Why do you care? What's it to us?"

"I need to know, Brian. It's our last connection to her. I need to know, why she was there, what the place gave her that she needed."

"What she needed? What about us? What about Dad? What about you? You were still a boy. You know, they didn't like us. They blamed Dad. And Julian and me. But it was precisely the opposite. She ran out on us. All of us. Without a word, without any warning."

"She had her reasons."

"But... Tim, this is not the way you do things. You talk. You discuss things, you compromise. That's the way it's done in our family."

Tim gulped his beer.

"Did you bring anything back? Letters, or pictures?"

"There were a few things. We gave them to Dad. He told us to do what we wanted with them. They're hidden away somewhere."

"I'd like to see them."

"Remind me. Next time."

Tim rose, empty glass in hand. Brian said he'd had enough. Tim went to the bar.

Back at the table he drank on his own.

"You know, Brian, you never came to visit me at university."

Brian sniffed. "You're sure raking over old times."

"But it's true. Julian did. Once."

"You were hardly very communicative yourself." His brother stared at him.

Tim knew Brian was right. He laughed.

"Do you know what my first day was like?"

His father had driven him down on that day of the first term. After dropping off bags at the hall of residence, they had gone for tea in town. Standing on the pavement afterwards, his father had gazed around him with a dour look, sniffed the air, and then, after a quick *Good Luck*, left Tim with a brisk wave and an envelope full of twenty pound notes. Tim kept his distance from then on. A few letters, one or two phone calls. He remembered, once, in the second term, he was called in by his tutor who spent half an hour telling him how much he respected his father's work and how lucky he was to live with a man of such immense talent.

"They all thought so much of Dad. I sometimes found it a bit hard. I remember wondering whether I was doing the right course. Whether to try something else, I might have been a bit more anonymous."

He might also have escaped from the geeks and dreary introverts he was surrounded by in his department. He recalled parties given by the self-assured young men and women he envied so much from across the cultural divide. Lawyers, linguists, playwrights. He recalled one night when he drank half a bottle of scotch and for once the blend of chemicals in his blood found a perfect balance and he felt a euphoria that did not dull his senses, he felt as smart and as witty as anyone else there, and he spent the night cuddling up with an older lady who said she was married but who said also he was cute and sexy. For a while after that he drank to excess every time he went out, he looked for that exquisite moment of release when he could leave the baggage of his conscience and personality behind him and walk up to anyone and everyone and win them over with a quip and a smile, but it became murky and debased somehow and he found he ended up instead asleep on a chair, or slurring and leering at the people he so wanted to impress.

"Do you still keep in touch with any of your old college friends?" Brian asked.

"One or two."

"Are you close?"

"Not really."

Brian had to leave early. As they walked out the door, Tim fished his car keys out of his pocket. He heard his brother clearing his throat behind him.

"Um. Tim."

"What's up?"

"Let's get a cab."

"Nonsense. I'll drive you."

His brother coughed again. "How much have you had this evening?"

"Not much. I'm OK."

They walked on. After a few moments Brian stopped.

"Tim. I'm telling you, think again."

"Brian. What's up?"

Brian looked at him under the streetlights. "I can't. I'm sorry."

Tim shrugged. "Fine. I'll drive. You take a taxi."

Tim turned and walked towards his car. Brian stayed where he was.

"Tim," he called out. He took out his mobile phone. "Tim, listen to me."

He stopped. Brian's voice boomed across the parking lot.

"I'm having a supper party this Saturday. The chief constable is coming. His wife and Sarah are both governors on the local school board. The four of us play golf together."

Tim turned. "What the hell does that have to do with anything?"

Brian stood there with his phone in his hand.

"Fuck you, Brian."

Tim marched over to his car and got in the driver's seat. He put the key in the ignition. He watched his brother in the mirror as he walked round to the back of the car.

Fuck you, he thought. He tried to make a calculation. Would he do it? Would the local cops give a damn? Here in London, on a busy night. He sat there. His brother waited. Tim sat in his car and calculated.

Tim met Sanjay at the casino. Sanjay asked him whether he wanted to gamble. He said that he didn't. After a while, Sanjay took him to his office and poured him a scotch. They watched the closed circuit TV coverage of the action at the tables.

Tim sat thinking of his brothers, and he thought of his future, of career paths and pay rises, of pension provisions and retirement homes. Of his unborn children, their education. Their orthodontics, their first cars, their dowries. He thought of his father, his powers fading, but his life complete with its fulfilments and accomplishments strung out like a thread of pearls shining in the night. Would they plan something similar for him, that he might look back at the end of his life in the same way? Tim looked to his own future, and the decisions he would have to make, the crises he would he have to resolve. His career, a long struggle ahead, with its peaks and hoped for successes, the status it would one day confer on him in the world that his father had created and his brothers now sustained. And perhaps his partner at his side, Imogen or some other, her children at his feet. The web of duties and responsibilities these people had created and which they now asked him to enter and extend, this web that now lay suspended in space ahead of him, each knot, each join of its strands, some hurdle that he would one day have to face. And the prospect suddenly terrified him, every knot lay like some cold stone in his bladder, some dead weight, his lot to carry about with him as he negotiated his slow way forward towards his future, his old age, his death.

After five minutes, there was a knock on the door and Michael walked in. He locked the door behind him. Tim observed Michael, staring at the screens on the wall, his look untroubled, serene, rooted in the present, in the here and now, in the achievable, in the exigencies of the moment he now experienced. This present moment, with its unpredictability and possibilities. Had he ever felt as carefree? And Tim remembered one distant night in Oxford, he and Sanjay crashing a college ball, the speed and the cocaine in his blood, and the curious rapture that he had felt for a few hours, when the cocktail of drugs had gently loosened, and then dissolved, one after the other, each knot in his stomach, the future revealed for once for what it was, a set of mere possibilities, to be relished or ignored as one preferred, of as much or as little importance as one chose to give to it.

Free me from the future, Tim thought. *Ask me whatever you want, but give me that in return.*

The three of them sat silently for a few seconds. Then Michael looked at Sanjay. Sanjay nodded and the two of them looked at Tim.

"There's something you want from me?" Tim said.

Sanjay turned to Michael.

We would like you to come and work for us.

We would like you to do a job for us.

We would like you to steal some money.

We would like you to steal twenty million dollars.

155

We would like you to steal twenty million dollars from the company you work for.

We will help you.

We will help you get away.

We will cover your tracks.

We need your expertise.

We need your knowledge and skill.

We will pay you.

We will pay you half a million quid.

We will pay you half a million quid for fifteen minutes' work.

We will look after you.

We will take care of you.

Sanjay looked at Tim.

"Say yes," he said. "It will be fun."

Part II

thirteen

On the first of August Tim Scott handed in his resignation.

His boss asked him what his reasons were. Tim said he wanted to spend some time off, travelling perhaps. He explained that his girlfriend was overseas. His boss said he was sad to see him go. He had four weeks' notice to serve. They agreed that his last day would be the twenty-ninth of the same month.

His boss told him to plan a handover schedule. He asked him to ensure that his work was fully documented. Tim said he might come in one or two Saturday mornings before he left to clear out the backlog.

It was Friday, and because the company always did the same on the first Friday of each month there was a fire drill at three in the afternoon. All staff, except certain senior company employees including the chief security officer, were required to assemble on the pavement outside and wait for their names to be called by designated wardens.

On Saturday the ninth, Tim came in to the office. There were two other staff from his department on weekend shift, carrying out maintenance work. They grunted hellos and then ignored him. He spent half an hour preparing some notes on projects he had worked on, and then logged on to one of the development servers. It was new. They had taken delivery of the box just months before. But it ran a proprietary operating system that had evolved out of research done in NASA labs in the seventies, it ran hierarchical databases and COBOL programs. Machines like these had once been the computing workhorses for a host of businesses. But as Open Systems were adopted across the industry in the nineties and as the internet began to take hold, it became apparent that its future was limited. The race was on for Tim's department to transport the applications on these machines to the Linux servers with their relational databases and their object-based programming tools.

That morning Tim began to look at the various accounts on the machine, and in particular those belonging to employees who had left the company. Bob Haldane, fired three months ago. Jane Smith, who moved to New Zealand a month before that. Paul Parfitt. Tim recalled he had found a better job in the City last year. For each, Tim listed the residual contents of their home directories. He paused at the last of them. He entered a command, and altered his default home area. He examined the files that Paul Parfitt had left. A few test scripts. A couple of games programs. Junk. Memory space, anonymous, forgotten. He began to type. He created a new file which he named x1, and started writing code.

On Thursday the fourteenth, four contract cleaners left Tim's office building at nine o'clock at night. Two of the men were Nigerian, the other two from eastern Europe. One of the Nigerians had a driving licence, and he drove the company van. He dropped off two of the men. As he drove through a side street in Stockwell in south London, a woman ran out into the road. The driver slowed. A thump, a sudden movement to the left. A man was running alongside. He grabbed at the door handle, pulled it open, and dragged out the passenger. A scream, a screech of brakes. Another man, his face hidden under a hood, jumped in from the right. He leaned into the driver and placed a blade at his throat. He grabbed the wheel. The van scraped against a metal waste container, and the engine stalled. The driver edged towards the passenger side, hands raised. He got out as the van came to a halt. He saw his friend lying on the pavement being kicked in the stomach. The two of them were told to take off their company jackets and trousers, and hand over wallets and keys. The hijackers got into the van and drove off. The cleaners sat half-naked in a heap at the side of the road.

Three days later the van was recovered by the police, vandalised and empty. They were at a loss to explain the theft of uniforms, tools, business cards. The company, embarrassed, said nothing to its clients.

During the week of the eighteenth to the twenty-second, Tim stayed late each night. He said to his colleagues that he was tidying up loose ends. He waited as they trickled out. Alone, he logged in and reset his home directory to that of Paul Parfitt. He coded. Program after program. Files x1 to x12.

He had prepared a small test database. At the start of each evening he re-created it from scratch with one of his scripts. Hours later, as he prepared to leave, he copied his scripts to diskette, and then erased the lot from the server.

On Saturday the twenty-third, he came in at eight in the morning. He carried out final testing. He created one more program which, when run, would delete the object and source versions of files x1 to x12. He tidied up. He was ready.

On Wednesday the twentieth, a man booked in to a hotel in Caracas, Venezuela. He used an Australian passport. It was early morning. Later, speaking accented Spanish, he visited the *Banco de Comercio y Crédito*, downtown in the financial district. There he opened an account, this time presenting a Panamanian passport. Citing a new multilateral free trade agreement between fourteen Central and South American states, the bank's commercial development manager opened the account immediately and without further checks on identity. The man deposited one thousand US dollars in cash.

When asked what business he was in, he said Oil. He said he hoped to be able to make a substantial deposit within the next few weeks. He assured the bank manager that there would be a generous reward if the transaction went through smoothly.

The man then walked one block to the *Banco Nacional de Caracas*. There he opened a second account, again with a deposit of one thousand US dollars.

The following day he left the country and flew to the British Virgin Islands in the Caribbean. He located the head offices of the *Traders & Merchants Bank (TMB)*, and opened a third account, this time using a British passport as a guarantee of identity.

On Wednesday the twenty-seventh, Tim visited the treasury staff on the third floor. The head of the department, a large lady in her forties, with a screeching voice and what was regarded by Tim's colleagues as an almost unbearable swagger and self confidence, teased him about what he was up to. She asked if it was girlfriend trouble. Someone told him that Jakob, their contact at the bank in Switzerland, with whom Tim had always maintained a good working relationship, wished him well.

On Friday afternoon he walked around the office with his camera. He said goodbye to people with whom he had worked, he took their pictures. They told him to keep in touch. He took a company phone list. Fixed and mobile. Later he would underline some key numbers in red. That evening he took his colleagues in the department out to the pub. They gave him a card. There had been a whip-round, and someone presented him with an ipod. He bought rounds of drinks.

He ended up with a few diehards at a curry house. At midnight, they said their goodbyes. As he left the restaurant he texted Sanjay. At five past midnight a black limousine cruised by and Tim got in.

He had left the company.

On Monday the first of September, Tim stopped shaving.

On Wednesday, he went round to a warehouse where Michael

and Bernie were waiting. There was a third man. They led Tim to a corner where there was a sink and a mirror and a chair. Tim sat down. The man tied a smock around his shoulders, and then connected up an electric hair trimmer. Tim watched in the mirror as his blond hair disappeared before his eyes. The man opened a carryall he had with him. He extracted half a dozen dark wigs. He fitted each of them in turn over Tim's scalp. Afterwards he looked at Michael, and he picked up the third one again, which he placed on Tim's head a second time. They nodded to each other.

The man opened a bag and produced a tray of spectacles. He made Tim try them one after the other. The lenses were without prescription. Tim glared at himself in the mirror. At the third the man placed a hand on Tim's shoulder.

He placed a number of tubes on a table. He opened the first and squeezed out some brownish-beige goo. He began to rub it into Tim's pale cheeks, and then some darker stuff into his stubble. The man looked at him for a second in the mirror. He rubbed in some more.

Later they examined pictures of the chief security officer that Tim had taken. He had reddish hair and a beard. He did not wear glasses.

On Friday the fifth of September at nine in the morning, Michael came up to Tim and shook his hand. *Just remember*, he said. *Have fun.*

At two-thirty in the afternoon, four men piled out of a van and went through the doors of Tim's office building. They were dressed in green overalls, with the label *Office Cleaning Ltd* on their backs. They signed themselves in at the ground floor, and then took a lift up to the first. There was a reception area. The leader of the men, a huge fellow, bald, walked up to the desk and leaned over it. The two men behind him were black. A fourth man, straggling at the back, Greek perhaps, or Turkish, had dark hair, week old stubble, and thick-frame glasses. The big man spoke to the receptionist. An accent, east European. He said they had essential cleaning work to do on the third floor. He showed her documents, ID cards. He asked if they could go up, he said he knew the way. She said she did not know anything about this, and called the office general manager. Five minutes later a flustered looking man with patches of sweat under his arms barged his way out of the lift.

"What's all this, then?" He looked at their papers. The men were silent.

"Wait here. I'm going to check this out with your office." He pulled out a mobile, but before he could dial it rang.

He scratched his head and muttered. "Damn. And there's the fire drill at three." He turned away from them.

"Yeah... yeah... OK." He flipped his phone shut. It rang again. It would ring continually for ten minutes. He shouted across. "Jane. Just sign 'em in, will you."

At two forty-five the four men ascended by lift to the third floor. At two fifty they knocked on the doors of the lavatories in the hallway by the swing doors outside the offices. They waited until everyone was out, and then placed a sign outside. *Out of Order. Repairs in Progress.* Inside, they unzipped holdalls, they took out toolboxes and briefcases. Two of them banged hammers against pipes. One started whistling loudly.

At three o'clock an alarm went. The four men heard a loud male voice, instructions to staff to tidy up and leave the office straight away, to use the stairs not the lifts. Swirling murmurs of people chattering, fire doors being opened. Footsteps fading. Then dying. Calm. The four men took out pollution masks. The big man pulled out a gas canister and opened the stopcock. An almost subliminal stench began to permeate through the lavatories. The fourth man, slow to don his protective mask, felt his throat gagging for a second. The big man looked out the door. The corridor was empty. He positioned the canister by the door to keep it open, and then walked through the swing doors into the treasury department.

How many of them will stay behind?

Tim had sat in a dark room two weeks before with Michael, Bernie and Alec.

Think, Tim, think.

Three, perhaps four. The head of security. The head of trading operations. One or two traders if they have a critical deal going.

He walked along the open plan office scanning to left and right. The chief security officer was checking the meeting rooms along the side. He stopped to watch the big man in his tight fitting uniform. He stared at the thing pressed to his face. Then he began to cough.

"Jesus. What the hell."

He coughed again, and then again.

"Sorry. Sorry. There is big problem. We fix it soon."

The head of oil trading ran out of his room clutching his stomach. He sneezed into a handkerchief. He struggled to stand upright.

"What the fuck's going on?"

There was one trader at his desk, coughing into his phone. He put the phone down and rushed from the room, his mobile in his hand, dialling as he ran. His boss followed him.

"Sorry. Sorry. We spill chemical. We fix. Five minutes. Is all. We fix fast."

The security officer pointed to the exit at the far end. He stumbled towards it. The big man followed. They walked through. As the door closed he began to breathe more easily.

"What in God's name is it?"

"Is cleaning chemical. We spill. We clean up. Fast."

"Jesus! You better. You incompetent fuckwits."

They walked back in again. There was no-one else there, the others had left.

"Here. Give me that." He grabbed the big man's mask. He walked the length of the office, and locked the doors to each of the rooms alongside. Back at the swing doors by the lavatories he handed back the mask. He coughed a few times. He held his nose.

"Right. You lot. Out of here. Follow me."

Outside in the hallway, the big man stopped. He spoke through his mask. "But. Is dangerous. We stay. We fix it."

He and two of his colleagues stood by, heads down. The security officer raised a finger and shook it silently. He was red with rage. He said nothing. Suddenly he was sick. He steadied himself on a railing for a second, handkerchief in hand, and then ran down the flight of stairs. The big man strode up to the lavatories and knocked on the door. The last of the cleaners came out. He had taken off his overalls. He had a suit underneath. He had also taken off his spectacles. His hair and stubble were a different colour, they had a reddish tint. A careful eye might have noticed the thing he gripped between his teeth. All four looked at each other for a moment. Then the big man pushed the man in the suit, and after him one other, through into the treasury department offices.

He handed a cosh to the remaining black man, and started whispering to him. Then he stopped.

"Oy. You lot." Two men, grey-haired, moustaches, in uniforms and peaked caps. On the stairs below, hands over their mouths. "Down here."

Do they have security cameras, Tim?

Outside. Not inside the offices.

How do you know? Management may have put them in secretly. To spy on staff. Bernie?

They wouldn't be high definition. Faces will be blurred. The wigs and make up should do us fine.

Through the doors, one of the cleaners, the black man, began to walk around the office. He checked jackets on coat-hangers, or on the backs of chairs. He examined pockets, opened drawers. He carried a bin-liner and threw stuff into it. Cheque books, watches, diaries, calculators. At the same time a man who looked curiously like the chief security officer walked up to one of the offices with a huge bunch of keys in his hand. He began to try the keys one after the other. He seemed to fumble.

Outside, the big man hesitated.

"Down here. Or we call the police."

He walked to the swing doors, peered into the offices and beckoned.

The cleaner with the bin-liner was standing next to the man in the suit. He took his keys away, bent to his knees and put his ears to the lock. He tried again. The door swung open. Then he rushed out into the hallway. Three cleaners began to descend the stairs slowly.

"Is that all of you?"

The big man took a chance.

"Yes."

Do we have to use a terminal in that room?

We must. They have dedicated router and comms links in there.

The man in the suit stood alone at the door. He walked in and sat at a desk. The terminal was logged off. He pressed return and was prompted for a username and password. He typed quickly, as if he had entered them many times before. He knew them by heart. He knew all the passwords by heart; he had set them all up on the database.

Tim moved fast. He pulled out a sheet of paper from his pocket.

He pulled down a screen for entering bank details, entered in the name, address, international sort code and other details for the *Banco de Comercio y Crédito* in Caracas. He pressed the enter button. A new serial number was assigned to the bank record.

Tim, what about unique serial numbers? If we delete the records we're creating afterwards, there will be gaps in the sequence numbers.

Alec passed his fingers through his hair.

Tell you what. Create the records, transmit them. Then change the details so that they are an exact copy of the transaction with the serial number one less. An honest mistake. Data entered in twice.

Tim opened a new window and logged on to the development machine. He pulled a diskette from his pocket and uploaded a set of files, then reset his logon account to be that of Paul Parfitt, and ran a script to compile a series of programs, with the names x1 to x12. He copied them over to an area on the live machine.

He returned to the payments system and looked at the number of transactions due to be transferred to the bank in Zurich. There were five. One was for two and a half million dollars, a second for a million and a quarter. The others were under a million. The target banks were Swiss, Japanese and American.

He ran program x1. The routine switched a status flag on the five payments from 'ready' to 'pending'.

He then pressed a button to go to the 'create payment' screen.

He breathed in and closed his eyes. *Have fun.* Who had said that? *Take a gamble.* Or that? *People do what they do, because they can.*

He began to enter in data.

The payee. The payee's account number. The bank. The bank's international sort code. Country, city. Caracas. The date. The amount. Twenty million dollars. *Twenty million dollars.* Comments and instructions. *Transfer funds with immediate effect. No mention of company or payee names.*

There was a button, *Press to calculate test code number*. He pressed. The code 127-DHH-2637-USD-9 appeared on the screen, appended to the record data. The code to authenticate the payment, the code that would guarantee the transfer of funds.

He stared at the code. *Jakob, you are going to calculate the precise same code. Aren't you? Please.*

He exited from the screen back to the menu.

There was a button which said *Send payments*. He paused over it. The skin of his finger brushed against the plastic, and then, as in a blueprint or wiring diagram, he saw in his mind the consequences, the causes and effects, the technology firing off, the lives of hundreds changing, the decisions, political, financial, human, all spinning and diverging off from this one act, this simple act of connecting metal plate to plate. There was a clock on the wall. He watched the second hand.

Tim's finger hovered.

One floor below, three cleaners fidgeted on the bottom step. The guards watched them. And then one of them got up and headed for the lavatory. The big man got up slowly. He whispered to one of the others, *Stall them. Upstairs, two minutes. No more*. He began to creep up the stairway.

Tim, how long will we have?
Fifteen minutes tops.
Assume twelve. Can we do it?

The big man loped into the room. He put an arm on Tim's shoulder.

Tim pressed down.

An automated sequence of actions began to take place on the screen. A list of transactions due to be transmitted popped up. There was just one. Total value. Twenty million dollars. Press to accept. He accepted. Progress warnings flashed in front of him.

Communication line being established.
Line now available.
Data reformatted.
Data transmitted.
Receipt signal awaited.
Receipt signal received.
Transmission complete.
Press accept to return to main menu.

Tim looked up at the big man. Tim's hands shook. He tried to give a thumbs up. The big man patted him on the shoulder again and left the room.

Tim began to run programs x2 to x12.

Program x2 altered the new bank record. It became an exact copy of another record entered just yesterday, a record for a bank in Osaka. It took three seconds to load and run.

x3 altered the payment record. It became a copy, a copy of a payment for seven hundred and fifty thousand pounds transmitted the day before at 11.30 am, test code 114-HJO-7334-USD-4. Identical. Except for a sequence number. Except it had test code 127-HJO-7334-USD-4. Except the status was cancelled.

x4 altered the status of the five 'pending' records back to 'ready'.

x5 altered the log of test code numbers generated.

x6 deleted the last record of the log of payment transmissions.

x7 reversed out the amount of twenty million dollars from the payments system P&L.

x8 deleted the last entries of the batch input file which, at the end of the working day, would be interfaced to the corporate accounting system.

x9 deleted all records on the login/logout logging file that had been created in the last fifteen minutes.

x10 reset all 'last update' data on critical tables to be half an hour earlier.

x11 did a remote access on to the router and deleted the log of the transmission.

x12. Files, records, entries. Purged.

Finally. There was a transaction log file that recorded changes to key datafiles. It was editable. If you knew the password. Tim knew the password. He found the file, opened it. He paged down to the last record. Deleted the last eight entries.

He then deleted programs x1 to x12.

He logged off the live system.

He returned to his window onto the test server. He deleted sources and objects for programs x1 to x12.

Tim got up and ran to the door. He stopped and ran back, picked up a diskette and a bunch of keys, and logged off the terminal. He stood there for an instant. The big man barged in, pointed to the watch on his wrist, and grabbed Tim by the shoulder. He forced him out the door, took Tim's keys and locked it. Tim ran, he crashed through office doors, he charged into the lavatories. His three colleagues waiting. He began to strip out of his suit. *Leave it on*, someone said, and handed him his overalls, his black wig, his spectacles. The big man hissed at everyone. He pulled something out of his pocket and opened the toilet door slightly. He took off his mask and breathed in deeply. He looked back in and nodded.

"Gas's clearing," he whispered. He waved the thing in his right hand. Tim stared at it. The gun not quite lost in his huge fist.

"Mick. No!" Tim shouted.

A hiss. "Jerome. Shut him up." One of the black guys was quickly at his side, a hand over his mouth. He whispered into Tim's ear.

The four of them froze. They heard voices below them. Two of the men began methodically to pack the gear. The third held Tim in a gentle grasp for a second. Then he let him go. He helped him with his coat, helped him adjust his wig. Mick opened the door, they all walked out the toilet to the lift.

They waited. The voices got louder. Steps. People on the stairwell. Shouts.

Jeez! That stink!

Christ!

I'm gonna throw up.

They waited. The lift appeared to be stuck on the second floor.

Crowds pouring up the stairs. People piling into their offices.

Get the fans on.

Turn the air-conditioning up.

They waited. They all looked back. They caught sight of the security officer in the centre of a crush of people. His face was grey. He saw them. The big man reached into the pocket of his overalls. *Don't, Mick, don't.*

"Here. You lot. I want to talk to you."

Someone called out from the other side of the swing doors.

"Hey. Ross. Unlock these doors. We need to get back in. Pronto."

The man swore to himself.

"Wait there."

He disappeared into the office. A synthetic bell-like sound. Lift doors opening. A mass of people staggering out. They waited. Men and women pushing, streaming by them. Suddenly the crowd was gone. The four men walked in and pressed Ground. The lift doors began to close. They stared outwards. The security officer burst through the double doors into the hallway.

"You lot. Wait."

The lift began to descend.

At ground floor, they walked past reception without looking at the doorman. They walked briskly through the revolving doors. Outside, as soon as they had moved beyond the view of the doorman, they broke into a trot. They rounded a corner. There was a van parked at the side of the road, its engine running. As they got close to it a side door opened. They threw their bags into the back and clambered in. As soon as the door was closed, three of the men raised their hands and shrieked at the roof.

172

The driver told them to shut it. He did a u-turn, then a hard left, and put his foot on the accelerator. The fourth man bent double. He was sick into his holdall.

*

In the office, the chief of security called the office general manager. He asked him about the cleaners. The general manager sighed down the phone, he had a member of the fire brigade facing him across his office desk. He said ad-hoc visits like these were not unusual. But he would double check. He was on the case. If he just had a few minutes of peace and quiet. The security officer let the matter drop, until, half an hour later, staff on the third floor began to complain about missing cheque books, missing jewellery. He felt a moment of panic, and knew in an instant that he had made a bad, bad decision. He rang the general manager again and insisted that he be given a contact number. He called the cleaning company's head office. He spoke to a secretary. She was evasive. Her boss had been at the pub all afternoon. She told the caller he was in a meeting. She said that there was no record of any planned visit by their staff for that afternoon.

He put the phone down and put a call in to the police.

At three thirty, the stench had faded. The four members of the treasury unit, seated in their own small room off the main open plan office, knew they had a deadline to reach. They had all logged back onto their terminals. They had to transmit payment data to Zurich by four if it was to be processed that day. Their boss had left early. The deputy manager listed the five 'ready' transactions on his screen.

"OK to send?" he shouted. He waited three seconds and looked around the room. "Angie, you as well?"

Angie frowned. She had been in the job just a few months. She noted that there was a cancelled transaction that came after the five. It looked familiar. She realised it was a copy of one she had entered the day before. Someone must have re-entered it, then seen the error and fixed it. She said nothing. Her colleague pressed the send button.

At four there was a call from Zurich. Jakob.

"Are you finished over there?" he said in his perfect English. "Thirteen payments today?"

There had been seven transactions in the morning, and, now, five in the afternoon. The deputy manager took the call. He was feeling a bit sick. The smell must have turned his stomach. He had been in a meeting all morning, but the numbers sounded about right. He gave the go-ahead and put the phone down. He went to get a coffee.

It was five o'clock in Zurich. Jakob looked at the thirteen payments. Total value, seventy-five million dollars. One big one. Twenty million. A lot. Not unusual though. He'd seen larger. He worked fast to process the payments. He did not want to stay too late. It was the weekend.

At eleven o'clock in the morning in Caracas, Alec waited at the offices of *Banco de Comercio y Crédito*. He was tired. He had flown in on Wednesday.

His Spanish had always been good. People seemed to buy his story about a Panamanian mother and an American father.

He had told the bank to expect a large payment into the new account, and an hour later the details began to trickle through. He took a coffee, he swallowed a pill. He waited. The day before he had explained precisely what he wanted the bank to do. They were to transfer all funds to another financial institution here in Caracas and then close the account. There would be an extra hundred thousand in fees if everything was completed that day.

At two fifteen he was called in to see the president of the bank. The man gushed.

Alec was told the balance of his account was now twenty million, one thousand dollars. Was he sure he wished to go ahead with everything as planned? After all, the bank could offer very favourable investment strategies for important customers like him?

Shut up you fucking prick face arsehole jerkoff creep. Just close that Jesus Christ fucking account.

"I'm sure," Alec said. The president of the bank sighed. He called in his senior operations executive and told him to proceed. Alec spent an hour signing forms. Then he spent half an hour in the lavatories of a McDonald's next door. Then an hour standing in the executive's office, drinking coffee and biting his lip. At four forty-five he was told it was done. They all shook hands, and Alec put a sheaf of papers into his briefcase. The president of the bank accompanied him to the door. If ever he wished to do business again, he knew whom to call. Alec walked out.

At a corner fifty yards away he steadied himself. He reached for a hip flask in his pocket and took a slug. He hailed a cab, they drove a block. He walked in to the offices of *Banco Nacional de Caracas* and asked to check the balance of the account he held with them. He was told it was nineteen million seven hundred and fifty two thousand US dollars. He asked to see the manager.

"Everything ready? We proceed as planned?"

"Of course," the man said. "First thing Monday morning."

At eleven pm in London, Michael took a call from Caracas. He listened silently for a minute. Then he put the phone down. Sanjay, Tim and Mick watched him.

Michael looked at the floor.

"I'd forgotten what it feels like. I'd forgotten how good it felt."

He said the same thing over and over. Then he walked over to the others and placed his arms on Tim and Sanjay's shoulders.

"You beauts," he said.

fourteen

At some point on Saturday Tim found himself staring up at a white ceiling and contemplating the state of death. His entire memory seemed to have been erased. He wondered whether he had entered that state.

He could not work out where he was. He knew only that he was in a bed.

He was still in his clothes.

After five minutes, fragmentary recollections of the previous evening began to trickle through. They had drunk champagne and cognac. Bottle after bottle. At some point things had gone blank. A panic flickered inside him. He felt his arms, his legs, his genitals, he moved his tongue around his teeth, as if he might have lost something during the night. He was shaking.

He pulled the blankets off and got up. He called out.

"Sanjay."

Somehow he knew where the bathroom was. He shuffled into it, sat on the toilet and then slid off and knelt, his face leaning into the seat. He coughed.

A voice. "Tim, you in there?"

The door opened.

"Jesus! What a mess!"

He felt an arm on his shoulder.

"Here. You go back to bed. I'll clean up here."

Tim was led back to the bedroom. He flopped down, felt the covers pulled over him. He could not stop shaking.

He was in Sanjay's apartment. Later Michael came to visit him.

"Tim, you've done everything we asked of you. You were

176

superb. It's over now. In a few days you'll have a ton of money in a Swiss account. So take it easy, unwind, relax."

The problem was he couldn't. He body was twitching violently underneath the blankets. He simply could not stop. He couldn't control his throat to speak or his eyes to focus on the man at the end of the bed.

After a minute Michael left. Tim heard voices talking outside the door.

fifteen

Some of the things that followed Tim would find out later. Others he would not, or perhaps only indirectly, through the consequences.

At eleven at night on Sunday the head of Treasury got a call at home. Suzi Blaine and her husband had entertained that day. They had just cleared up, she was a bit drunk, and she watched late night TV with her feet on the coffee table and a tumbler of scotch in her hand.

It was late. Her husband sighed as he picked up the phone.

"Honey, it's Steve. Steve Roth."

She took the call in her study. On the other end the director of trading operations sounded jumpy. He said he had had a text message alert an hour before. Something had triggered it, some shortfall in their positions, he couldn't figure out what it was. He had logged on remotely to the office mainframe to review their trading statements. They looked in order. But something apparently was not right. Somewhere there appeared to be a discrepancy.

She said she was confused.

He asked if there had been anything unusual the previous Friday.

She said no, the nature and the volume of payments going through the system was by no means out of the ordinary.

He said he was wondering whether to take a taxi into the office.

She said there must be some computer glitch.

He hesitated for a second. "OK. But let's meet early tomorrow. At seven thirty?"

She swore as she hung up.

A tension swept through the company the next day. Twenty-four hours later rumours began to sweep through into the outside world of their partners and competitors, and by the end of the week articles began appearing in the *Financial Times* and the *Wall Street Journal* gossip columns about possible business irregularities in this famously secretive firm.

It started in treasury on the third floor and spread that morning to trading, operations and accounting. In the afternoon it seeped down into IT and personnel on the second floor, and spread upwards into metals and grain departments on the fourth. Few initially knew what caused it. Everyone felt its effects. A mood of expectancy settled. People whispered to each other, they told no jokes. They held their breath and waited.

At eight in the morning, Suzi Blaine and Steve Roth held a conference call with one of the bank's senior systems analysts in Zurich. They asked him why the text alert had been received. He explained that there were various technical measures of so-called critical alert status, which they had devised for all their major account holders, and that one of these had crossed into the red. He examined the log of last night's messages, and told them that a formula existed, based on patterns of business activity over a long period, which determined what level of credit line they might need in order to meet trading commitments expected during the coming week, and that the software had determined there might be a risk that it could fall short.

Suzi Blaine called in her second in command and asked him to prepare a position statement from their own systems. He instead rang down to IT, who set up a terminal in the meeting room so that she could see it herself.

At nine o'clock, still hooked up on the conference line, she protested to Zurich that their trading statements looked entirely satisfactory. The systems analyst in Zurich said he could only answer for the workings of the bank's computer systems, and asked for a fifteen-minute break whilst he brought in Jakob and his line manager. At twenty minutes past the hour, they reconvened. Jakob checked his figures. He said that the alert was justified, that on a preliminary review the credit lines did look alarmingly close to exhaustion.

"Didn't you know?"

There was silence. And then, "But they can't be." And, "OK. Read us the figures you've got on your system over there. Totals, payments and receipts. Monday last up to Friday."

In London they listened to Jakob's glacially perfect enunciation. He recited figures. For Monday. Perfect. The correlation exact on all currencies. To the cent. As expected.

Tuesday. Wednesday. Thursday. Friday.

"What?" A pause. "Let's have those figures again."

Jakob's voice once more.

London. "Look, we're going to put you on hold for a few seconds."

Zurich. "Fine. We'll wait."

A mute button pressed. Around a table in London, three people stared at each other. They whispered.

"Twenty million seems to have gone up in smoke."

"How? Where? Zurich must have screwed up."

"Jesus Christ. We're in deep shit."

"Hold on. Let's look at their figures again. Let's get a breakdown."

Someone reached down onto the phone and pressed the keypad.

"Hi. We're back. Listen, we need more details of those Friday figures. Any way we could see those?"

"Hang on." The analyst. A pause, then Jakob's boss.

"We're just trying to set you up a remote link. Give us five minutes."

"OK. Listen, in the meantime. Jakob, can you read out for us the figures you have. We'll tick them off against our own."

"Sure. Here, let me see." The perfect accent again. "Number one. Seven hundred and fifty thousand. US dollars. Payable to First National, Seoul. Next. Three million. Swiss Francs."

They listened. One, two, three, four, five. Six, seven. A pause. Eight.

"Twenty million."

"What?"

"US dollars. Payable to Banco de Comercio y Crédito." Silence. "Hello? You still there?"

Between ten and twelve, London time, senior management held crisis talks with their Zurich counterparts.

"When can we contact this mob in Caracas?"

"They're five hours behind."

"Who's our agent there?"

Papers fluttering, a directory being scanned.

"What about the bank in Zurich? Should we suspect them? Foul play?"

In Zurich, Jakob and his boss were ushered into a cold, grey room with three senior officials from the bank's supervisory board. They were informed that a serious breach of the bank's normal practices had occurred. So serious, the bank's reputation could be fatally compromised. There might be criminal charges.

Jakob spluttered. There was nothing he could think of to say. He had followed procedures by the book. As he had always done.

At twelve noon in London, Graham Turtle, in charge of IT, was called in to see Steve Roth. He was told that an unauthorised payment had been made from the treasury system last Friday. It was of absolutely critical importance that he determine what had happened immediately.

Turtle protested. He said he needed more details if he was to uncover the problem.

Ross Williams, the company's security officer, was sitting in the room also. He asked Turtle to leave for a minute while they conferred. He stepped outside.

A minute later he was asked back in. Twenty million, he was told, twenty million had been lost. He was given the bank name, the account details, the test code number. He sat in silence for a moment, mouth open.

"Twenty million?"

Half an hour later, the head of IT sat alone with his three senior people. He told them that what he was about to say was in the strictest confidence, on pain of instant dismissal. He told them to drop everything else they were doing. Straight away. Everything.

At one o'clock London time, they were able to speak to a junior account manager at the bank in Caracas. It took a while for him to realise the seniority of the people at the other end of the line. He then said he could not give out confidential client information. He became flustered. He said he would need to wait for his boss to arrive in an hour's time before he could say more.

They put in a call to the company's agent in Caracas. He was told to take all and any steps necessary to find out more about this bank account. If he needed money, he was to ask. Resources, people, anything. He had merely to name it. He was given a direct access line to London that he was to use at any time of the day if he came up with anything.

At three, they spoke to the president of the *Banco de Comercio y Crédito*. He was reluctant to divulge any more information than had already been given. They warned him that he was playing with fire by denying them reasonable cooperation. His mood became prickly. He was silent for a few seconds, and then stipulated that a court order would be required before any more details could be given. On this, he said, his word was final.

Another call to the agent. Move heaven and earth, he was ordered. He called back an hour later. It would take forty-eight hours. Forty-eight hours before the papers could be presented to a magistrate and the necessary signatures obtained.

*

At nine o'clock in the morning in Caracas, Alec presented himself at the offices of the *Banco Nacional de Caracas*. He was immediately ushered in to see the bank's president.

"As agreed?" Alec was asked.

"As agreed," he replied.

"You sure you would not like to re-consider?"

It took three hours. The account was closed. Alec left the bank. He returned to his hotel, checked out two hours later and headed for the airport.

He arrived in the British Virgin Islands at ten at night. He knew that for the remaining years of his life it would be unwise ever to set foot in Venezuela again.

*

That evening in London, six men and women sat down in a conference room. They remained in constant touch by video link with a parallel meeting going on in Zurich.

They knew that the company had seen twenty million dollars of its money prised from its grasp. They knew where it had gone, but they couldn't get it back.

They had not the faintest clue as to how or why the money had been spirited out. They argued. The only consensus that they seemed able to reach was that there were three broad lines of further investigation.

It was either a problem with the firm's London office. Or with the firm's Zurich office. Or with their bankers.

The Swiss were angry.

"It can't be us. It has to be London treasury. Or it's software."

London. "Hang on. We cannot exclude anything. Or anyone."

They agreed that managers in both offices would begin hostile interviews of all relevant staff, starting first thing the next day. Especially all IT staff. Especially all treasury staff. And they would demand that their bankers conduct an investigation of the very highest urgency straight away.

Someone mentioned the police.

"Should we be calling them in now?"

The chief of security operations in London fidgeted in his seat. "They've been in to see me today. For something else."

Five pairs of eyes turned to him.

"We had some stuff stolen from our offices. Friday last. It was the cleaners. People posing as cleaners."

Silence.

"Why in God's name didn't you mention this?"

"I'm sorry. It's an entirely separate matter. This was petty theft."

"So what happened?"

Ross Williams explained. As he did so, as he looked at the five people facing him across the table, as he looked at the video link and the faces staring out from it, he began to imagine an alternative life, a life in the Algarve, spending his hours playing golf, hoisting the mainsail of his yacht. Gin and tonics with his wife as the sun went down. A part of his mind began totting up his assets. His pension, his savings, the value of his home. He subtracted the preposterous costs of maintaining his three teenage children. He felt a sigh trembling in his soul. It could never work. But it would have to. For he knew he would never ever work in the security business again.

A face appeared on the video link. Nico Geldman, founder and chief executive. Williams had never met the man, though he recognised his features from newspaper articles. Fabulously wealthy. Fiftyish, tanned, good looking. A young wife. He had not left Switzerland once in five years. The rumour was that he had one wish before he died, to taste a New York hamburger, freshly prepared, from a particular deli a block down from the office where he had first set up on Wall Street.

"Hey look, you guys. Listen. No police."

The regulators in New York had recently got tough. The charges against him had been ratcheted up to include racketeering. The type of thing they used against the Mafia.

"Remember Enron, WorldCom," he continued. "I don't want the authorities crawling over us like they did them. We'll fix this ourselves. So far it's just an accounting problem. It could even be our own bank. Perhaps they've fucked up."

There was a pause.

The head of security spoke.

"Ahem. Excuse me. Sir. What do I do about the thefts? In the office."

"For Christ's sake. Let's stay focussed on the big picture."

On Tuesday morning Graham Turtle held a meeting for all his staff. He told them that a breach in company security had occurred, and that the head of office security wished to interview all IT personnel over the next two days. Half hour slots would be scheduled. He himself would be the first.

At nine fifteen he presented himself to Ross Williams. The door was locked behind him, a tape player was switched on.

He was asked what he knew about the treasury system. Very little of the technical detail, he said. He delegated that to his staff. Who were the experts? He gave names.

"The guy who wrote it, he left just recently," he said.

"Oh? Who was that?"

"Tim Scott? You may remember him."

The head of security made a note. He moved on to current system safeguards. Were they lax?

The head of IT said he didn't think so.

Who had access? How often were passwords changed?

He said he did not know precisely. Again, that was delegated to his lieutenants.

"Besides. This system is being re-written. It's one of the legacy systems."

"Legacy?"

He explained. Williams frowned.

"One of our key applications? Running on old technology?"

"Complex systems can't be written in a day."

The man across the desk took more notes.

At ten, the director for corporate governance arrived from Zurich at the London offices. His brief was to interview treasury staff, and then, more informally, to interview all senior managers. No one was above suspicion.

He hung up his coat, took a cup of coffee from a machine, and began with Suzi Blaine at treasury at ten thirty. By twelve he had worked his way down to the most junior member of the department. Perhaps twenty minutes later, in front of a screen, the young woman mentioned the duplicate transaction.

"What's that? Let me see it. Show me on the terminal."

They stared at a screen.

"How can this happen?"

"Two of us get presented with the papers. We enter it twice. Independently."

"Does this occur often?"

"No. Once in a while. We always spot it. The second entry is always cancelled."

"So who entered it in the second time?"

"Uh. Don't know."

"You didn't check?"

He called in the other members of the department. He asked them who had entered in the cancelled payment. They all gaped at it. They shook their heads.

"Well, someone must have done."

In Zurich, Jakob and his immediate superior spent a further two hours being questioned in minute detail about what had happened the previous Friday. Jakob appeared to be in shock. He had to disappear to the toilets every half an hour. Despite this, the paperwork, the computer data, his own records, all seemed to be in perfect order.

The bank's compliance officers gave them a clean bill of health. This was reported to the bank's president, who had taken a call that morning urging him to leave the police out of the investigation. It was an internal matter, a matter between the bank and the company. No-one else need know.

It somehow offended his Swiss sensibility, not the fact of keeping the affair quiet – after all, discretion was part of the fabric of his country's banking industry – but rather the fact that the discrepancies seemed so lacking in any coherent explanation. It hinted at incompetence, a kind of throw-away, third world approach to banking. It just wasn't the way his people did things. But he had no choice. The business that came their way from this customer was so huge.

*

In the British Virgin Islands, Alec walked in to the offices of *Traders & Merchants Bank (TMB)*. As soon as he declared his identity, he was shown in to see the company CEO.

He explained that he wished to disburse funds to a number of accounts in Switzerland and Moscow. He wished this done immediately.

"These are large sums. Let me see, nineteen and a half million. Plus change. Are you quite sure?" he was asked.

He sighed and asked how long it would take. He discussed the bonus the CEO himself might receive if it could be all completed by the end of the week.

*

On Wednesday afternoon, Caracas time, the company's agent, armed with a magistrate's signature, finally managed to gain access to the details of the offending account. In London they waited.

It was late evening when they received his call. He explained to them that the account had been closed, all funds transferred out.

"To where?"

"Another account. Another bank. Here in Caracas."

"So, what next?"

"Another magistrate, another court order. Another forty-eight hours."

"Jesus. It's slipping away from us."

"Do you want me to go ahead?"

On Friday evening, by which time it had become apparent that the money had vanished from Venezuela, the founder and chief executive of the company made an address to senior management in Zurich and London. He spoke again by video link.

He said to them that an elaborate act of corporate theft had been carried out against them. They had lost twenty million dollars.

The company could take the hit, but this year's figures would be sharply down. He said that their bankers had assured him they were not to blame. He said he did not entirely trust them. Yet, to sever links might raise suspicions in the commercial markets. They were wedded to each other for the time being.

He ordered department heads to continue with their own enquiries. He ordered a fundamental review of company security and especially IT security. Where necessary, staff would need to be replaced, more able staff recruited.

The police would not be called in. Instead, an appearance of calm and 'business-as-usual' was to be presented to the world. It was important also to counteract the rumours that were appearing in the financial press. He urged directors of public relations to issue the appropriate statements to the media.

He said finally that he was calling in an external company to conduct an independent review and to carry out its own investigation of the affair. He urged everyone to extend to them every possible assistance. These people would arrive Monday.

sixteen

Tim spent three days in Sanjay's flat. The first day floated by him, his consciousness barely registering the passing of the hours, the lightening and the darkening of the sky at the window.

Sunday afternoon, daydreaming. He heard footsteps in the hall, and then the front door slamming. After that, quiet. He got up and wandered around the rooms alone, in a dressing gown Sanjay had left out for him. A cold tidiness. Flowers, dusted surfaces, polished wood. No clutter, no old clothes on the floor. He searched the kitchen. No food in the fridge. On a shelf he found a bottle of scotch. He watched daytime TV and got drunk. He was in bed when Sanjay returned.

Monday. The same.

He returned to his own flat the next day, showered, had a shave, a change of clothes. He sat on the sofa in his living room, and waited in silence for the police to arrive. They never did.

Sanjay called round in the evening. He made scrambled eggs and toast. *That's all I can cook*, he said. Then he told Tim gently that he had to snap out of it. *Try to change your attitude*, he said, *try to think about what you've experienced over the last few weeks in a different way. Try to re-think what you are*, he said.

Imagine a new Tim. See him relishing the things he has done, see him celebrating the audacity of what he has accomplished. Step into that man, become that other Tim.

They had all done something remarkable, *he* had done something remarkable. He should take pride in the achievement. A tiny window had opened for them all. How they had stepped through it. With what skill, what aplomb.

For heaven's sake, he said, *you were brilliant. Someone will write a book about it one day.*

He took Tim to meet the others. Michael, Mick, Bernie, the other lads. Later, Alec. They seemed to Tim to float on air. They would burst out laughing, for no reason. Or stop to hug each other. He saw that moments like these were what they lived for, that here and now, for a short period, a holy fire burned inside them. It had been a good trick, a sweet, sweet con. Made the sweeter by the planning, the scale, the timing, the precision.

Tim watched them.

Why can't I feel like that? he thought to himself. *Why can't I burn with the same fire?*

seventeen

Dan Becker arrived inconspicuously at the London offices at eight thirty in the morning the following Monday. The three other members of his team were waiting for him. They were taken up to see the managing director of London trading, who provided them with an office and issued them with the authority to see anyone in the company, at any time, in any department. A memorandum was sent to all department heads that their co-operation was required.

Becker remained in the background as they were shown round, he let the others do the talking, although in fact it was he who had decided on the strategy that they would follow. In the evenings, the four of them alone, when they collated what they had uncovered during the day, it was he who sat back to try to make sense of it all, and who determined which staff they would interview next, whom they might call to see a second time.

His employers rated him highly. Since Becker had moved into the private sector he had worked behind the scenes on a number of high-level cases of corporate espionage and malpractice. He brought with him the expertise and the contacts he had acquired over the years in two very different, though both equally demanding, espionage milieux. He had started off his career in the bowels of one of the CIA's huge electronic eavesdropping centres. He learnt about technology, about programming, about data trails, he learnt how to sift through vast amounts of white noise in order to pick out the tiny irregularities that transformed the signal stream from the random into the meaningful. Later in Israel he began to master the techniques necessary for human intelligence gathering, the psychology of desire and motivation, the subjectivity of perceptions of truth, the deconstruction of belief systems, of self-image, of the forces that may stiffen men or break them. They rated him. And he loved his work.

Becker was intrigued by this case. The kind of case where it was not even certain from the evidence that there was a solution. This case he would enjoy. And while he and his colleagues would in due course be preparing a report for senior company officers, he might also at some point be presenting his own findings to the most senior. Outside the official channels. His own personal thoughts, his own conclusions. He had a contact number, in Zurich. A number that was not on any company phone list.

Perhaps. He would see.

That Monday, he started by busying himself with the data, the transcripts of interviews, the minute analysis of the events that had occurred that day. He constructed a time line, tried to figure an exact sequence of events, and which events were causes, which effects. He was disturbed by two things outside the ordinary. The thefts carried out by the bogus cleaners. And the cancelled duplicate payment.

The cleaning company, with whom they no longer did business, had, he suspected, not been entirely forthcoming. They denied that the burglars were their people. And yet how did the men acquire the uniforms, the badges, the credentials? How did they know about the fire drill, or when the office emptied?

The duplicate payment. Everyone denied entering it. Had someone forgotten? Surely not. And the sequence number. The same as for the missing funds. Had the bank in Zurich done something crooked? Had they found out about the copy, and substituted their own illegal transaction?

He had a number of tentative suspects. Jakob, in Zurich. Ross Williams, chief of security. Graham Turtle at IT. Suzi Blaine. Yet there were significant problems. Jakob, it seemed to him, would never have had the balls for something like this. Williams. Something was not quite right with the man. His hair was dishevelled, his tie loose. His eyes stared. Too weird. This job needed a steady nerve.

The head of IT. A man with a home in the country, a large family, the eldest child at university. Comfortable. Settled. It seemed unlikely. In addition, like many technology managers, he had let slip his grasp of fine detail. Would he have had the technical knowledge to attempt something like this? The head of treasury. Would she have had the necessary systems knowledge?

Becker thought some more. Perhaps, if not one, then two of them? Three? Working together?

He was puzzled also that there seemed to be no obvious way to tie up his suspects with the other events that had taken place that day. What linked his suspects with the bogus cleaners? Was the duplicate payment a coincidence? If Jakob was the perpetrator, then were events in London irrelevant? If he was not, then how was the false payment communicated to him from London? And by whom?

He began to look at network traffic between the two locations, but he was hampered by the incompatibilities between the different computer systems. The technical guys showed him there had been traffic throughout the afternoon of that Friday, even during the fire drill. Email, remote links, automated transmissions, but they could show him only overall volumes, not the contents of the data packets.

Becker had Turtle at IT install a piece of software he had brought, which enabled him to peek into the operating systems of the legacy software they ran, into the file and directory headers, the actual disk addresses, the action dates for file creation, the deletion bins.

He was presented with a piece of film, taken by secret cameras in the trading areas. The existence of the cameras was known only to two or three senior managers. He was fascinated by the time period covering the fire drill. He looked again and again at the grainy black-and-white shots of staff exiting the building, then men in head-to-toe uniforms walking through the offices. The cleaners. There they were. The big man, talking to the head of security. Two minutes to three. Then four minutes past, one of the other ones. A black guy. Again, with Williams. Becker had gone over this with him in some detail.

"They spilt this chemical. I was furious, I was shouting at them. There. You can see me."

"And this second time? You're with another of them this time?"

"Yes. It's me again. I can't remember what I said. There was some swearing I should imagine."

Becker stared at the man talking to him.

He had retained the services of a private investigation firm. He made a mental note to ask them to include this man in the list of people they had under surveillance.

*

"Sanjay."

"Tim."

"They want to see me."

"Who?"

"Work."

"Who?"

"The guys. The guys I used to work with."

"Why do they want to see you?"

"To talk."

"What about?"

"Work."

"What about work?"

"The stuff I did. The systems I used to work on."

"So?"

"Something's up, Sanjay. I can feel it. What shall I do?"

"Calm down. Explain to me. Slowly. What did they say?"

"They've got some questions. Questions they need me to clarify."

"Technical questions?"

"Yes."

"Is that a big deal? Weren't you a guru of some kind?"

"Yes, but..."

"You're seeing your ex-colleagues? Not the police? Not the company's security people?"

"The guys I worked with."

"So, there's not a problem."

"Sanjay. I can't do it."

"Tim. Listen. Meet them. Don't go to the office. Meet somewhere neutral. Speak to them. Answer their questions. Then leave."

"Are you sure?"

"Tim. Play ball, play their game. And then walk away."

*

Ex-employees. Disgruntled ex-employees. Becker began to widen his search. He looked at ex-traders, accountants, treasury staff.

He began to poke around in the directory areas of the IT staff who had left the company, stuff that should have been deleted long ago. He found files, test scripts, junk left lying around. There were a few letters, to bank managers, girlfriends. Some porn.

There was a directory header record held on the system, not normally available to system administrators, which contained detailed information about file usage in the directory. He, Becker, was able to look at it. His software was able to open up the operating system. Bob Haldane, Jane Smith, Paul Parfitt. There was a register that contained the last activity date for the directory. He began examining this register. Paul Parfitt. And now a surprise. The last activity in this directory, it was the fifth September. The date of the theft. Yet this person had left over a year ago. Becker looked at the files in his directory. All a year old. So what was this file activity?

He spoke to the operations manager, and asked him how often backups were done. *Full* every Sunday morning, he was told, *incremental* every day. He asked if it was possible to restore the directory for Paul Parfitt for each day, going backwards from the fifth September, for one whole month. Then two, if necessary.

The operations manager frowned.

"It'll take ages," he said.

"I have time," Becker replied.

He began with the fourth of the month, and then slowly worked his way back. Day by day the directory remained unchanged. No files were added, modified, or deleted. Becker persisted. The operations manager was not happy.

There was a register called the High Water Mark. It indicated how much disk space allocation had been utilised against a given directory. Becker saw it unchanging as he worked his way back. Then, retreating further during the week of the twenty-second down to the eighteenth of August, he noted that it rose. Day by day. Yet the files were unchanged. The implication was clear. Someone had been creating files, and then deleting them before the backup occurred. There had been activity against the account. But not by Parfitt. He was long gone. So. By whom?

He sat in an office with the head of IT and his deputy. They discussed employees who had left. They had photographs, copies that security had made when each employee had joined the company. Becker asked about Bob Haldane, and why he had been fired. They looked at his picture. Becker made a note. He would ask his PI firm to check him out. They moved on. They came to Tim Scott.

"We could have used his help," Graham Turtle said. "Th was his area."

Becker looked up. "When did he leave?"

The IT people looked at each other.

"After the twenty second of August?" Becker asked.

"End of August. That's right isn't it?" Turtle spoke to second in command. They looked at the photo.

"He looks so different now," his deputy said. "I met him for lunch yesterday."

They all stared.

"He's not got another job yet. He's cut off all his hair."

"Demob happy?" his boss joked.

Becker began to think. He remembered colleagues who had suddenly and drastically changed their appearance. In the US. Midlife crisis. A divorce. A younger woman. Some became Buddhists. Or in Israel, those who had joined one of the orthodox settlements on the West Bank. A change in life, a change in direction. A change in appearance, sometimes shocking. A shaved head, a clearing out of the wardrobe. An act of self-deception, Becker often thought, the new outer image the proof of an inner regeneration. A kind of imagined baptism into a new faith. People in their forties, their parents dying, when they were beginning to realise that their own time was running out, that their own workaday lives had a hollowness to them. Tim Scott. What had his life lacked? In what way had he desired to change? Straws in the wind. Becker decided to keep a watch on him as well.

Weeks passed. The trail cooled.

Becker spent time in Zurich. He spoke to Jakob, studied the documentary record of the actual transaction that Jakob had received authorising him to set up the payment to the South American bank. He struck Jakob off his list.

He flew back, knowing that he had wasted time out there in Switzerland. He was beginning to run out of steam. He had felt so fired up when he first arrived, yet his three main suspects remained as near to or as far from guilt as they had always been. There was just one development that interested him. The behaviour of the chief of security. Williams was getting worse. His personality seemed to be disintegrating in front of their eyes. He was increasingly erratic. He sat in his office alone all afternoon, then emerged to have shouting matches with his

subordinates. He started initiatives and immediately cancelled them. Becker wondered how long it would be before the company pensioned him off.

Yet Ross Williams's life outside office hours was without blemish.

Becker had accumulated substantial files on the half dozen people his private investigators were following. He examined the reports and the photographs. He had information on where they lived, whom they went out with, their wives, husbands, children. Their secret lives. Secrets that were so often a bit sad and tawdry. The head of IT, it seemed, had a taste for Soho strip joints. Bob Haldane, who had been fired, now ran a gay nightclub. Tim Scott was revealed to be an occasional visitor at an upmarket gambling den. Williams, however, seemed beyond suspicion. He commuted. He saw his family at nights and at the weekend. He seemed to switch off at home, as if he left the confused personality of his daytime life locked away in his office.

Becker sat with him. They talked. The man's answers to Becker's questions were mumbled, sometimes contradictory. It seemed as if a thread was beginning to unwind. And then Becker realised that he was trying to string it out as long as possible, that he knew his time was up. He had screwed up. Becker guessed that he saw his career was over, that he just wanted to maximise what he might get out of the company before they booted him out.

Would he leave with a hidden secret?

Order and chaos. The logical and the random. Becker knew that there was a place for both in his methodology. He had a set of photographs, pictures prepared by the private investigators. Pictures not of his suspects, but rather of the people with whom they associated. Shots of a street in Soho, a club visited by the head of IT. Then friends and relatives of Jakob. Of the head of treasury. People arriving and leaving her home for a dinner party. Some people that Tim Scott had been seen with. Associates of Bob Haldane.

Becker was not sure what he expected. He sat with Williams, photographs scattered over his desk. A pause, a raised eyebrow, a sudden blush. A recognition, secret, momentarily unmasked. And he got all of those, though they told him nothing. The man's responses had an unpredictability, and Becker found himself distrusting his own instincts.

At lunch he began to wonder how long he should continue on the project. He hated to admit failure. The forfeit of his bonus was an irrelevance compared to the sense of incompleteness he felt at a case unresolved. And yet the trade-off between time and progress was beginning to move against him. Perhaps he needed a break, a few days out. Back home, if he could swing it.

At five in the afternoon, he received a call from the chief of security. He was asked to bring the pictures he had been showing earlier in the day. Becker went up to his office, and saw Williams playing and re-playing the film that had been taken of the bogus cleaners. The man asked for the photographs. He riffled through them and picked one out. He placed it on the table, and then slowed down the video player. There was an image of a big man, head shaved, in cleaner's uniform, moving in slow motion jerks across the office floor. He froze the picture.

"Well?"

Ross Williams pointed to the photograph on the table. There were three people in the picture, a man with greased back hair and sunglasses. Next to him a huge man, bald. The third man, black. The three of them were looking at each other, smiling. He pointed to the big guy in the middle.

"That's him."

Two days later Becker sat with another report from his investigators. He had been on edge these forty-eight hours, he had pushed his men hard, but now he had names for the faces. Michael Palmer. The good-looking one. The second man, a string of names, aliases. He was referred to just as Mick. He worked as a bouncer. A security consultant. Becker smiled at the pompous deception in the term. The man had a criminal record. Palmer, his sometime employer, was the owner of the casino where Tim Scott had been spotted. The third man. Boxer, petty criminal.

Becker felt his instincts twitching. Yet at present he had very little. What connection did Tim Scott have with these men? Were the three men working together? Or had the man called Mick been doing some freelancing with the office takedown? He studied the report on Palmer. His business interests were varied and colourful, and in many cases just this side of the law. Legitimate, nevertheless. It was hard to imagine someone whose dealings featured in the business pages pulling off something like this.

He sat in front of his PC and ran Palmer's name through the search engines. Thousands of hits. The first few pages seemed to be focussed on his dealings with a pair of Russian businessmen. There were reports in the financial press that things were not going well. Becker knew of the Ivanovs. The Twins. Like so many of the oligarchs, it was the speed with which they had acquired their massive wealth that surprised. They had picked up fire-sale bargains from the disposal of energy assets by the government in its teetering lurch towards capitalism. They had diversified into media and property, and now carried the vulgar profile of the new super-rich. The customised Mercedes, the retinue of blonde, waif-like, catwalk girlfriends, the bartering for power and governorships in the remote Russian hinterlands. Perhaps the people he now worked for had traded oil with them. An irony.

It was late. He tapped at the keyboard, rode the search engines. He stopped. He rubbed his eyes.

He typed.

M-I-C-H-A-E-L P-A-L-M

The phone rang. His colleagues in the next office. They were packing it in for the night. He put the phone down. He rubbed his eyes again. His fingers brushed the keys.

Return.

He cursed. A typing error. Three thousand four hundred and three entries. He read idly.

"...born June 8,1882, son of **Michael Palmier** and..."

"...de gauche a droit, Lafitte **Michael, Palmier** Jacques..."

"...a brief biography of General **Michael Palmier**, and his role in..."

"...fetish, studs who love it up the ass, porn star **Michael Palmier**, ..."

"...for whatever reasons, dropping the i, changing his name from **Michael Palmier** to Michael Palmer, proved an astute move..."

He looked again. The fifth entry down. He clicked on it. A press article, July nineteen ninety five. A reporter by the name of, who was it, Pete somebody, he scrolled up. Becker read on. He began to laugh, at first to himself, and then out loud. Someone else's secret life. He began to read about the secret life of the man once known as Michael Palmier. His uncle, the drugs trading, the six months in jail. Robbery, GBH. Suspicion of murder. His breakout into the business world.

Dan Becker was still laughing. He thought about the evening ahead, about what he might do after work. He would join his colleagues for supper. Who knows, he might even have a drink or two, something he avoided while working. Just to be sociable. He would be giving them a surprise, he would tell them he was leaving them, it was time to hand the project over. He wondered whether his colleagues would ever figure out what he had uncovered. In truth he did not care. From now on his methods and theirs would diverge. They would prepare their own report. The authorised report. Some of the things he now knew would remain out of it. Others could fine-comb the existing evidence, uncover the final proof if it existed, the smoking gun, as the Americans said. Others could lay blame, could exact redress using the official channels. But he knew he had one end of the thread in his hands. For now that was where it would stay.

He took out his phone, and entered a Zurich number, a number he kept in his memory and not in any address book. He waited for the line to connect.

*

A few days later, two men arrived at Heathrow airport with Swiss passports, though they looked more Mediterranean than Teutonic. They took a taxi to an address in north London. They waited for five minutes. They were given some keys. An address on a piece of paper. A call was placed with a local firm for another car. The two men asked to be dropped off near King's Cross. They paid the driver and waited until he had driven off. They hailed another cab and went this time to the west of London. They were met by a man with whom they seemed on familiar terms. They were handed a dossier. Then a suitcase and a medical bag. The suitcase contained a number of firearms. The bag contained various medical items, drugs, syringes. The two men were pleased. Dan Becker offered them a drink, which they accepted, and the three of them began to chat about old times. About undercover operations under a Levantine sun, in the heat and the dust of hollowed out cities, about drops and insertions and blown cover, assassinations and interrogations. About fundamentalism, conscience and the bald mechanics of pain and sudden death. The interwoven terror and exhilaration of the secret life. The two men stayed for three hours. They then took a series of taxis to a third address. An empty house. Inside, they opened the dossier and began to examine photographs.

Part III

eighteen

Tim met a couple of his old colleagues for lunch.

He had paused and taken a few deep breaths as he picked up the phone and first recognised the voice. The tone had been apologetic. His old boss. They had some questions, his boss said, questions on systems Tim had written, they would be grateful for an hour of his time. Instantly he was sweating. Cold droplets slid down his back. He said he would get back to them when he had checked his schedule. He rang Sanjay. Afterwards he called the office again and agreed to meet at a café nearby at one o'clock the next day. That night he lay on his bed measuring the slow movement of the shadows across the ceiling, wondering whether it was all unravelling.

He sat with two programmers from the department over coffee and sandwiches and they talked software.

"There's been a flap," they said. "We've been told to accelerate the re-write of the payments system."

Tim mumbled. He explained with a thin smile that everything he had written, all the work he had done for them, it was already beginning to fade from memory.

He tried to answer their questions. Later they asked him about Imogen. In America, he said. They asked him about his plans. He was going to travel, he said.

His colleagues looked at each other. "You and your charmed life," they grinned.

As they paid the bill, one of them paused.

"Oh, by the way." He fished out a card from his pocket. A local police station. There was a detective's name written on the back.

"He's been interviewing everyone. He was interested in you. He wants you to give him a call sometime."

Tim stared at the name on the card. He swallowed and asked what it was about. They said it was nothing. They were in a hurry to get back.

Twenty-four hours later he called the station. The detective was out. The reception desk asked for a contact number. Tim said instead he would ring back.

He put the phone down and called Sanjay again. There was no reply. He thought of phoning Michael, and then experienced a failure of nerve. He did not know what to do. Apart from wait. After an hour he tried the station a second time.

A voice, bright and sunny. The officer thanked Tim for calling. He explained that there had been some thefts at the office where he used to work. Wallets, cheque books. Had he had anything stolen? In the months before he left? Tim listened intently. He hung on each word. A part of him strained to detect another meaning, a different set of questions embedded in the ones that he had just been listening to, an off-tangent line of enquiry cloaked and hidden, somewhere in there.

"Hello? Are you still there?"

"Yes. No. No, I never had anything stolen."

There was silence. The policeman asked him if he was sure. Tim said he was. He said he had left the company now. There was really nothing further he could add. There was another pause. The policeman thanked him and told him to give him a call if he thought of anything else.

Tim hung up.

*

They sat in Michael's offices, looking out over the city skyline. They were alone.

"How are the twins?"

There was a look on Michael's face, a stillness, a Buddha

208

smile, that Sanjay found faintly disturbing. Michael did not alter his gaze as he replied

"We've got 'em by the short hairs."

They discussed progress in Moscow. It was much better.

Later Michael asked Sanjay about Tim.

"We've not spoken for a while. He left a few messages."

"Do you think he'll be OK?"

Sanjay thought about the question for a few seconds.

"He and I, we've been through this once before. He's fretting now, but soon he'll begin to wall off the experience. Place it in a far, far corner of his mind and ignore it. It may take a while. But there'll come a day when he'll begin to act as if it never happened."

Michael looked at Sanjay, as if appraising.

"Fucking straight people," he said quietly.

*

He told himself to make a clean break with his old life. Get away from it all. He felt suddenly that he no longer understood the city in which he lived, it was almost an alien place, populated by people whose lives and motivations were incomprehensible, a race of beings who had arisen from nowhere, or from cracks in the pavement, to replace the society that he had once known. He tried to contact Sanjay, but he was always unavailable. He tried and failed one evening to find the pub that Bernie had taken him to. He crossed over into south London and drove around, looking for landmarks. He checked the map, tried alleyways and side streets. He stopped to ask directions, and then realised he did not know what he was asking for. After two hours of searching he gave up.

Once he called Michael, but he was brusque, he said he had a meeting to go to.

Tim was stung.

I was part of it all, he thought, *I helped you.*

He had received enquiries from recruitment agencies and headhunters, and for a while he spoke to them and discussed his future. But then he began to stop returning phone calls, to leave emails unanswered. They cautioned him, saying it was easy to lose touch in the fast moving world of the emerging technologies, but he knew that a connection to their world had been broken, that their assumptions, their goals, the very language of their corporate world, all these were beginning to seem out of step with the person he felt himself becoming. He had fallen in with Sanjay, and through him, with Michael, Mick and Bernie, and then Alec, and they moved to a different beat, they reeked of something more fast-paced and spontaneous, something freed from the constraints of the over-ordered world in which he had grown up, a way of living that offered satisfactions and excitements that were unimaginable to the suits and the penny-counters he had once surrounded himself by. But this new world was passing him by as well, it had offered him a glimpse, a leg up, and somehow he had fluffed it, he had missed his chance. It was true, his nerve had failed. As he looked at the underbelly of Sanjay's world, at the squalid violence that bubbled beneath and occasionally erupted into the daylight, he felt a terror which became a barrier he could not cross. It would always prevent him from stepping inside.

He remembered Mick, the last moments of the sting, the gun in his hands.

Just in case, he had said later. In case of what? Tim thought to himself. He had felt for a few moments the glamour and attraction of their world. He had been seduced. But he could never step inside.

The underbelly. He began to collect press cuttings. A police raid on addresses in north London. Families of thugs, the final link in a modern day silk trail from Kabul to the West, trading heroin, prostitutes, slaves.

An old house with a hidden room behind a brick partition,

shackles on the wall, chains on the floor. A body, concealed in a cupboard, dead for months.

A gunfight in a crowded nightclub in south London. Crack house territory. A hundred people inside. Two dead. No witnesses.

The torso of a child washed up in the river. Ritual slaughter.

A jogger. Raped. Murdered.

A dead baby. In a bin liner.

One morning, as he travelled on the tube in the rush hour, he spotted three youths, with pudding basin haircuts and shell suits. They walked towards the barriers and suddenly they were rolling in a mass on the ground throwing punches at each other. A glimmer of metal. One of them, an eight-inch blade in his hand, and the crowd of bystanders rippled out and away from them. An elderly lady, schoolmistressly tones, standing her ground and ordering him to put the weapon away. The youths scarpering, a Nike blur.

He sat now, caught in the pivot between the two worlds, looking in on both, ignored by both. He felt himself erased, his tread, his shadow, his footprint somehow shrunk and fading, drying up in the sun. There were two maps to this city of his, two stories it could tell, but his presence was increasingly irrelevant to both.

He took to driving, the length and breadth of the country.

Once, to Cambridge. He went slowly past his brother's offices, but he did not stop. He went further. To Yorkshire, the Lake District. He would stay a night, then drive back down to London. As he escaped from the city he felt his tension easing, and then, as he returned, he felt the nervousness fermenting and acidifying in his guts. He remembered one day that Imogen's godparents owned a holiday cottage in Scotland, outside Inverness. Imogen had taken him there once, the spare key was always left under a plant pot at the side. Expats. The place would surely be empty. He started to drive up, but then, in Edinburgh, had second thoughts. He got drunk in a bar, and knew suddenly that he would go mad in the isolation. He slept in the back of the car. The next day he started back down south.

He arrived back to find he had a letter from Imogen. She described how they were halfway through the tour. They had arrived in Boston and had played in concerts up and down the eastern states. They had been mobbed in Texas, where they were now performing. She said she loved it. They would soon move on to Colorado and the west coast. Seattle, LA, San Francisco. The letter was hand written. Take care, she wrote.

After Edinburgh he began to lose the will to rouse himself. He stayed in mornings, and then wasted the afternoons in a café at the end of the road where he lived. He read her letter often. He hid himself away in a corner, unwilling to share tables. More and more, as he drank his coffee, he threw quick glances to the other people sitting around him. He did not know why, but he did. Taxi drivers. Builders. Two businessmen, briefcases open on the table. He might catch the eye of one of them. They might return his glance or look away.

He began to lose his judgement. When he went out, he had arguments, over petty things, over imagined slights in restaurants, or disputed parking spaces, or the change he received in shops and bars. His friends stopped ringing.

He thought occasionally of replying to Imogen. She had left a forwarding address. Once or twice he composed a few lines in his head. They were never quite right.

Days passed. Weeks. He sat in his café and stared out over his coffee cup. He kept her letter in an inside pocket.

Then one day he had company. He walked into the café one afternoon, found his usual place in the corner and picked up his paper. Bernie was sitting two tables down, a mug of tea in front of him. He smiled and waited. After a minute he got up and placed himself in the seat opposite Tim.

"Mind if I join you?"

A waitress squeezed by. Bernie shifted his seat forward. Tim was perturbed that he had not immediately noticed him. His mass, his presence.

"Why are you here?" Tim said.

Bernie shrugged. "We'd almost forgotten about you. I thought I'd see how you were getting on."

"I'm doing fine," Tim said. He looked back down at his newspaper.

Bernie unwrapped a chocolate bar. He broke off a chunk.

"You been up to anything?" he said between bites.

"Nothing much."

"Been away at all?"

"No."

"How's the girlfriend?"

And Tim looked open-mouthed at the bulk of the person sitting facing him. He had a sense of the ludicrous that Bernie was sitting there asking him about his love life. This man who, just months before, would have represented something that he would have feared and detested. Whose presence, facing him across a table, in a conversation of sorts, would have been unthinkable. Tim half-frowned, in irritation that Bernie was there, his presence a distraction from a different kind of dislocation he was grappling with, something less precise and manageable, but no longer embodied in the character of the person sitting opposite. He could not help a sardonic smile as he thought of Bernie's form, his past, the things he had done, things that even now Tim would hesitate to ask after.

"Did Michael send you?" Tim said.

"Doesn't know I'm here. He's given up on you."

"Sanjay?"

"That prick."

"He's my friend."

Bernie shrugged again. "You were there that day. He wasn't."

Bernie drank more tea. "You know," he said after a few moments, "I never thought you'd do it. First time I saw you. I told Michael that." Bernie put down his cup. "Guess he trusted his instincts. He guessed right." He licked his lips. "Mate, you're one of us."

Tim stared. Those words. *Just words*, he told himself. He reached into his pocket and felt Imogen's letter. Those last words. They seemed to represent an admission that Tim simply dared not make. That he simply could not yet allow. He pushed his chair back.

"Piss off." He stood up. "Fuck you." And instantly Bernie was standing as well, chest out, his chair crashing behind him, the lithe rapidity of the movement as shocking as its threat. But a moment later he was shrugging and reaching down for his chair. Tim grabbed his things and walked out the café. He waited for the sound of Bernie shifting his weight back onto his seat. When it did not come he thought for a moment that he would not make it out the door, although he did, but then, more strangely, he stood for a second wondering which way to go. He headed out fast onto the high street, marched past the shops, and on towards the tube station. He bought a ticket, a one-day pass, and then, at the barrier, he stopped. There was nowhere to go. In this vast city, he knew that everywhere was the same, the same as the place where he now stood. Every street, every landmark, contained its own menace, there were no hideaways, no safe houses, every face that he saw seemed to observe and assess and threaten in equal measure.

He turned and began to walk back. Bernie was still at the same seat, he was still drinking from the same mug. He was smiling. Tim sat down.

"People don't usually say that to me," Bernie said. "Not to my face."

Tim looked at him. "So why are you here?" he said.

"Dunno. Curious I guess."

"About what?"

"About you."

"Why?"

"You're not like the rest of them."

"What are they like?"

"Like someone like me."

"Like you?"

"I don't know. Someone with history."

"History? I have no history?"

"Not like mine."

Tim grimaced. After a moment he looked up at the ceiling, pulled his lips back and emitted a soundless scream. He rubbed his eyes, got up and ordered another coffee. As the waitress wrote down his order, he asked for a mug of tea as well. He sat down again.

"So you've not told Michael?"

"About what?"

"Coming down here."

"He's not my fucking nanny. Anyway..." The waitress brought over two cups. "He's tied up with business."

"He's not worried?"

"About what?"

"Being found out?"

"By who?"

"The police?"

"Are you?"

"What?"

"Worried?"

"I don't know." Tim rubbed his forehead. "I just don't know. It's... I just think there's a whole world out there that I don't understand."

"So?"

"I can't believe it won't strike back some day."

"It's all looking fine at the moment."

"You say that."

"I know that."

"How?"

"'Cos I can spot these things."

"How?"

Bernie looked at him. "'Cos I can."

"Well, that's great. So you'll warn me?"

"Warn you?"

"If they ever do decide to strike back?"

Bernie smiled. "OK," he said. "I will."

Tim smiled also and put his heads in his hands again. "Good." He got up and walked out the door a second time.

The next few days Tim turned up at the café in the afternoon. Sometimes Bernie was there, drinking tea from a mug at the same table. They would say hello, Tim would order coffee. At first their conversations were brief. Tim did not speak about Michael, or Sanjay. He asked nothing about Bernie, his life, his past. But gradually Tim found himself talking about other things, about football, the latest computer gadgets, about the news or the political gossip. It started cautiously and then seemed to gush out. Tim found himself chattering without stop, as if it were a pleasure he had once enjoyed and had suddenly rediscovered. They stayed at the café for a couple of hours, they talked, and in the evenings, alone, back at his flat, Tim tried to remember anything of what he had said earlier on, and he knew it was of absolutely no importance if he could not. He felt a strange kind of release, and then began to feel almost embarrassed at the anticipation he felt each time they met.

One day Bernie was not there. Nor was he the next. Tim waited. He sat alone at his table, took out Imogen's letter and started to re-read it. He smiled as he read. *Bernie*, he thought, *you've saved my life*.

*

Dan Becker looked at a sheet of paper. There was a list of names, in descending order of importance. He picked up a red pen and drew a line through the last one.

The guards at a South London tube station began to sense something stirring below the mouths of the escalator shafts just as the first police sirens became audible. Flickering shadows on the walls, shouts, whooping, screams, just beyond the lip of two shafts, both up and down. They looked at each other and crept forward, and then turned and began to retreat towards the ticket office, slowly, but moments later at a run, and as they hurried, there rolled up the shafts a slow motion wave of teenagers, a wave that exploded and crashed through and over the barriers, caps, hoods and trainers darting in asymmetric fluidity, fists and boots smashing windows, machines, kiosks. The guards gaped. Then, a thwack, two hands smacked against the glass. And a face, screaming at them, as if the volume on the PA was suddenly switched up to max, its bloated features inches away, lips swollen and snarling.

Thirty metres below, a hundred passengers staggered out of the train nursing cuts, bruises, and the loss of wallets, purses, mobile phones. They carried two men onto the platform, the men's stomachs heaving, wet, dripping crimson.

Later these same hundred people would number their attackers as being as few as ten and as many as fifty, figures the CCTV - vandalised, left unrepaired - could neither confirm nor deny. What was certain was that one of the youngest, whom police would identify later only as Wesley, was thirteen years old, and it was the image of his youthful features, gap-toothed, doe-eyed, that the papers would run the following day. Wesley was already trailing behind the others when he made his first mistake and chose the down escalator to flee the platform, and his breath was short as he stumbled to the top and the gang evaporated into the streets outside. He charged out the exit himself, he ran and ran, amid swirling blue lights, until he remembered a side road where his friends usually congregated. Rows of broken houses, empty doorways, smashed windows. An old bridge, underneath it a skip, overflowing, rat infested. The melancholy gleam of a single working street light where they would share crack and gear and stuff. Where they sometimes dragged girls. But police discounted the boy's claim that two men, two white men, big guys, speaking a weird language, marched past him, one either side, as he sprinted to the end of the road.

The two men saw the glint of the boy's new trainers before he noticed them. They looked at each other. One of the men extended a finger and traced a line slowly across the stubble over his Adam's apple. They headed towards the boy. The man looked at his partner. The other man's expression was indecipherable in the shadow.

The man whispered. "Well?" he might have said.

They walked fast. His partner stared ahead.

He whispered again. More urgently.

The boy came close. His partner turned. In the half-light, a gentle shake of the head.

The two men edged apart and glided left and right past the boy.

Wesley ran, and then walked, alone and silent under the bridge, and he knew that he was wrong, that the older kids had met up elsewhere, and as he realised this, as he reached the high metal edge of the rusting skip, he sank onto his knees and began to cry. And, a minute later, as streaks of blue light shimmered and then raked down the far end of the road, he stood, and reached up to the wall of the skip. He grunted and pushed, hauled his left leg onto the edge, and tumbled inside. A roll of carpet broke his fall. Something else as well. Next to his face, something smooth, cold, ridged. Hairy. And slowly his vision adjusted, and light and shade began to arrange themselves around him, and he saw two eyes, human eyes, inches from his own, staring straight at him. He screamed and thrashed but an arm pawed at him, or so he thought, until, an age later, a beam of light shone from above and two uniforms leaned in, reached down and dragged him out. But not before the lingering torchlight illuminated what lay below. Male, black, a boxer's physique, odd shiny patches over chest, arms, genitals, though whether these indicated cause of death or merely the later attentions of the street's rodent population was unclear.

Wesley's gang lived to rampage another day, and the police changed the focus of their enquiry to murder.

nineteen

Sanjay and Alec looked at each other across the conference table as Michael continued to ignore them.

"Can we get back to business?" Sanjay said. "We've still got a few items to get through."

Michael turned to him for a second, and then back to Mick and Bernie. They had been out the previous night, celebrating Mick's birthday. The three of them laughed. They were unshaven, their clothes were crumpled.

Sanjay put his pen down and walked to the water cooler. He had a momentary impulse to ask Patti to find Michael a tie.

"Sanjay." A shout to his back. "I'm thinking of taking up boxing again. What do you think?"

He poured.

Something was playing at the edge of his mind. A wrong note somewhere.

"Where was Jerome last night? I need him to give me some coaching."

"Fuck knows." Mick's voice. "No one's seen much of him the last few days."

"New lady friend?"

A concern, a doubt. Something.

Sanjay sat down next to Alec. He looked at the spreadsheet they had been discussing, and then began idly ticking off the numbers at the end of each row. The businesses, the clubs, the magazines. Spain. All profitable. And growing. Moscow. Michael's project. Especially Moscow. He had played a long and subtle game with the twins, and the balance of advantage had now moved in his favour. He was negotiating new terms, taking more control in the venture, nominating his own managers. Somehow, amazingly, it had all turned out right.

Sanjay thought back to the last few months, the changes that had occurred in all their lives. A chance meeting with Tim. And then a sudden, unlooked for opportunity. How narrow, how insignificant it had seemed, and yet once he, Sanjay, had figured out how to persuade Tim, once he had been able to exploit his weakness of character and tie together the unique position he had in his company with Michael's purposes, how smoothly the whole thing had worked out. Now they stood, staring across the continent of Europe at their two partners, their opponents, these two overweight buffoons, like figures from the days of the Tsars, these clowns who just happened to have access to the levers of power in modern Russia. And for Michael, his was the upper hand, it was in his power to move things forward.

Things were good. So the others said. He really wanted to agree.

Sanjay had dined a few nights back with an old acquaintance from his university days, someone with the centuries of authentic pedigree that took him right to the core of the British establishment – or so he pretended to Sanjay – and yet who seemed, like the ever decreasing number of his peers, destined to flit impotently around the fringes of the new, characterless elites who ran the modern day institutions of state.

They met at his club. Quentin had talked, of trekking with his cronies in the Sahara, of his new Porsche. Or perhaps it was his new wife. Of new business ventures in Brazil. Sanjay listened, amused. He had the suspicion that he was being sounded out. His friend said there was money to be made. Later they had discussed Michael.

"I'm surprised you're still with him," his friend said.

Sanjay had smiled at the comment. "Why?" he said. "I think we're doing just fine."

"He'll come unstuck." His friend was smoking a cigar. "Eventually." He exhaled. "Where's he from anyway? Greece?

Sicily?" The blue smoke seemed to sharpen Sanjay's concentration. "These Mediterranean types, they all blow it in the end. They haven't got the temperament."

He had said nothing.

"Look, Sanjay, at the end of the day, he's just not one of us."

Not one of whom? Sanjay thought.

He gazed across at Alec, who glanced back and appeared to shrug. Even he had changed, it seemed to Sanjay, since his short stay in South America. The exhilaration of the front line. It had rubbed off on all of them. Except him. He, Sanjay, had played merely an enabling role in the whole affair. He himself had not lied to anyone, or threatened anyone, or intimidated, or stolen. Perhaps he should have done. Perhaps this was the cause of his unease, that he was somehow excluded from an inner circle, a circle that comprised the other four people sitting around this conference table.

"Yeah. Jerome," Michael said. "Where the fuck is he? He's got a helluva right hook, that kid."

The swearing, Sanjay thought. He was sounding more like Mick every day.

A week later, at home, he had not yet left for work, Sanjay read about the death in the paper. The victim. Boxer, nightclub bouncer. The article mentioned police fears of a resurgence in gangland violence. The body had been found in a rubbish heap under a tunnel. The authorities were refusing to indicate cause of death. The article appeared inside, under domestic news. What made Sanjay gasp was a small picture at the side of the piece. In black and white, faces indistinct. But recognisably those of Jerome and Michael and Mick.

After a quarter of an hour, the phone started ringing.

Tim thought it was strange being rich. But then again, he wasn't really. Half a million pounds was not a lot of money these days.

Still. Ten years' salary. Tax-free. Available, ready and waiting, in a bank in Switzerland. He hadn't contacted them, for some reason it had not crossed his mind to do so. But perhaps in a while he would. He would run out of cash soon. He had bills. His flat, his car. Perhaps he would have to take an interest.

And then one day a message from Sanjay. On his voicemail.

"Tim. Call me when you have a moment. Call me, soon as you can." Tim smiled. The first time in a while Sanjay had made an effort to contact him.

He sat in his corner reading a book, a coffee in front of him. A novel. He had not read anything like it for an age. He had almost forgotten how.

His phone rang. He wondered whether to let it go. After ten seconds he decided to pick it up.

"Sanjay?"

"Tim. Hi." A pause. "Did you get my message?"

"What's up?"

"You OK? What've you been doing? You are OK, aren't you?"

Tim said nothing.

"Have you been reading the papers?" Sanjay again.

"Not specially. Should I have?"

"No. Just checking. Listen. Tim. Do you know anywhere out of town, out in the country? Somewhere where you could get away for a while?"

"Why?"

"No. Nothing. It's just that..."

"Sanjay. Should I be worried?"

"No. No. Look, let me suggest something. If you can, take a holiday. Use up some of that lovely money. Just go somewhere."

"Sanjay. What are you saying?"

"And if anyone unusual approaches you, be cautious. Just be careful."

There was silence.

"Tim? You still there?"

"You know, I've been seeing a bit of..."

"What? A bit of who?"

But Tim had second thoughts.

"Who?"

"Sanjay. It's nothing. It's not important."

"Tell me more."

"Sanjay. It's nothing."

Tim listened to him breathing, fidgeting.

"Listen, Sanjay, I'll be careful."

"OK." A pause. "Just think about what I was saying."

Sanjay was agitated. It surprised Tim to hear him sound that way. As if a balance between the two of them had changed. He was surprised but not alarmed. And he had an intuition that the sense of equanimity he felt was somehow rooted in his meetings with Bernie, that Bernie had somehow burst a bubble of anxiety that for weeks had been growing inside him. He, Tim, had taken something important from men of power, from the kind of people who made things happen in the wide world out there, and for weeks he had been expecting them to hit back. But he realised now that this whole hypothesis could be false, that, in truth, because these men operated in the shadows, he had no knowledge of how they might behave, what they might know, how they might react. And the theory was probably wrong, for when a reaction of sorts finally did arrive, it came in the shape of his new friend Bernie, cuddly Bernie, an overweight, middle-aged man, in a leather jacket and a 4x4 who drank mugs of tea and read the sports news in the tabloids, and with whom Tim could talk about the TV and the weekend's football. There was a harsh world out there, Tim knew. More than one. There were different worlds, different circles of people, moving, competing, acting independently of each other, like the planes stacked up in their flight corridors above London, one on top of the next, a mere few metres apart, and yet pursuing their own routes, their own purposes and destinations.

He sat snugly on his own, no longer able to understand why

Sanjay was concerned about him. These differing worlds, hostile or benign, they were all ignoring him, and he ignored them. Perhaps he was stupid, but he had begun to trust one voice only in all this confusion around him. He said goodbye to Sanjay and carried on reading.

The next day Bernie called him and told him things had changed.

He rang early. Tim was still in his dressing gown.

"You know the Royal Festival Hall?" Bernie said.

"Sure."

"Go there. Drop everything. Go there now. Find a bar or restaurant, somewhere in the open. Buy a drink, sit down, just wait. Wait for me to call. Might be a few hours. Might be more. Just do as I say."

"Sure, Bernie, but... Where are you now? What..."

A click, a dial tone. He waited uselessly for another five seconds.

Tim finished his coffee. *Why should I do this?* he thought to himself. *Why should I listen to what he says?* But he did. He got dressed, locked up the flat, and walked to the tube. He took the same route that he had taken months before with Imogen, crossing the river by the same bridge. There were high glass doors at the front of the concert hall. He stopped outside and peered in, then walked through, bought a paper and coffee from a machine, and found a spot in clear view of everyone in the huge foyer. He sat. He waited.

He watched the tourists coming and going, and then the lunchtime crowd, office workers looking for an agreeable place to meet and gossip. In the afternoon he considered getting up and exploring the bookshop, but he decided not to. A security guard walked by, looked him up and down, and strolled on. An hour later, he had to stretch his legs, and he went outside and spent fifteen minutes standing at the embankment looking out over the river. He came back inside, bought a sandwich, and sat down in the same chair. Early evening, bars opening, concert goers arriving. It began to get crowded. And then, as the five-minute bell started to sound and the mass of people began to move, his phone rang.

"Mate. Take the side door. At the western end. Turn left. Some concrete steps there, fifty yards in front of you. Go up, and then down the other side. Wait there. Got that?"

Tim stood up and walked quickly. He knew the building well, knew the exit that Bernie meant. He found the door, and elbowed his way past latecomers hurrying in. Light fading, the first autumn chill in the air. He trotted towards the stairway. At one point he stopped to look back. *Stupid*, he told himself. He faced forward and continued on. At the bottom of the steps, he looked around. He waited a minute. The crowds had disappeared, or perhaps they had got to where they wanted to go. Traffic was light. He squinted at each car, until one of them, coming up fast, sidelights off, came to a smooth stop fifteen yards away. Tim hesitated for a second, and then began to walk towards it. As he got close the passenger door opened out. He climbed in. Before he had closed the door, the car was gliding forward. They drove in silence.

After fifteen minutes, Tim looked at Bernie.

"Where are we going?"

"My surprise."

They drove around the centre of London for a couple of hours, accelerating and slowing, Bernie wary, alert. Eventually they headed east. Above, low cloud reflected the dull glow of the city.

At nine they crossed over the river at the Tower. Side roads winding through the ranks of building projects along the southern bank. Old wharfs and warehouses, now re-fashioned for a new working class of previously unimaginable wealth. Apartment blocks. Glass and brick, balconies suspended over the grey sludge of the Thames. Cobbled streets, gated carparks holding rows of Porsches and Range Rovers. Empty pavements. An area caught between the ages of steam and silicon. Curiously lacking the spirit of either.

Bernie pulled into an underground carpark. They took an elevator up to the fourth floor. A hallway, a line of doors leading off. Bernie led Tim towards the last of them, and pulled out a set of keys. They walked in. Darkness, Bernie fumbling with the lights, Tim's eyes adjusting. A massive living-room, white walls. Empty, apart from the sofas and the huge flat-screen television. Bernie pulled back curtains. Tim saw the towers of Canary Wharf across the water.

"Make yourself at home," Bernie said.

He went into the kitchen and returned with two bottles of beer and a litre of scotch. He placed everything on the floor.

"Why are we here?" Tim said.

"You hungry?"

Tim said nothing.

"I'll be twenty minutes." He tossed Tim a bottle opener. "Here, help yourself."

Later. Pizza and garlic bread lay half eaten in cartons strewn across old newspaper laid down on the carpet. Bernie had switched on the TV. He opened the bottle of scotch.

"Why are we here?"

Bernie played with the remote. "We'll talk tomorrow."

"I'm not staying."

"Tomorrow."

After five minutes Tim got up. Bernie pointed him to a bedroom.

The next morning, Tim awoke late. He showered and dressed. The flat was empty. He checked the fridge. The milk was off. It was the only item of food there. He found some coffee and drank it black. He returned to the living room and watched the bright sun playing on the river.

Bernie returned at midday. He laid a few bags on the settee.

"I got you a few things. Toothbrush. Some t-shirts. Groceries." He went into the kitchen.

Tim shouted after him. "Well?"

Bernie returned. "Let's go for a drive."

They headed further east, out of the city. Flat lands, pylons stretching away. Later they stopped at a small estuary town with a beachfront. They parked beside the promenade, and Bernie broke the story about Jerome. Tim gasped.

"Could be local turf wars," Bernie said. He smiled. Bad news, the bleak thrill in its revelation. "But there again... Best be careful."

Tim gazed out to sea.

"Sanjay? Alec?"

"Mick's got 'em covered."

They drove back.

"Bernie," Tim spoke at one point. "Can I ask you something?"

Bernie drove.

"Why are you doing this? For me?"

Bernie dropped Tim off at the flat. He said he had some business to look after. Tim read the papers, he explored the living room, kitchen, glanced round Bernie's bedroom. No pictures, no books, ornaments or diaries. Blank walls, a model-home sterility.

Bernie returned in the evening with Chinese takeaways. They ate watching TV. Tim felt somehow relaxed, cocooned. He was curious.

"You live here on your own?"

Bernie nodded. After a minute he spoke. "Wife's place. Ex. She's in Oz. With her sister. She isn't coming back."

Tim waited for more. It never came. He asked Bernie about Sanjay, how long he had known him. Bernie mumbled, his mouth full. Tim drank beer and began to talk, of how he had known Sanjay when he was much younger, of how they had met again by chance, just months before. He spoke of the time in the casino when he had talked half-drunkenly about the work he did, and their increasing closeness from that evening on. He described how later he had met Alec, and then Michael.

"But you know all this, don't you?"

Bernie nodded.

Tim sighed, and his tone became dry and matter-of-fact. He recounted the meetings they all had together, the discussions, the evolving plans. In a low monotone, he recounted the events of the big day, the day of the job itself, that day, the most extraordinary day of his life.

Bernie listened in silence. He waited until Tim had finished.

"So why did you do it?" he said.

Tim shrugged. "I don't know. Yes. I do know. Many reasons. It's complicated."

Bernie got two more bottles of beer. "I guess Michael just couldn't resist one last walk on the wild side," he said. "Can't say I'm surprised."

Bernie drank.

"He was very different when I first got to know him," he said. "I met his uncle first. He was the one who introduced me to Michael. The kid was tough, out of control. Perhaps he's become nostalgic for those days." He paused for a while. "He was smart though. He sorted himself out. I watched him shift the business into all these semi-legit areas. He was the one who recruited those city boys like your friend.

"But for me it was the end of something when they all arrived. I stuck it for a few years, but... Not my scene, sitting in conferences with me brolly and pinstripes. Began to put me off. I had friends in South Africa."

"But you came back?"

Bernie stared at the television screen. "I got old."

After a while he collected up the plates and took them into the kitchen.

Tim called out after him. "Bernie, how long do I need to stay here?"

A shout back. "Dunno." He walked back in. "Look, mate. Just wait. Just see what happens."

*

Michael Palmer had a meeting that evening. A detective, they met for a drink. An older man, he liked a pint or two. He had known Michael's uncle. He was talking about retirement, of buying a small place in Spain. Michael made a mental note to look out for somewhere suitable when the time came.

"You're not serious, Mike?" he said. "About the boxing."

Michael smiled. He bought more drinks.

"That kid, Jerome," the policeman said. "He was one of yours, wasn't he?"

Michael nodded. He agreed it was a bad business.

The policeman took his time before continuing.

"I wanted to speak to you about it, Mike." He sipped his drink. "Do you know how he died?"

"It was the drugs, wasn't it?"

"His heart stopped."

Another pause. Another sip.

"I spoke to the coroner. They did things to him."

"So?"

"Experts. It must have taken a long time. It must have been nasty."

"He's not the first to end up like that."

"He had bits missing."

"Yardies."

"Is anyone out to get you, Mike? You got any enemies?"

"I always have enemies."

"No. Seriously."

Michael said nothing.

"It was drugs. But not the usual. The type of thing you only get in hospitals. I've got the name written down somewhere. I can't pronounce it."

Michael had looked away.

"Look, mate, I once made a promise to your old man. To keep an eye out for you..." The policeman leaned closer. "Mike, tell me, there is something, isn't there?"

Tim slept well that night. Bernie was up early, making noise, washing dishes. But when Tim got up, he had gone. There was a note and a key on the kitchen table. Tim did some shopping, he walked along the waterfront. Bernie returned late afternoon. He said he would cook. Steak, chips, vegetables. Then television and bottles of beer.

They watched news, documentaries. Images of war. Of troops in Basra and Kabul.

Bernie became animated. He turned the volume down low, and talked about his childhood, of alcoholic parents on the dole, of teenage years scrapping in the streets and nicking cars, and then meeting a mate who was in the army and joining up himself almost as a kind of dare, and Tim suddenly knew he was hearing a story that was centuries old and had been repeated a thousand times, and involved an institution inextricably embedded in British society as the final stop for all the misplaced anger, the inebriated, uneducated, mindless violence that festered around the coarser edges of the nation's disaffected youth. Tim remembered demonstrations in his student days against precisely this type of symbol of the state, and he saw now how meaningless they would have seemed to young men like Bernie for whom the army had become the framework and the focus for everything he was and aspired to be. That desperate aggression, tempered, harnessed, directed somewhere useful, even benign. He described driving a tank and learning to ski, and jumping out of aeroplanes. He described jungle training, and his mates leaving scorpions in his boots, and losing his footing once when crossing by ropes over a streaming torrent and being dragged two hundred yards by the current and ending up half-dead and entangled in the roots of a submerged tree trunk.

He described the first time he had shot a man. It was a sniper hidden away behind a hedge in the remote countryside of South

Armagh. He wasn't sure at first whether he had got him, but his sarge was crouched down at his shoulder, whispering, *good man, good man*, and he had wondered for months what it would feel like, and in a way he felt nothing that day because they had trained and trained for exactly this moment, and his instincts had just kicked in without even thinking, but in another way he felt something he had never experienced before, a sense of the moment, the sky and the fields and hedgerows around him, his mates at his side, the hallucinatory quality of the puff of smoke in the bushes two hundred yards away, the exhalation of life, and the imprinting of the moment on his soul, a kind of branding in fire that set him apart, as one of the army's own, and he knew he could never be the same kind of person again.

He described an action on the slopes of a hill outside Port Stanley, a cold blackness all around, streaks of fire racing overhead, men shouting and firing, shouting, firing, a spray of shells, the earth rumbling and bouncing under his feet, an explosion at his side, and then a feeling that suddenly he did not know what was up and what was down, and for a while, he did not know how long for, he stared at the stars and seemed to rotate in the sky with them, but it stopped and he was back on the ground, encased in mud, willing his legs to move, and his mates were shouting at him to get up. And he did, and a part of him died for a while, or perhaps it became submerged in something else, this band of men, this pack, with a single unified will driving itself forward, destroying everything in its way.

Tim asked him why he left the army, and Bernie mentioned defence reviews and cutbacks.

"Some of us had trouble back home," he said. "Wives hated it. Mine," he chuckled, "my first, she ran out while I was away in the South Atlantic. Our boy was a couple of years old. Later I heard she married an officer."

They drank beer and watched the news. The announcer cut to a reporter in an African country, they saw militiamen in jeeps, bodies in the street.

"Many of the lads couldn't live with the memories. Others needed the buzz again. They'd felt it once. They'd do anything to feel it one more time." Bernie laughed. "Guess that was me." He laughed again. "That shock you?"

The reporter was telling the world that war was hell. "It's rubbish," Bernie said. He swore at the television. Tim stared at him.

"It's not hell. It's the fucking opposite." His voice rose. "If it was hell, they'd stop it, they'd stop it in twenty-four hours."

They watched grim-faced aid workers, lines of frightened women and children.

"It's bollocks," Bernie said. "They do it because they love it. Those men, those soldiers, the ones on that truck, they're addicted to it. It's the most exciting thing that ever happened to them."

They watched a man spraying machine gun fire into the sky.

"Look at him, see that guy." Bernie was still chuckling. "Look at that guy. He's loving it. Every moment of it."

The next day it rained. Again Bernie was up and out before Tim arose. He wasted the day staring at the wind churning up the river below. Evening, the pattern of the last few days began to repeat itself. Food, basic and filling. Beers, TV.

Bernie was quiet. Later he opened the scotch and began to talk about Michael's uncle.

"He helped me, that old man. He looked out for me when I left the army and didn't know what I was doing next. A gent. Old school."

Tim asked him what Michael's uncle had wanted from Bernie.

Bernie extended his legs and then turned down the volume on the television. "I think he wanted me to keep an eye on his nephew. And Mick and the other lads."

He described the first few years he spent with them. He laughed. "There were some psychos amongst that lot. I tried to change it all."

"And Michael?" Tim asked.

"He changed as well," Bernie said. "He changed a lot after he went to jail. Perhaps it was the age he was at. Twenty-four, twenty-five. You're not a kid any more. He met some girl soon after, some Sloane with a rich old man. He had plans. He wanted to straighten the business out. He saw what the other lads were like, they'd get their hands on some dirty money, spend the next few weeks getting high or doped up, living in shit in some Brixton dive, until the money ran out and they were back to where they started. He couldn't stand all that. He wanted to build something, something that would last."

Bernie pushed his fists into his pockets. "Michael began to realise there was a right and a wrong way to do things." He closed his eyes. "Sometimes you'd get some guy, he'd be making trouble, not just for you, but for everyone. Perhaps he's always high, he's antagonising people. We had tons of this white stuff coming in from South America. Everyone made money. As long as you were cool about it. Some guys weren't. Mick always wanted to go for the spectacular, make an example. But I would persuade Michael to be a bit more subtle. One night we might pick up the guy, quietly. We drive somewhere, he disappears. They usually have no papers, no one hears of them again."

Tim stared. "But..."

"Look, mate..." Bernie opened his eyes and chuckled. "...there are no good guys in this business. We all go into it with our eyes open. If you behave like an arse-hole, you pay the price. Everyone knows that."

They were silent. They drank scotch. Bernie began to talk about Africa. Guerrilla wars, mercenary wars. Anti-insurgency operations. Protection for the diamond companies.

"I was there, five years. You know, out there, it's... it's hard to describe... it's..." Bernie rubbed his eyes. He mumbled. "You cross borders, you go where you want. You don't know where you'll lay your head that night. You don't know if you'll be lying in a ditch with a bullet in your brain. There are no rules, no frontiers. You're free. To do what you want until someone points a gun at you and tells you not to. Sometimes they mean it. Sometimes they don't. It's just your luck that day."

Later Tim would wonder whether he had heard these things, or whether he had made them up.

Open plains, grasslands extending to every horizon. Blanched skies, burnt landscapes. Short sunsets and cold nights. Tropical downpours. Each day, a crimson dawn, a rebirth. Jungle trails, swollen rivers. Every acre of land, every square inch, shared by a million species, each clamouring for its right to existence, an existence predicated on the hunting, the slaughter, the devouring of a thousand rivals in the struggle for another day of life. Each day of life a contest whose stakes, life itself, made every other consideration pointless.

Men in land rovers, rifles always at their sides. Patrolling weeks on end, sleeping where they would. Brits, South Africans, Australians. Veterans from Chechnya and Iraq. Men who had felt the moment of death and the negation of their own existence, and the exhilaration of passing out the other side, whole and alive. Men for whom the constraints and regulations of civil society were a disenfranchisement, not a benefit.

Atrocities.

"They once took some villagers, poor farmers. We chased them into the jungle." And Bernie paused. "They have this thing about machetes."

Dirty wars, summary executions. Child soldiers. Slavery. AIDS.

"Why were you there?" Tim said.

"Money."

"Is that all?"

"It's what I do." Bernie sighed. "That shock you?"

"Is there a solution?" Tim said.

"No."

"So what's the point?"

"They told us we could fence it in. Prevent it from spreading. Sometimes we thought we did."

Tim said later, "Your son. I guess he's grown now?"

"I suppose."

"You never tried to trace him?"

"Why should I?"

"Don't you care?"

"He's probably like you. College education and all that. Probably wears a suit to work."

"Bernie, I could help you. I could help you find him."

Silence.

"Bernie, I know how to do things like that."

"Why bother?"

"The internet. Government agencies, bureaucrats. I know how to talk to these people."

The TV was still on.

"I could trace him for you. There've got to be records. Somewhere. I can track these things down. I know how the system works."

Channel hopping. Tim half caught its fractured narrative.

"Bernie?"

It was late, but Bernie started to talk again, and Tim wondered what compulsion seemed suddenly to be driving him. As if he needed to take Tim to some place he had inhabited all his life and which had faded and greyed with over-familiarity. But Tim began to realise that this was a place he already knew.

"I suppose it's another world for you?" Bernie said. "The kind of life I've lived.

"Tell me. Tell me about normality. I need to know. What's it like to work in a regular office? To pay taxes? To believe the other guy's not out to get you?"

Tim went to the kitchen. He got another beer from the fridge and sat down again.

"I did something myself once," he said. "When I was at university. When I first knew Sanjay." He drank. "We decided one night to drive to Oxford. The pubs were closing, Sanjay had friends up there, and he said he knew of a party. We were pissed, but you know how it is, at that age it doesn't bother you. I sometimes did stuff, and for some reason, that night I bought a whole load of speed. I thought if we were staying up all night, we might need some chemical stimulation.

"It was... I don't know, one, two in the morning when we arrived. I had driven. The streets of the town were empty, but the party was still going strong. It was at one of the colleges, bright young things in evening dress. Pretty women, their arrogant boyfriends. You know the type. Or perhaps you don't. It's another world. We crashed their party, I'm not sure Sanjay in fact knew anyone. They gawped at us, we got drunk. I got high. I just remember this, all of them just staring, not saying anything. Sanjay desperately trying to make conversation. But I was so drugged up I didn't care.

"It was beginning to get light when we left. We had nowhere to stay, we had to drive back. Sanjay slept, I put my foot down. As we got close to Bath it started to rain.

"There was this place outside town, this kind of camp, just by an old rubbish dump. It was where the tramps hung out. Bag ladies, alcoholics, drug addicts. I've no idea how many. I don't think anyone ever did. But there was a short cut into town that took me right through the area. I wanted to get home, I'd had enough. The drugs weren't working any more.

"There was a cloudburst. The rain was pelting down, visibility was just a few yards. There was so much shit in the streets round there. Rubbish, bottles, mud. So much shit, we were skidding all over the place.

"There was a face. In the headlights. In front of us. I... Sanjay was suddenly awake, I remember his screaming. I was hitting the brake pedal, but... I don't know..."

Tim paused. He swallowed, took another swig of beer.

237

"There was a bump. I felt something being dragged underneath the car for a second. I slowed. It was pouring with rain, in the mirror I could see this lump in the road behind. We didn't stop. I knew we should have done, but I just couldn't. We just drove on. I couldn't even get out of the car when we got back. I couldn't because I knew I didn't dare look at what we'd see on the front bumper. Sanjay had to drag me out. And there it was. Blood. The rain hadn't quite washed it off. Something else as well, flesh maybe.

"And then Sanjay took over. He garaged the car, cleaned it up. I was a wreck. I went to bed, and stayed there twenty-four hours. The booze, the drugs, the trauma of what had happened. I didn't leave the flat for the next four days. I just sat there, waiting for the police to call, thinking that my life was over, I'd spend the rest of my life in jail. I asked myself why I didn't at least stop at the scene of the accident. That was unforgivable. And then something amazing happened. Or rather nothing happened, and that was amazing. No one called, the phone didn't ring. Life went on. The fifth day I stepped out, I went to some lectures. I checked the university notice boards. Nothing. No one asked me anything, my tutors ignored me as they always did.

"A week later, exactly seven days later, I went back there. Back to the rubbish dump. I walked around. There they all were, these hooded figures in their rags, scowling at me, some begging, some just telling me to fuck off. I saw where they lived, their cardboard boxes, the shelters a few of them had constructed out of the piles of rubbish nearby. And then I saw a body. Someone dead. Our guy. Or someone else perhaps. Dead. Or dying. Or perhaps just asleep. I walked up. The body was face down, I didn't dare turn it over or check any more closely. But it didn't matter, because I suddenly understood something. That no-one cared. No-one gave a damn. This was where people came to die. We had just helped someone on his way. I don't know what they did with the corpses. Perhaps they buried them themselves. Or perhaps the authorities came by once in a while. But it was nothing to do with me. I just walked away. I just..."

Suddenly he was coughing. "I just..."

Coughing, doubling up. He went to the kitchen and got a glass of water, came back. He waited a minute.

"But a part of me didn't escape from it that easily. For months I had nightmares about the accident. I stopped sleeping, I felt depressed. I never socialised. And then one day the dreams just stopped and... I know it sounds strange... I just put the whole incident totally out of my mind."

Tim cleared his throat. "I hardly ever saw Sanjay after that. He just seemed to be getting on with his life, but it was a life that excluded me. I don't know, he didn't seem at all affected by what had happened. I would see him on campus, but we never spoke. He disappeared before graduation and that was it. Until this year."

Tim was silent. After a while he got up. He went to the toilet. He sat on the seat and put his head in his hands.

He had a hangover next morning. Recollection of the previous evening came back in fragments.

He was alone in the flat. He made coffee and tried to recall the things he had told Bernie. Things he had told no one else. Things he should have told Imogen.

Mid-morning a memory came crashing into his mind. The previous night, late, very late. Pale skin, grey-flecked hair, emerging slowly out of the dark hallway like form and shape on developing film. Bernie stood at the door of his room, staring, watching him sleep. Tim could not figure out whether the image was dreamt or observed.

He stepped out onto the balcony one last time and felt his head clear. The image should have disturbed him, and yet it didn't. Instead he sensed in himself a kind of gratitude, not so much for what Bernie had done, as for his agency. He felt a strange completeness. He went back inside and wrote out a note, thanking him for everything. Then he collected his things and walked out the flat.

It took him a while to find a station, he did not know the area. He got back to his place about noon. He dumped his stuff, showered and changed. Then, on a whim, he picked up his keys and got in his car.

An hour later he hit the M4. He drove, machine-like, the needle steady on seventy-five. After ninety minutes, he took a turning for Bath. He spent a couple of hours walking, observing the students, admiring the old terraces, revisiting a favourite coffee bar. As it began to get dark, he drove around the outskirts of town. At one point he stopped and looked around. *The same as it always was*, he thought. He got back in his car and headed back to London.

twenty

At some point that day Mick woke up suddenly. He tried to open his eyes, and couldn't. It puzzled him for a few moments and then he tried to turn over, but he realised he did not know which way he was facing, whether the bedside table was to the left or to the right. He moved an arm, but it was numb, something that always happened when he slept uncomfortably. He tried to flex his fingers, but he could not feel them. Instead he became aware of something sharp, at his cheek. Sharp, very sharp. It was painful, excruciatingly painful. He probed with his tongue. There was something in his mouth, it tasted unpleasant. Dust, or something. And then he felt it. A stone. Or glass perhaps. The thing that was hurting his cheek, it was inside his cheek.

He thought. Where was he? At home? At the club, on the sofa? He tried to remember the previous night, and it seemed he could. He could remember clearly getting into his own bed, under his own sheets.

He heard a voice, someone calling him. From a distance.

He remembered his own bed, and then he knew that he had already got up, he had got out of his bed already. It was hours and hours ago, he was sure of it.

The voice was there again, a man's voice, repeating something. Then a hand, feeling his forehead, his face. He twitched, he tried to flick it away, he swore.

He started coughing, gently at first, and then he opened his mouth and began to heave, and a ton of stuff seemed to explode out of him.

His eyes were open.

He lay on glass. On glass and stone, the shards were on his eyebrows, his eyelashes, his hair, and he twitched again and a hand, gentle, so gentle, began to smooth away the glass, a million fragments, on his skin, his eyes. Pricking, biting, alive.

"Wait. Stay still." The hand was so soft, and for a second he felt a weariness. Then he remembered something else, something that explained how the glass was in his hair. He remembered hitting the glass window of the shop, he remembered he was two foot up in the air, travelling towards that glass, his arms waving, trying to stop himself. But he had not been able to. He had tossed his head and writhed, and he hit the glass and it shattered over him and he crashed to the pavement outside.

And Mick began to scream.

It had been a beautiful day.

"Mick, give Vicky a hand this morning, will you."

He had parked early outside the shop. There were no customers, not even any traffic wardens. He knocked on the door, then opened it.

"Chauffeur her round, can you. She's got some stuff to pick up."

Vicky always looked so great, she always dressed so great.

"Sure, Michael"

She was inside, the back room, the hat room. There were parcels, boxes. She pointed. Mick picked up a handful and began to walk back to the car. He opened the boot and dumped them inside, then went back into the shop.

"How many to go?"

"All of them," she said. "Please." A wide smile.

He picked up another bundle, turned, and walked back towards the main door. And then a memory came back to him, out of the blue. A memory that he knew had begun to haunt his dreams recently, of himself as a boy, in the country, running. Just running. He was small, and unimaginably thin, and light, and his feet caressed the ground below. Weightless, so thin, the warm grass beneath his naked feet, it felt so exquisite. Floating. He felt it now. He was lighter than air. He was bathed in bright light, warm air. He was travelling through the air. He was travelling towards the pane of glass at the front of the shop.

Mick turned and hauled his body onto an elbow.

"Don't get up." The voice again. "Lie down. The ambulance is coming."

Mick tried to swat something away. The hand. Again.

He made as if to get up, and his legs seemed odd and bent.

"Calm yourself. They're on their way."

And then Mick grabbed the hand. "Fuck off!" he shouted. He looked around. A crowd of people on the pavement, backing away. He tried to stand but he could not raise himself above his knees. He saw a hole in the building. Where the door had been. He began to crawl. Dust. Something to the left. On fire. A whole pile of things on fire. Glass, more glass, fragmented, a sea of glass, beneath his hands and knees. The back room, ahead of him. A darkness. Dust.

"Vicky!" he shouted. "Vicky!"

The back room ahead of him. Black. A hole in the wall. He could see nothing beyond. Absolutely nothing.

*

Michael Palmer looked around the conference room. His secretary stood at the door.

"I'm so, so sorry," she said.

He was silent for a while.

Then, "Patti, why don't you take the day off. We're not going to get much done here."

"Are you sure?"

He nodded.

"The tickets to Zurich. I don't know if... " She paused. "If you decide to go tonight... they're on my desk."

Half an hour later, Bernie arrived. Then Sanjay, Alec.

"How's Mick?" Michael looked across at Bernie.

"He's OK. Cuts and bruises. They want to keep him overnight at A&E. Don't think he'll stay."

Michael waited for the others to settle.

"Right. Let's try to be quick. I have to go in half an hour. They need someone to identify the body."

Everyone was silent.

"Well, guys? What the fuck do we do?"

"Let me say, Michael." Alec. "We're so... If there's anything..."

Michael frowned. "Yeah." Then, again, softly. "Yeah."

"They're after us," Bernie said. "Someone's got it in for us."

"OK. Let's hold it a second," Sanjay said. "I know it's difficult. Let's think it through for a moment."

"Think about what?" Michael said.

"Are we absolutely sure?"

"Sure of what?"

"Well. With Jerome. A squabble over drugs? And now this. What are the police saying? A gas leak?"

"For fuck's sake..."

"Michael, Bernie, I know things are bad. But let's not rush in."

There was a pause.

Alec spoke. "Sanjay may have something. Wait, I'm not taking sides. But, well, think about motive. If it's deliberate, what are they after? What do they achieve by this? If these people, *they*, are in fact behind it?"

"What d'you mean?"

"Michael, I... I don't really know how... how to say this..." Alec looked down for a moment. "Vicky?"

"For Christ' sake," Bernie said. "It was Mick they were after."

"Jesus, why did I...? Years ago, she asked me years ago." Michael stared at his hands. "She wanted to move out of here. Why did I let her stay in this godforsaken fucking town? Why didn't I just set her up somewhere..."

Sanjay got up. He walked over to the water cooler.

"So." Michael, behind him. "What do we do?"

Sanjay poured himself a cup. "You know, there is something we could try..." he said. He turned to the others. "This chap Geldman."

"Who?"

"Bernie, the guy that... you know... the oil trader..."

"Sanjay what are you saying?" Michael broke in.

"Michael, if we assume it's him. We can put out feelers. Alec has the contacts. We can sound out a few people..."

Michael slammed his fist on the table. "Bernie, give me a cigarette." Bernie fumbled in his pocket. "Quick, what have you got there?" He lit up and took a puff.

"Sanjay, that guy's just shot up half my organisation, and you're talking about getting into bed with the fucker..."

"Michael. Whoa! I'm not talking about alliances. I'm talking about interests. Just think for a second. The big picture. What do we want? What are we after? It's this whole project in Moscow, isn't it? It's the company, it's the success of this business of ours. And also Spain, and London, and everything else we've worked to achieve. I'm talking about our interests, Michael. And if we need to bend with the wind once or twice, well, that's fine, we do it."

And Michael was charging towards Sanjay, the cigarette falling to the carpet somewhere. "Jesus! Vicky's lying on a fucking slab, and you're suggesting we roll over like..."

Michael had Sanjay by the lapels and was pushing against the wall.

"Michael, Michael." Bernie stood up. "Mike. Calm it." He was at Michael's side, a hand on his shoulder. "Calm down."

*

Sanjay worked in his office at the casino that evening. He was disturbed by a call from his secretary.

"The man from the BBC. He's waiting in reception."

Sanjay cursed. "When did I agree to this?" He had forgotten. He knew it was months before. Before... all this. He asked for the man to be sent in, and then realised that he had never agreed. Sanjay looked him over. The front. Young, sharp. In a suit. A contrast to the shabbiness of so many of the TV journalists he had met. But he knew that a new wave of second generation Asian producers was shaking up the corporation.

The man took a seat, presented his card. He began to talk about his brief, to design a package of new shows, programmes to reflect the nature of modern Britain. He wanted to profile a number of Asian businessmen, and a few women, who had been successful in their adopted country. He spoke smoothly, enthusiastically.

At one point Sanjay interrupted him. "Excuse me, how did you hear about me?"

"You were... recommended."

"By whom?"

The man would not say. He continued. He said he wanted to highlight the difficulties that such people had faced, the culture shock they had overcome. Sanjay listened to his voice, his accent flipping every so often from a measured newsreader-blandness to south London twang, as if defining a final level of assimilation to which he would not climb.

He asked Sanjay questions about himself, his family, their difficulties.

"Difficulties? What kind?" Sanjay said.

"You never felt part of a wider struggle?"

Sanjay said he was slightly bemused by the use of that phrase.

"Well, were you picked upon? As a child."

"Possibly. No more than any other."

"Your parents. The prejudice they faced. Was it ever a factor for them? Even if indirect."

"My parents worked hard. They raised a family."

"What did they do?"

Sanjay paused. He looked at his interviewer. "I think that's my business."

"Do you ever feel you have obligations to a wider community?"

"Which community is that?"

The producer paused for a moment.

"Did you ever feel personally disadvantaged?"

"In what way?"

"Because you were seen as an outsider."

"What kind of outsider?"

The man smiled. "You know what I mean."

Sanjay said nothing. The man began to ask questions about the company, about Michael Palmer, his past.

"Look. Sanjay. Let me be frank. I guess what I'm trying to explore is whether people like yourself still face a glass ceiling. Real or imagined. Whether they feel they can only go so far in whatever they've chosen to do."

Sanjay began to drum his fingers on the desk.

"I've heard one or two things about your boss..."

"Such as?"

"He has a colourful reputation."

Sanjay said nothing.

"There was an explosion today. In town. I understand Palmer owned the premises."

"How do you know that?"

His interviewer laughed. "I'm a reporter."

Sanjay leaned forward into the microphone at his desk, and asked his secretary to get his visitor another coffee, and then a taxi when he was ready to go.

"Someone was killed at that shop," Sanjay said.

"I'm sorry, I didn't mean..."

Sanjay excused himself, saying he had another meeting to attend. He led the man into the reception area.

As he paced around the tables that evening, Sanjay thought about Mick. And then Jerome. He had been spooked when the body was found. They had argued at the time over what to do with Tim. Michael didn't give a damn. *The kid's lost his bottle*, he had said. *Nothing we can do about it.* But Sanjay had urged some caution, there was a lot he could give away. If the wrong type of pressure were exerted.

Pressure from who? The police? They've got nothing. Where's the evidence?

Michael was missing the point. There were other threats out there. He thought about Vicky, the shop. Michael's outburst.

Sanjay watched the punters at play. He spoke to his managers. It normally relaxed him to watch the pattern of success and failure on the floor in front of him. He looked across at the money being gambled and lost. Here, in this club, in other clubs like it, in Spain, in Moscow. This was the way forward. This was the future. He had come a long way with Michael, and here, at the moment of their triumph, it seemed to him that Michael was in danger of forgetting all that he had learnt.

He thought about the TV producer. A relic of old class wars. He remembered the demos and marches of his student days. Not that he had attended any. That was where that reporter should be. Not here in the real world.

*

As he drove to London Tim thought about Imogen's letter, now discoloured and torn along the folds. He arrived back at his flat at eleven. At home he read it again. He knew there was something he wanted to do. Something he needed to do. He had calculated the time difference and guessed it was early afternoon over there. He sat on the phone and waited as he was bounced around for five minutes, and then he got through to a man who identified himself as the west coast tour manager. Tim introduced himself. He asked for Imogen.

A pause.

"I'm afraid she can't come to the phone just now."

"Oh?"

"She's been a bit indisposed."

"What?"

"Nothing serious. No need to worry."

"Where is she?"

"She's been staying with my wife for a couple of days."

"Is she a doctor?"

"No. It's just, she went through much the same, before her..."
Silence.

"Yes?"

"Excuse me, who did you say you were?"

"My name's Tim."

"Are you family?"

"I..." He was thrown by the sudden change of tack. For a second he thought of lying. But he knew he could absolutely no longer do that. "No."

"A friend?"

"Yes." Softly. He rolled the question around in his mind. He cleared his throat. "Yes," he repeated.

"I see."

"Can I speak to her?"

He sensed an indecision. And then. "Does she have your number?"

"Yes."

"Good. I'll pass on a message."

"Wait..." He knew he had to add something, he needed a few seconds to think. His mind lurched.

He thought of Bernie, of Sanjay. Of his past, of his other life.

"I'll tell her you called."

"Please." Tim felt useless and inept. "Please do. Make sure you do."

In the silence he stared at the letter, his fingers resting over the redial button on the phone. Then he stood up. He wondered if he could try again the next evening.

He wasn't tired. He fretted, he needed something to do, someone to talk to. He thought about his day. Bath, the town, the bars, the streets.

Places he and Sanjay had once known so well.

Half an hour later, he was parking his car down the road from the casino. Sanjay always worked late.

Tim was asked to wait in his office. Sanjay was not long. He poured Tim a scotch, and then himself a larger one.

"How's things?" Tim looked at him. Sanjay's suit looked, for once, crumpled, ill-fitting.

"Let's get out of here," Sanjay said. "You eaten?"

They took a taxi into Soho – Sanjay insisted even when Tim produced his car keys. They sat in a small Italian. Tables tightly packed. No music. Sanjay was on familiar terms with the owner. Tim noticed a line of second-string celebrities at a table in the corner. Sanjay ignored them. He concentrated on the wine list, talked vintages with the waiter.

"God, I needed to get away," he said.

"I was thinking about you today," Tim said. He began to talk, about his trip, his day off. "It's not changed," he said. "The place is the same as it always was. That old charm is still there."

Sanjay studied the menu. "I'm glad you came," he whispered. "I really am."

Tim was silent for a moment. "I said, it's not changed. At all."

The wine arrived. Sanjay tasted it and nodded. The waiter poured two glasses. Sanjay swallowed impatiently.

"You really couldn't wait to get away from there, could you?" Tim said.

Sanjay looked at him. "You remember Jerome?"

Tim's mind shifted a gear. He recalled a moment of panic long ago, Jerome's hands on his shoulders, over his mouth, calming, soothing.

"You heard what happened?" Sanjay said.

"Bernie says it was some drugs thing."

Sanjay poured himself more wine. "It wasn't. I wish it had been. I wish. I wish..."

"What does Michael say?"

Sanjay shook his head. "He's seeing the Ivanovs tomorrow."

"That's something, isn't it? Isn't that good?"

"The twins. The cause of this whole mess."

"Mess? What do you mean? This is your game, Sanjay. You've won. You've got everything you wanted, haven't you?" *Everything you wanted*, Tim thought. *And I've got my money. For me it's now over.* And he thought about the call he had put through to the States earlier on, and when he would be able to try again.

"Tim, where are you staying these days? You being careful?"

"Listen, Sanjay, I'm out of it. I'm not part of it any more."

"Don't be a fool. You're not out of it. None of us is out of it."

"Sanjay. This is your scene, not mine."

They still had not ordered. Sanjay turned to the waiter. He asked him for the special of the day.

"Sanjay, walk away from it. If you don't like it, just go."

"How?"

"It's easy. Follow me."

"I spent my whole childhood walking away from one life." Sanjay stared at him. "My student years walking away from yours."

"OK. So. Stick it out with Michael." Starters arrived. "Your choice."

They ate.

Later, over coffee, brandy. "Tim, where are you staying tonight?"

"You asked that before."

"There's a bed at the casino."

"I'm going home."

"Look, I'm meeting Bernie tomorrow. At my flat, late afternoon. He's arranging for his boys to keep an eye on things."

"And Mick?"

"He's... he's out of action for a few days."

Tim looked across the table.

"Something's happened, hasn't it?" He bent close. "Tell me. Something's happened."

"Meet me. Tomorrow. Bernie'll be there. He's got keys."

Tim had to laugh. "Sanjay. For God's sake. How can you be surprised at the way things have turned out?" He looked at Sanjay's untouched dessert. He shook his head. "How can you possibly be surprised?"

"Don't say that. It wasn't supposed to..."

"What?"

"Just don't say it. Don't say anything."

Sanjay was calling the waiter. He struggled with his wallet. Credit cards fell across the table. He swore.

Sanjay was drunk. Tim found a taxi back. Things were winding down at the casino. Sanjay was unsteady on his feet, just about able to find the keys to his office. There was a backroom with a sofa bed. Tim helped Sanjay onto it, and then decided he was too tired to go home himself. He found a drawer with blankets and pillows. Then he remembered his car.

"Sanjay, I'm going to get ticketed tomorrow."

But Sanjay was asleep.

Tim left the office. The lights over the gaming floor were low.

Outside he spoke to the doorman. He asked if there was twenty-four hour parking anywhere close by.

twenty one

Michael Palmer stepped into the lift and pressed the button for the twentieth floor. The top floor. The penthouse rooms. He would not have expected anything else, the twins had a certain taste for conspicuous displays of extravagance. It did not surprise him. What interested him instead, as the doors closed, was why they had asked him to come and see them in their own private rooms. Moreover, to come alone. No Sanjay, Alec. No Bernie. It had occurred to him that he should worry, but he dismissed his fears. He had not even mentioned it to anyone, they had enough to deal with back in London. It did not bother him. On the contrary, he relished the prospect.

He clenched and relaxed his fists as the lift ascended, wondering what it was the twins wanted. He rocked backward and forward on his toes. He guessed that there was a camera in the lift. *Let them watch*, he thought. *Let them watch.*

They had meetings lined up the next morning, at a conference suite in the basement of the twins' Zurich hotel. The twins, their advisors and translators. On his side, Alec, flying in tomorrow. Yet the twins had seemed only half-interested when he discussed the agenda on the phone earlier.

He was met at the top by a man in a dark suit who waited with folded arms by the entrance. They walked to the end of the corridor and through a set of double doors. Michael was led into a large reception area that spread out over two levels. Two other men stood by and watched them enter. He wondered for a moment whether he was going to be searched. One of them approached and asked Michael what he would like to drink. There was an extensive bar to one side. The other man asked Michael to follow and led him up three steps to a lounge area with high windows looking out over a dark city. There were three armchairs spaced around a small table. Borzoi and Chergo sat in two of them.

"Michael," Borzoi said.

"Please sit down, take a seat," Chergo said.

They spoke English. They did not get up.

They chatted. About the night view from the window, about the hotel, about Zurich. There were two bowls on the table, a bowl of nuts, a bowl of olives. As one spoke, the other pawed. Michael studied them carefully. They were young, early thirties perhaps. Their puppy fat rippled around their chest and their bellies. He remembered that tactic of theirs, that they never introduced themselves, they left it to the visitor to guess which was which. But, Michael knew, Borzoi's left ear was missing its lobe, a jagged scar remained only. Chergo's hair was thinner, greasier.

A drink was laid in front of him. The twins looked up and the assistants disappeared.

"Gentlemen," Michael said. He raised his glass. "What can I do for you?"

There was a pause.

"Do you like Tel Aviv?" Chergo said. "Have you ever been there?"

Michael shook his head. He looked from one to the other.

"Perfect weather. All year round," Borzoi said.

"We go there often."

"We are not Jewish, you understand. But we like to go there."

"Lots of Russians there. Some go for holiday. Some go to live."

"Many Russians have Israeli passports. They are Israeli citizens. Many have gone since the fall of communism."

"Some are Jewish. Some aren't. Did you know that?"

"Lots of Russian businessmen. They like the climate. They like the way they do business over there."

"They have money, these men. They are big men. Successful. A bit like us, perhaps. They like to have somewhere to go. For rest and recreation. To escape for a while."

"They are thinking, also. They are Russian. They think deep things. They have a sense of time, of history."

"We Russians, we love our history. We love to think about our history. Of course, we have so much of it."

"The Mongols, the Tsars. Lenin and Stalin. Men with vision. Men who loved power."

"Putin, you like him?"

"A good man. He has done a lot for Russia, he makes it easy to do business. He can be good for men like us."

"He too likes power. You understand, perhaps it is in the blood. He doesn't like anyone to threaten."

"So some of our friends, they are thinking. Is there a bit of the spirit of the old Tsars there? Of the old commissars?"

"You see, some of our friends, they are in jail. You know why?"

"They are too successful. I tell you, that's it."

"Good men. Family men. Their only crime is that they know how to make a few dollars."

"So they need a place to go. If things get nasty. Some of them are Jewish."

"Some are not. But these days you can find people who can change things. Change history."

"An uncle, a great aunt, a grandmother. These things can be made up. You can buy these things. Isn't that amazing?"

"You can make up a past. There were lots of pogroms. Some bad things used to happen. Perhaps your ancestors, they were killed there."

"We have cousins. In Pittsburgh. For us it's OK. If things get bad."

"But we go to Tel Aviv, to meet our friends, to do our business. And we talk."

"Everyone talks there. We go to cafés, we listen."

"Traders of all kinds there. Food, diamonds. Currency. Gas. Oil."

"Oil traders. Many of them. Some of the biggest."

"Russian. Armenian. American."

"We heard a story there, a very remarkable story. Can you guess what it is?"

"Who knows if it is true? A man, a trader, one of the biggest, he lost some money recently."

"Not in a speculation, you understand. Not in a bad speculation."

"No. This money was stolen. They were very clever. It was done right under his nose."

"His own company. His own people. People that he trusted."

"They say it was a lot."

"They say it was twenty million dollars. Can you believe that?"

"They say whoever did it must have had help."

"His employees, these youngsters. IT whizz-kids. Hackers. We have them in Russia."

"Thin and spotty. They don't chase girls. They spend all their time in front of screens. No idea about life. They are not practical, these men."

"They can't do things like this on their own. They need help. From bad guys, men who know how to steal."

"Or perhaps from men who need money. Businessmen perhaps. Businessmen with plans that have gone bad."

"Our friend is angry. He wants revenge. You can understand that."

"Anyone can understand that. Don't you think?"

"He knows some people. People who can fix things. Violent men. Killers. He has been speaking to these people."

"He's not like them. But he can't help it. He cries out for answers. These men tell him they can give him answers."

"You can understand that. Can't you? Anyone can."

The twins paused. They scooped up nuts and olives and shovelled them into their mouths. Chergo turned to look at Michael. Borzoi wiped crumbs from his jacket lapel.

You dirty fucks, Michael thought. *You dirty, filthy fucks.*

He got up. Immediately two men appeared from the shadows, but Borzoi waved them away. Michael stood by the windows for a moment. Then he sat down again. He took a sip of his drink.

"This friend of yours," he said. "He's a good business man?"

"One of the best," Chergo said.

"And when you're a business man, you have to take risks. Isn't that so?"

"Of course. We all understand that."

"You have to make judgements. About risk. About people."

"That's true," said Borzoi. "Well said, Michael."

"But this friend of yours, perhaps his judgement was not perfect this time. Perhaps he made a few bad choices."

"Michael, this was rotten, this has a bad smell," said Chergo. "How could he have expected this?"

"Perhaps one day the smell will clear," Michael said.

"Leaving what?" said Chergo.

"Surprise, perhaps. Astonishment, even. If this man is so clever. If he lost so much."

Borzoi chuckled.

"Or, admiration. At the skill of the people who did this. At their audacity."

"Perhaps there you go too far." Borzoi was smiling.

"Let's face it," Michael said. "Sometimes when you have been successful for a long time, you think it will never end. You can get careless."

"I agree," said Borzoi. "You can never afford to relax."

"Let's face it," Michael said. "Business is business. You can't afford to hang around. We all know that. Opportunities must be grabbed, as soon as they appear."

"Fair opportunities, Michael," Chergo said. "Fair opportunities."

"My friends, what's fair? Is there a law that says what's fair? Do we need another law? Do you want another law, another piece of red tape?"

"That's right," Borzoi said. "There's too much of that already."

"Do we want men like Putin to tell us everything? What we can and can't do?"

The twins looked at each other.

"All I know is, when I see a chance, I go for it. I know that if I don't someone else will. That's how it is, that's how it's always been."

Borzoi smiled at his brother. They spoke Russian for a while. Michael looked out over the city lights. After five minutes, the twins suddenly burst out laughing. A private joke. They turned back to Michael.

"We like you," Chergo said. "We like the way you do business. We always recommend you. To our colleagues and our associates."

"I'm sure our friend would admire you as well."

"We have been suggesting to him some opportunities in Russia. Oil. Gas. Who knows. Property even."

"He will be a valuable partner. He has a lifetime of experience."

"He will join us. He is actually quite excited by the chance of working with you."

"We think we can persuade him to forget his loss. Or perhaps think of it another way. Debt for Equity, you might call it."

"But our friend is an emotional man. He needs something. Something to assuage his anger."

Michael smiled to himself. *Let's have it, you shits.*

"He talks of revenge."

"We think we can persuade him that that's not the best way. Not civilised."

Chergo spoke. Borzoi leant down and picked up an envelope.

"It would help so much," Chergo said, "if we could just offer him something. A token, perhaps, to show how concerned we are for his unfortunate situation.

"This situation. You see, we ask ourselves, what kind of man could think up such a thing?"

Borzoi opened the envelope and laid some photographs on the table between them. Of Jerome. Then Mick. One of Tim Scott. Of Sanjay.

258

"The man who thought it up...the man who planned it... he's a bad fellow."

Michael looked at the picture of Sanjay. He was standing outside a shop. Vicky's shop. There was a shape, blurred, by the window in the background. A human shape. *Oh, Vicky*, he thought.

"Which one is it, Michael?" Chergo said.

Michael twirled a pencil between his fingers.

"That man should not enjoy our support," Chergo said.

"He's not one of us. Don't you agree?"

"No. Not one of us. He should not enjoy our support. Or our protection."

A token? An offering? Is that what you want? Michael thought. He lay the pencil down, on top of the photograph of Sanjay. *One day I'll have you two fucks as my own to offer up, as and when I choose. Just give me time. I'll storm the fucking gates of Moscow to get you. Some day. Some day soon.*

*

I need something to do, Tim thought. *Something to occupy my time.*

He and Sanjay got up late. There was a shower room in Sanjay's hideaway. They left the casino to get an early lunch. Sanjay apologised for his behaviour the previous evening, and then was silent as they ate. After fifteen minutes he got up abruptly, saying he had some paperwork to sort out. They arranged to meet back at his office in a few hours.

It was a fine day. Tim explored. He found an internet café, switched off his phone, and idly began to scour the web. He began with a look at postgraduate courses at the city's universities, and then, to probe further and more arbitrarily. He found a few speculative opportunities for which he thought he might be suited. He fired off half a dozen emails.

Later he thought about Imogen, and then about Sanjay, about

his growing paranoia. He checked his mobile. There were three text messages.

"Whr are u mate? B" Then.

"Mate?" Then.

"?"

Sanjay lived in a mews road a short distance from the casino. Tim decided to accompany him home. They walked. Tim found that he was noticing small details about everything around him. In the streets, the crowding, the smell, the sweat. He began, for the first time seriously, to consider leaving his city and trying somewhere else. As they strolled, he looked at the buildings around him, and he knew he could leave without regret.

Sanjay unlocked the front door of his house. They walked down a hallway. The place had for Tim the familiarity of a dream. He had stayed here. He had been semi-conscious most of the time. Sanjay fiddled with a door handle. It was stiff. As the door opened they looked through into the living room and saw that it was dark.

The curtains were drawn.

Tim stared. The television lay upside down on the carpet. Books and papers were scattered around it.

There was a man standing in the middle of the living room. He stared at them for a second. His shirt was torn. There was a cut above his left eyebrow.

A presence behind. Tim felt arms wrapping themselves round him, tightly, and then one hand over his mouth. He tried to cry out, but couldn't. The man ahead of him marched forward and punched Sanjay twice, once on the face, once in the stomach. Sanjay fell. The man held something in his other hand, something black, bulbous, shiny. He knelt down, and, seemingly casually, hit Sanjay on the chest, neck, head, the chest again. Tim stared, paralysed. The man then got up, walked forward and punched Tim in the stomach. Tim doubled up. He was winded and started coughing. The arms around his chest tightened their grip and he felt his torso being jerked up. He tried to free himself, he squirmed and twisted, his fists flailed. The man who had hit him then came right up and did something with his knuckles against Tim's nose that made him almost pass out with pain. He felt tears streaming down his face. He cried out. The person behind pushed him forward towards the sofa and forced his face into the cushions. After ten seconds he pulled him up and the first man plastered a strip of tape against his mouth. He tried to scream, he screamed as hard and as loud as he could, he closed his eyes and yelled. A muted whine. He was dragged over to a chair at the side of the room, and forced down onto it. His arms were wrenched back. His head jerked around and he saw Sanjay, inert, on the ground.

And then something else, something that for a second made him still, very still, and then made him retch. He tried to spit, realised he couldn't, and swallowed his bile. He pressed his eyes shut, but his head span, and he had to watch as the first man ran roll after roll of thick tape around his body, his arms, his legs. After a minute he tried to move. He was pinned to the chair. Again he tried to yell. Another subdued moan. He tried to bounce the chair up and down. The two men walked up to him quickly. He shut his eyes and braced himself. They grabbed the chair and rammed it against the wall. His head cracked against it. For a moment his vision was blurred. He came to. One of the men stood in front of him with a finger against his lips. Tim watched them. They stood, hands on hips, heads bowed. Their clothes were dishevelled. One had a nosebleed. They started talking. Tim listened. He could not understand what they were saying. He thought the language was Arabic but then knew it was not.

He returned his gaze to the doorway. A second body lay in a heap to the left, its bulk nestling at an angle in the crook of the wall and the wardrobe standing against it. The left half of the face was covered in blood, it had dripped onto a ripped jacket. The body's left arm was bent back underneath. There was no movement.

Tim started moaning again. The two men looked at him but

did not react. He tried to bite off the strip of tape, but he could get no purchase. He began breathing heavily, and then felt a panic as he sensed that he was not getting enough air into his lungs. His heartbeat quickened, his nostrils flared, he sucked at the tape over his mouth. One of the men walked over to him, grabbed him by the hair and pulled his head back. He studied Tim's face for a moment, and then, as if satisfied, let his head fall. Tim willed his heart to slow. His breaths became more regular. The man lost interest in him. Tim closed his eyes and let his head bob on his chest for a few moments. The men started talking again, in quiet voices.

He thought about Jerome, whom he had met just a few times. During the planning for the big day. And then the day itself. They had hardly spoken to each other. He was Mick's boy. How did he die? he wondered. What did they do to him? He thought about himself. Why had he gone along with it? Why had he listened to Sanjay? How could he ever have believed that afterwards he would walk away from it unaffected? Then he thought about the body by the wardrobe. It was still. As if life had left it. And hope with it.

Fifteen minutes earlier, Bernie had stood at the front door of Sanjay's house. He rang the bell. He stood waiting for ten seconds, rang it a second time, and then waited a further minute. He backed away a few paces, and glanced up and down the front of the house a few times. He turned and began walking back to his car parked down the street. He had gone twenty yards, and then, as if coming to a decision, he stopped. A few seconds later he was at the front door again. He had some keys in his hand. Without ringing again, he began trying each in turn. The second took him into a hallway. On a small table there were piles of letters. He examined them. A staircase ascended into darkness above. At its foot to his left was another door. Closed. He walked up to it and tried the handle. He pushed the door open, moved slowly across the threshold. Dark. He gave the door a firm shove.

It swung round until it caught on something. He stared inside, sniffed, walked forward slowly. The television was on. He saw that it was the news. A politician was making a speech. The sound was off.

He sniffed again. He stood still. The air was close. There was a shadow on the carpet. He wondered why the door had jammed.

There was a clock on the wall. Tim stared at it. The second hand had moved and yet time did not seem to pass. He stared and stared and yet it seemed to remain at the same minute past the hour. His head drooped for a moment. He looked up, and fifteen minutes had gone. He could not figure it out.

The men talked quietly. One time, they stopped suddenly and their expressions became concentrated. Tim heard a door outside slamming shut, and then footsteps on the street outside. Neighbours. The men waited half a minute, and then relaxed. Later, one of them began to look around the living room. He opened drawers, checked an airing cupboard. He pulled out something from inside. The ironing board. He assembled it in the middle of the room, and plugged in the iron. He pulled something out of his jacket pocket. He laid a knife and then a gun on the board. He nodded to the second man, who left the room. Tim heard the front door open slowly, and close. A minute later he was back with a leather valise, what looked like a doctor's bag. He began inspecting the contents. He pulled out a syringe, and after that a series of small vials, each containing a clear liquid. Tim watched the two men, in horror, in fascination.

One of them looked up at Tim and smirked. He laid a finger on the lid of the first vial.

"These drugs will do strange things to you." He had an American accent. "Not all of them harmful. This one will stop your heart." He pointed at the next bottle along. "This one will make you unconscious."

The other man punctured the lid of the second vial, and began to fill the syringe.

263

"In a moment, we would like to ask you some questions," the man said. "You. Your friend. You were the ones. You thought it up, didn't you?" He waited for his companion to finish.

"Actions have consequences. You know that, of course. We are the consequences. Of your actions."

Actions and consequences. Had Tim forgotten that? No, he had not, but the problem was that he never knew what kind of consequences there could possibly be, he had always been the child playing with fire, the savage watching thunder roll and lightning strike, and having neither the knowledge nor the experience to guess that there might be a connection, a link between action and reaction, between desire and retribution, between greed and violence. His old company, its billionaire bosses, or men like Michael, even Mick and Bernie, they had a place in the world, a role, with a reach and a capability, they made things happen, at their say events changed, people listened to their commands and obeyed them. Men like that understood cause and effect. They knew that actions had consequences, because it was their will that caused the consequences to happen. Men like Tim were not like that, they grazed with numberless others in placid herds, wanting no more than the freedom to carry on grazing, that day, the next day, the rest of their days. But the carnivores patrolling at the edges of the herd would never allow it, not while there was a world to manage, to manipulate and exploit, to make their own. The carnivores were now here. For reasons that he could never understand, they had picked him out. They were here, now, in this living room.

The man with the syringe suddenly sniffed, and blood began to drip from his nostrils. He put a finger to his upper lip. He shrugged, put the syringe down, and walked towards the bathroom. The other man looked at the items arrayed on the ironing board, and Tim knew that his time was up. And he closed his eyes and thought of Imogen, and he imagined himself at her side, her hand in both of his, as she lay back with her legs propped up, and people around them whispered to her to breathe and to push. He wanted to cry, and he opened his eyes.

And then as he watched, the body in the heap by the wardrobe was suddenly standing and advancing on the man at the ironing board with two fists raised, and Tim saw a glint of metal between the fingers of Bernie's right hand, a key perhaps, and the man turned and, mouth open, glanced at the gun and hesitated for a fatal moment and then turned to strike out at the figure coming at him, but Bernie seemed to bend and twist and for one miraculous second to become thin and the blow sailed by him and his own right fist hit the man on the left cheek. Tim saw two things happen to the man's face, it was as if the left side suddenly exploded and opened out in all directions, and also the face immediately turned crimson, it just became another colour, and the features were distorted and not quite human. The man sighed and crumpled, and then the second man came sprinting back into the room, silent, fast, arms outstretched, and Bernie and he were in a kind of embrace, faces close, lips snarling and biting, arms thrashing, fists, fingers, poking in eyes and throats, and they hit the ironing board and it fell, and the bottles and syringes and the bag crashed to the floor, and the two men rolled around, and Tim closed his eyes and began to wail and to stretch his muscles as taut as he could, to push and tear, and his chair toppled. He screamed, but lying there on the ground he was useless and immobile. He just could not move. He. Just. Could. Not. Move.

There was silence.

He opened his eyes. There was no movement. But there was movement. A figure crawling towards him.

Sanjay came close, he whispered, "Tim." There was a knife. On the floor. On his knees he began to scrape, and then he picked up the knife and tore at the tape around Tim's legs, his arms, his body. Strands hanging off him. Tim hauled himself up. Bernie, somewhere, face down, pawing at the carpet. He pulled Sanjay to his feet.

"I'm OK."

Tim pressed forward. But Sanjay stopped. He turned back. The gun was on the floor. He bent to pick it up. The second man lay on his stomach a few yards away. A low moan. There was a syringe by the gun. Sanjay picked up gun and syringe. He walked to the man, raised his right arm and plunged the syringe into the man's back. His body bucked and trembled, and then was still. Sanjay lurched back to Tim and grabbed his arm. "Help me." They knelt at Bernie's body. Sanjay heaved a fleshy wrist over his shoulder, Tim took the other. They dragged his bulk, feet trailing, out of the living room and into the hall, a couple of yards, till the weight slipped down Tim's back and Sanjay fell and clutched his stomach.

"Jeez!"

Tim tore the strip of tape off his mouth, wincing at the sting. He twisted and picked Sanjay up by the shoulders, marched him to the front door, opened it. He looked back. Bernie stared into mid-distance. Tim dithered, then bent and whispered into his ear, and stepped out into the street. *My car*, he thought, *my car*. He looked to his side.

"Sanjay, where are you parked?"

Tim gasped. Sanjay's eyes were rolling.

They stumbled forward. After ten yards, Tim turned to Sanjay. "Look at me. Look at me. Sanjay." He slapped him across the cheek. "Sanjay, do you have a car?"

Sanjay's vision seemed to stabilise. He nodded. He pointed.

"Keys? I need keys."

They moved on, and Tim saw Sanjay's BMW. They pushed towards it and he leant Sanjay against the passenger door. He fished around in Sanjay's pockets. Bunches of keys. Car keys.

He tried the door. He flashed the keys. He turned and looked back to the house. Where were the men?

He opened the door.

"Sanjay. Inside." He pushed him in, and then looked up. *I promised*, he thought, and took two steps towards the flat, but something changed his mind. There was a report, like dry timber cracking. He turned and rushed round to the other side of the car. He climbed in and started the engine. He looked to his left.

"Close the door. Sanjay, close the door!" he shouted. Looking in the mirror, he could see a man coming out of the flat. He was crawling. The left half of his face was somehow all wrong. The man hauled himself up against a concrete post. He had something in his hands that he was trying to point.

The left hand car door was still not closed. Tim put the car into gear and twisted out of the parking space. The door hit the car ahead and slammed shut. They shot forward. Tim pressed on the accelerator.

He drove fast and aimlessly. Sanjay was silent. Tim looked over at him. His eyes were closed.

"Sanjay. How are you feeling?"

He mumbled. "It's OK. Just carry on."

"I'll find a hospital."

"No. Don't." Sanjay opened his eyes. "Just drive."

"Where?"

Tim thought about his flat. "Sanjay, did they take your wallet?"

There was no reply.

It came to him to make for somewhere far away. He thought of Bath. Tim headed westwards. They had reached the motorway. They continued for a few miles, and then he thought better of it. He swung north. They skirted around the edge of London. An hour later they hit the M1. It was getting dark. After a while Tim pulled in to a service station. He positioned the car away from the lights and stopped. He thought of Bernie. On the carpet looking up at him, his eyes as slits. For thirty seconds his arms shook and he could not grip the wheel, and then it passed.

There was an outside lavatory ahead. Tim started the engine and went up close. Inside, he waited until everyone else had left. He walked quickly back to the car and opened the passenger door.

267

"Sanjay, let's get you cleaned up."

Tim helped him inside, and positioned him in front of a sink. He grabbed a fistful of paper towels, soaked them in water, and gently washed Sanjay's face. He examined the bruising above the left eye and bathed a gash above the hairline.

"Do you need the loo?" There was no reply.

He helped Sanjay back into the car. He went to the cafeteria and bought coffee, sandwiches, cake. He found a chemist and bought aspirin. In a shop he bought a thermos, then went back to the cafeteria and got five more coffees. He poured them one after the other into the flask. Back at the car he saw that Sanjay was nibbling at the food. He handed him the flask.

They got back onto the motorway. They continued north. Tim drove all night. Sanjay slept. At five in the morning, near Edinburgh, he stopped at another service station and bought maps of Scotland. He continued up to Inverness. Outside of town, he stopped at a lay-by, and sat staring for fifteen minutes. He took a swig of coffee and tried to recall the route to the house that Imogen's godparents owned. He drove into town, and then headed out west. After twenty minutes, he stopped and headed back. There was a turning. If only he could remember where. He tried successive side roads.

On the third attempt he knew he was on the right track. The road rose, it passed through a small village, the shops vaguely familiar, and suddenly Tim knew where he was. It was not far. He came out the other side. Another turning soon after. The narrow road led him through woods and then back into open land. He saw the cottage ahead. Hedges around the front, the woodland encroaching right up to the back.

He stopped at the side of the road. Sanjay slumbered. Tim scanned the drive for cars. Nothing. He prayed to himself. That the place was empty. After a minute he started the car and drove up to the cottage. He walked to the front door and peered in at the windows. He walked around to the left, then the right, and rolled aside a thick earthenware pot. Keys. He opened the front door and walked around. The power was off, the place looked tidy and unlived in. Tim went back out and parked the car round the side. He patted Sanjay on the shoulder.

"Sanjay, we're home. Come on, out the car."

Sanjay slowly opened his eyes. He reached forward, grabbed the dash and pulled himself forward. He groaned. Empty cups and wrappers fell to the floor.

Tim helped him out. They stumbled through the front door. He led him through into the living room and on to the sofa. He found a blanket, lay it over him, and then spent fifteen minutes figuring out the electrics. He turned on the hot water, he checked the kitchen. There was a box of tea bags, some sugar. He made two cups of sweet tea.

It was early afternoon. Tim sat in a chair opposite Sanjay and drank his tea. He waited for Sanjay to drink his. He felt his eyelids becoming heavy. He dozed.

Tim awoke suddenly. Hours had passed. He looked across at Sanjay, who was sitting up and rubbing his face in his hands.

"How are you feeling?"

"Where the hell are we?"

Tim got up. He took the cups to the kitchen. He called back, "The water's hot. Why don't you have a bath?"

*

Dan Becker stood at the end of the mews looking at the police activity beyond the blue tape. After a few seconds he turned away. He knew it was unwise to remain there for too long. It was said they sometimes videoed people stopping at crime scenes.

He walked on. He was disappointed. With the way things had panned out. And the new instructions that had arrived that morning.

He was confused. Shifting alliances at the top, enemies becoming friends. He felt as if he had been cut loose. There was an untidiness about it. And then, the curious rider attached to his orders concerning Palmer's associate. The Asian.

But the man's whereabouts were unknown. As were those of his colleague, Tim Scott. Becker wondered how he could get into the house in the street he had just been observing, to poke around a bit. It might be too difficult. But Scott's place. There were no policemen there. Perhaps one of Becker's men might be able to sneak a look.

*

Later Tim drove back to Inverness. He found a supermarket and bought groceries. He was back at the cottage at eight in the evening. Sanjay was sitting on the sofa watching television. Tim looked him up and down. Sanjay stared in silence.

Tim cooked something to eat. Afterwards he opened a bottle of wine. Sanjay sipped at his glass for a while and then nodded off. Tim prepared a bed. He stayed up alone for a couple of hours, thinking, drinking a little, and then turned in himself. He slept little. He kept thinking of Bernie, collapsed on the floor.

At four in the morning he was woken up by Sanjay's coughing. He went next door. The sidelamp was on, Sanjay sat propped up in bed, his stomach heaving. Tim got him some water. After five minutes the attack began to subside.

Sanjay had taken off his shirt, and Tim saw his stomach. Red, bloated, raw.

Tim sat at the breakfast table drinking coffee at eight in the morning. His fear had left him, and he asked himself why this was. Perhaps it was that they were alone, undisturbed, they could stay here, no one knowing a thing about them, for as long as they wanted. As long as they were careful. Unlike London, where despite its anonymity you left traces, you left your trail, everywhere you went. In the shops, in the pubs, in the people you met, in the closed circuit television whose field of vision you crossed. It seemed strange that despite their animal conspicuousness, despite the fact that they were almost intruders here, intruders in a land of birds and fish, sheep and deer, in this world they were safe.

But he knew this was not the only reason he felt better. He felt something else, a subtle sense of atavistic purpose. He could no longer afford to worry. He had something, someone to protect. The paradox, that the urge to protect another's life was more powerful than the urge to protect one's own.

Sanjay appeared, bleary-eyed but awake. Tim brewed a pot of coffee.

"So, where are we? You never said."

"How much can you remember of last night?"

"Just driving."

Tim filled him in. The journey north. The cottage, Imogen's godparents.

Tim made toast. They had breakfast.

Later he asked, "Who were they?"

Sanjay shook his head.

"Will they come after us?"

Sanjay thought for a second. "Yes."

Tim was silent. He had dared hope for a second that it was over. He began to plan. At least here they had some time. After a while he spoke again.

"Sanjay, why did you..."

"Yes?"

"You stayed, you untied me."

Sanjay ran a hand through his hair. "Bernie saved our lives." He poured himself more coffee.

Tim looked at him.

"Tim, you did what you could. You couldn't go back."

He thought, *I simply couldn't do it. I couldn't force myself to walk back there.*

"Bernie once told me something," Tim mumbled. He looked away. "Something about his son."

Sanjay sat staring into the mug in front of him.

Tim suggested a walk in the afternoon.

"You go, Tim. I'll stay here. I'll watch TV."

Tim was concerned, but then he thought that perhaps it would be a good thing if Sanjay rested. Here, for now, he was safe. Tim took the car and found a spot by the lochs. He marched up and down the slopes of the surrounding hills. A cold wind gusted. This far north, summer long gone.

That evening Tim cooked again. Later, wine, television. Tim could not concentrate. Eventually he broke the silence.

"Sanjay, you need to go to hospital."

"I'm all right."

"I mean it. Look, I saw what they did to you. Your insides may be all fucked up. You have to see a doctor."

Sanjay turned to him. "I'm not going to jail, Tim. I just... I just can't do it."

Tim frowned. "Well, perhaps if I could find someone. A friend, a medic, someone who could take a look at you. No paperwork."

Sanjay's attention was on the programme they were watching. Tim got up from his chair.

"For Christ's sake. We can't stay here forever."

"You go, Tim. I can make it on my own."

The next afternoon, Tim suggested another hike in the hills. He felt better when Sanjay said he would come, but it began to rain as they found a spot and parked. Sanjay stayed in the car while Tim walked. That evening Tim asked him if there was anyone he could call.

"Michael? Mick?"

Sanjay shrugged.

"Lily?"

The following day, Tim drove into Inverness and paid cash for two pay-as-you-go phones. The lady in the shop asked for a name. Tim made one up. She asked for some identification. He said he would bring it the next day. When he got back, Sanjay was sitting on the sofa with the gun in his hands. There were rags and newspaper on the table in front of him, a bottle of wine on the table. "Remember Spain?" he said.

"Yes." Tim said. "I was good. You weren't."

"Bernie once showed me how these things work." Sanjay gazed down the barrel. "Bernie." And then, after a minute, "You're right. Perhaps you should have it."

"Don't be ridiculous."

"Perhaps you need it more than I do."

"Neither of us needs it." Tim looked at the bottle. Three quarters empty.

"Tim."

"Can I get you some coffee?"

"Tim, there's something I have to say..."

"Sanjay, why don't you hand me the gun?"

"Tim, I must say it now."

"Let's have it."

"We never really talked about it. I don't know why."

"Talked about what?"

"That time years ago, when we drove back from Oxford. You remember. Afterwards."

"Let's forget it. It's in the past."

"No. Tim. We must talk now."

Tim leant forward. Sanjay began to whisper.

After a few minutes Sanjay stopped talking and there was silence. Tim thought he was going to hit him, he wanted to grab his face and rip and tear. But he didn't. He got up and walked into the kitchen and screamed.

He pulled opened the drawers. There was a half-empty bottle of brandy. He poured himself a shot, and then another. And then he screamed again. He wanted to destroy something with his hands, to rip something out of himself, to make up for a decade that suddenly seemed useless and wasted.

He threw the glass he held into the sink and marched back into the living room.

"You fuck, Sanjay! Why didn't you ever say?"

Sanjay had the gun in his hand. He looked at Tim, raised the gun to his right temple and smiled. He pulled the trigger. There was a dry click. He smiled again. Tim stood there blinking. Sanjay laughed. He picked up the magazine and loaded the weapon.

Tim stared. "Jesus, Sanjay!"

Tim grabbed the gun and walked out the front door. He stood outside for five minutes. He opened the car and put it in the glove compartment.

The next morning Tim went walking again. By himself. He took one phone and left the other. He drove aimlessly for a few hours and then found a spot off the road where he could park close to a lake.

He was alone. He thought about what Sanjay had said the previous day. The anger came in waves.

No other cars passed along the road. Tim took the gun, put it in his pocket, and walked over to the water's edge. He sat. He took the gun out his pocket and thought for a second that he might chuck it into the lake. He looked up at the hills around him. Not a sign of human life. He looked again at the weapon. It had a certain beauty, a kind of clean design, a symmetry along the line of its barrel, a balance in the grip. Polished metal, precision tooling. The elevation of function to a principle of aestheticism. The function was so clear and simple. It carried out that function so perfectly. This machine was his. He could not get rid of it just yet.

He walked along the lakeside. Trees rustled in the wind, birds flapped and disturbed the calm of the surface of the water. There was a cliff ahead of him. Ripples flickered against the rocks at the bottom. And then, as he scrambled past a hollow in the rock face, all sound seemed to die. Tim paused mid-step. The air itself seemed to press in against him. He walked a few yards back, and heard the wind again, the trickle of water against stone. He walked forward. Total silence. An absolute stillness. A magic threshold. His spot. He had discovered his secret place. If only he could find it again.

He sat for fifteen minutes, and walked on. He returned to the car and drove to Inverness. His rage simmered. He found a coffee bar and read the paper, and then rang Sanjay. A dozen rings. The voicemail cut in. He picked up his paper, but his attention wavered. His thoughts began to settle on the image of Sanjay with the gun to his head. Anger and concern, in a shifting balance. It was mid-afternoon, already getting late, when a kind of resolution began to emerge and he thought about heading back. He knew that at this northern latitude the sunset would be drawn out, there would be a few hours of daylight left. He drove. The route was now familiar. The turn-off. The village.

There was a car a few hundred yards behind him. It stayed in his mirror, and then disappeared. He slowed as he came up to the cottage. He decided to drive on. He continued for five miles, and found a lay-by. He waited. For the car to catch up and overtake. After five minutes he began to stare at the second hand of his watch. At fifteen he started up the car and turned round. He felt a chill. He headed back slowly, looking out for lights, vehicles. For a second time he drove past the cottage. He parked a few miles beyond and thought for a few minutes. There were no turnoffs. No side-roads. He took a moment to steady his breathing. He stared ahead. There were no farms or buildings nearby. Apart from the cottage. He picked up his phone and dialled. Voicemail. Straight away. The other mobile was switched off. He put his phone down on the passenger seat, looked up, and then gasped. Two eyes in the shadows. He swore. A fox stared at him from the trees.

He switched on the engine and pulled out onto the road.

Time. He needed time. He wondered if he should contact Michael. He thought about his flat, about the papers scattered around his drawers. An old address book. A letter from Imogen's godparents. A postcard.

He saw a signpost back to Inverness. *What shall I do?* Perhaps it's nothing. Perhaps they turned back. Perhaps they didn't. *What shall I do?*

He stopped the car and looked in his mirror. The sun was setting in the west behind him. A pinkish grey in the clouds. He twisted his head and stared. The colour was almost unbearably beautiful. He felt a sense of privilege, a divine privilege, that he was able to sit, that he had eyes to see, and to watch the sky. Changing colour. Just for him.

It was getting late. For the third time he turned the car round.

There were some woods, about a mile or two short of the cottage, through which the road ran. He slowed as he passed through them, he searched for a path or a clearing, and then drove off the road and parked as far away from it as he could get. He switched off the engine and checked the glove compartment and the boot. There was a torch which he pocketed. He began to walk. He knew the woodland curved around to the back of the cottage. Also, that daylight would not last too much longer. More than an hour, less than two. For fifteen minutes he walked by the side of the road, up to the edge of the woods, the point where the grassland began. There he struck off to the right, into the trees. A wind came up. It got cool. That suited him. The wind might cover the sound of his movement. On the other hand it might carry it, he thought. There was no knowing. He walked. He stayed close to the edge of the trees. From time to time, he walked right up to the grassland itself, and then retreated. There was a gentle rise between him and the cottage, and for a while the house lay out of sight. It had to be there, just beyond the slope, he thought, and as his path bent round, it came into view, the front of the house, in open land, a hollow in the far distance. He stared.

There were no lights on. Nor could he see any car in the drive, or signs of life around. He continued walking, five yards back from the tree line.

The light was fading. It was becoming increasingly difficult to pick out a path ahead. He felt branches and leaves brushing against his shoulders, his hair, his cheeks. He had to slow, he walked with his arms ahead to shield him. It occurred to him to use the torch, but he knew the risk was too great. He marched on, ten minutes, twenty, thirty. He looked out for lights, for activity. Nothing. It could be, he thought, that the house was empty. The trail twisted and bent, the side wall of the cottage became visible, a distance away, and then, later, nearer, as he moved round, the back windows, the back door. He heard a crack. Twigs underfoot. He stopped. Waited. And then decided to take off his shoes and walk in his socks. He stooped, undid the laces, stepped out of them and left them where they stood. He took one pace and winced. A stone. He moved on.

Imagine, my darling...

He was a hundred yards from the back door. It was almost dark. He could just make out the shape of the building, and also, his senses sharpening, a faint bluish light that permeated through the back windows, as if thick curtains had been drawn. No movement. No sign of life. He stopped, and felt the gun in his pocket. He felt the safety catch, then pulled the gun out, and slipped the catch off. He slid it back on. *Off. On. Off. On.* He raised his arms carefully in front of him and felt for branches. He brushed them gently aside and pushed forward. The trees cleared. Mud underfoot. Then plants, weeds. Thirty yards from the house, twenty. He knew there was a lawn. And that he was close. He began to crawl, feeling each movement of hands, knees and feet against the grass. Anything he could not identify, he circled round. Seconds, minutes passing, and suddenly he hit concrete, under the palm of his left hand. He stopped. He had come up too fast, he was there, at the cottage, three yards from the door. He waited for a moment, and crawled leftwards towards the windows of the back room. He positioned himself underneath and listened. And then squatted, one ear raised. Silence. No. Something. Traces of a low murmur. Human, but indistinct. The television perhaps. He felt in his pocket. *Off. On. Off. On.* He tried to peer in, but all gaps between curtain and glass were sealed. He thought, and then began to crawl around to the side. Wind dragging the leaves. The darkness in the sky deepening. He edged his way round the corner.

Imagine the man you want to be.

A sound, a scraping sound. He stopped. He stopped breathing. He froze. Darkness. He waited a minute and then edged forward again along the side of the house. The next corner. He stopped and peered round. Noise. Again. He pulled his head back. Curtains being drawn, and then, around to the front, the sound of a window being opened. He felt a draft of air, hot, sweaty, tinged with a faint tang of urine. A voice again. In the blackness. Soft, but this time he could make out a few words. An American accent.

"We'll take a break." It faded and then swam back in. "...fifteen minutes..."

Imagine the man you want to be...

And then he heard something else. A moan. He felt in his pocket again. *Off. On.*

... And be that man.

He began to crawl on his stomach, his neck twisted, eyes peering up. He crawled around the corner until he was positioned under the open window, and there he waited. He listened. The man talking again. A door opening, movement, footsteps. A faint light, as if from the kitchen or the back room.

Be that man.

Tim closed his eyes. *I want it to be over*, he thought. *How can I make it all finish? Now?* And he remembered, himself aged eight, or nine, at the swimming pool. He saw himself watching the older boys diving from the high boards and one day he had followed them, up one ladder, to the first board, the bouncy one, then the second, the one that he dived from once before and he had belly flopped and he had almost drowned when in the shock of the impact he had swallowed a mouthful of water but he had struggled to the surface and the edge of the pool and suffered in silence and said nothing, and then on up, and he was standing now on the highest board, looking down and he couldn't jump, but nor could he climb back down, the others were watching, and he thought to himself, *I want to end it now, I want it to be over,* and he heard the other boys coming up behind him, daring, mocking, and he stepped right up to the edge, and he peered down. *Imagine.* He had to get down to there. From here. *Off. On.* He heard the man talking. Above him. There. Just there. *Off. On.* Off.

He stood up and looked through the window. Dan Becker was standing, his head was turned. He talked to someone in the back room. Tim raised his arms. *Look at me*, he thought. *Just look at me.* The man talked. Tim pointed. The man turned his head and looked. A crack, sudden, sharp. Light. For an instant. The man slowly turned and began to run. A flash of light, again. He fell. His body bounced. It bounced again. And again.

Tim's ears sang. Bells clanging, loud. And then they seemed to quieten and fade and he heard the whisper of the leaves in the wind. He clambered through the window and walked over to the body. It was frozen in what seemed to Tim in the half-light a moment of rage. The arms crooked, the face distorted, teeth bared. Eyes, staring at the floor. Tim turned and walked into the other room. Sanjay was flopped out in an armchair, his shirt open to the waist, the sleeves rolled back, his head lolling at his side. There were bruises. Many of them. On a table nearby, in the light of a side lamp, Tim saw a leather bag. Syringes.

"Sanjay. Jesus, what's been going on here?"

A moan.

"Sanjay. Can you hear me?"

The head righted itself, eyes slowly opened. A slight smile.

"What are you doing here?"

279

Tim took him by the shoulders and slowly attempted to move him a little.

"Is this more comfortable?"

Sanjay grimaced.

"Sanjay. I need to call an ambulance."

"Fuck it. Don't you ever listen?"

Tim pulled out his phone and punched three nines, but Sanjay put a hand on his arm.

"Please."

Tim lowered the phone.

Which service? A machine-like voice, faint, fading.

"Please."

"They'll trace the call."

"Not here." A cough. "Hicksville."

Tim sighed. He got up and walked out towards the kitchen. He looked at the body and gasped. It lay frozen still. But it had moved forward two feet. Tim was sure. In the faint light he saw a trail of blood. He paused, and stared as the two hands began to move infinitesimally, in a crablike motion, as if tearing at the carpet. He could not go near it. He tensed, and then leapt over the body. He looked back. Spittle gathering at the mouth, the eyes flickering. He turned away and switched on the kettle. He made tea. He stepped back over the corpse's arms. He propped a cup in Sanjay's two hands and helped him raise it to his lips. He found towels, which he wetted. He wiped Sanjay's face and neck. He found a blanket which he placed around him. He pulled a chair close, sat down, and watched.

"Why did you come back?"

Tim said nothing.

"Did you get him?"

Tim nodded.

"Good man." Sanjay's eyes closed. Tim sat and waited. He watched Sanjay breathe slowly and steadily. After an hour he got up and went back into the other room. He looked across the carpet. The body was sprawled on its front at the entrance to the kitchen. Tim opened cupboards. There was some brandy left. He picked up two tumblers and returned to Sanjay's side. He poured.

"Sanjay? Sanjay?"

No reply. Tim drank from his glass.

He dozed. Hours later, mumbling. He opened his eyes. Sanjay was staring at the ceiling. He was saying something.

"Sanjay, what is it?"

His eyes moved slowly from left to right, and then back again.

Tim bent and listened, and for a moment he thought it wasn't Sanjay. He had difficulty with the words. He felt a sense of displacement, as if it was another person's fake testimony, as if the figure in front of him was pretending this past and this history that they shared, in some complex and grotesque deception. But he listened again, and he knew suddenly that what had fazed him was the accent, and as he listened he knew it was in fact two accents, traces of northern, traces of Indian subcontinent, accents that had been scrubbed out of the person Sanjay had presented to the world, but which now re-asserted themselves as that history was peeled back.

"I must pass something on to Michael. And Alec. They need to reschedule some meetings." Silence. "Although I think they'll do fine on their own. I wonder how the twins are. I'm sure Michael will get his way in the end. He always does. Divide and rule. That was his philosophy. He..." Coughing. Then, more quietly, "Divide and rule. It always worked for him. He...."

Later.

"My brother. Can you believe it? He once visited me in London. My father sent him. How ever did they find me."

"Sanjay, don't tire yourself."

"You know, when my mother died, it was the day I'd taken delivery of a new car. A Merc. A monster. A beautiful monster. I drove up the motorway to Leeds. And then when I got close, I just carried on driving. To Scotland. Glasgow. There was a girl

I knew up there. I spent a grand to stay with her that night. The next day I just drove right back down to London."

His eyelids quivered, the voice trailed off. His glass was untouched. Tim got up and made himself a coffee. He drank some more brandy. He stretched and walked for five minutes and then sat down again.

Sanjay was speaking again. A whisper. Tim bent down close. He listened for a while.

"It's in the past, Sanjay. Everything's fine now."

The air was chilly. He sat and watched, and later saw light seeping in from outside, and finally he slept, waking once or twice as he felt his body slipping off the chair. Each time he started, looked over at Sanjay and then drifted off again. But finally he looked up and Sanjay's eyes were open, and dull, and still. His mouth hung open. Tim leaned forward and felt his forehead. It was cold.

He shivered.

He sat there for one more hour and then got up. He looked around the house and wondered what to do next. He found a bin liner and collected all his things. The mobile phones. He found a cloth and began to dust all the surfaces. He did not know why, but he had seen it in films. He dusted the gun, and then left it in Sanjay's hand. He had one last look at everything. The body by the kitchen, its skin grey, limbs twisted. Sanjay, staring up at the ceiling. Looking calm, surprised almost.

Tim turned and walked away. As he reached the front door he glanced down at his feet and smiled. He needed a pair of shoes. He walked out of the cottage and locked the front door. He placed the key under the pot at the side. He walked round to the back, found a stone and broke a window.

He headed off down the road. A few minutes later he stopped and sat in a ditch. He put his face between his knees. His shoulders shook. After a while he got up.

It took him twenty minutes to get back to the car. He started up the engine and began to drive south.

twenty two

Tim drove Sanjay's car to Edinburgh. He parked a few blocks from the station, then took his things out of the boot, wiped down the steering wheel and the dashboard with a cloth, and lowered one window a fraction. He left the keys in the ignition, got out the car, and walked away. He took the next train down to London.

His flat was a mess when he arrived back home. It didn't surprise him. He spent a couple of hours tidying up. Later, on the way out, he passed a neighbour.

"Burglars," Tim said.

"What did they take?"

"Nothing valuable."

He went over to Michael's offices. His secretary told him Michael was out on business. Tim made an appointment to see him the following afternoon.

He was shown in at three the next day. The door closed behind him. He was alone. He looked at the books on the shelves and pulled down a biography. *Erwin Rommel*. He sat at the conference table and leafed through it.

After five minutes Michael walked in. He sat down, two places away, and looked at Tim.

"Michael," Tim said. "I want out."

Michael got up and poured himself a glass of water. "What do you mean?"

"I'll give it back. All the money. Whatever's left."

"Give it back? Who to? To me?"

"I want it to end. Now. I don't want to be part of it any more."

"Part of what?"

"You know what I mean."

Michael grunted.

"So why are you saying all this? Now?" He got up again and stood by the windows. "You know, I've just made a deal with some people. It's over. We're done. Everyone's happy now. We're all fucking ecstatic."

Tim frowned.

"What kind of a deal?"

"Look, mate..."

Tim shouted. "Michael, please don't..." His voice went quiet. "... don't 'mate' me."

Michael stared at him for a moment. "Yeah, well, perhaps you've heard a few things. You've read stuff in the papers. I can tell you, Tim. It's sorted out."

"Jerome? And the others?"

"Which others?"

"Jerome?"

Michael said nothing for a while.

"Yeah. Jerome and the others," he said. "This lifestyle of theirs, the drugs and all that. What can I do?"

Tim was silent. There was a loud knock at the door. Mick loped in. He sat down. Tim stared. A row of weals coruscating along cheek and neck.

"Hey, guess what," Michael said. "Tim wants to give us half a million quid."

Mick said nothing. Michael sat down next to Tim.

"Tim. Keep it. You earned it. Your job's done. It's over. We did it. We all got what we wanted."

Michael looked down at the book for a moment. "You know, Tim, I think I always underestimated you."

Tim got up slowly.

"Here. Keep the book. A souvenir. I don't have time to read these days."

"I don't think so."

Mick rose as well. He extended a hand. "Look after yourself, mate."

Tim looked at him. His bulk, his chrome-top head. Tim walked to the door. As he reached it, he turned.

"Mick, listen, is there anywhere I can send... Bernie... You know, flowers or something..."

Mick said nothing.

Tim opened the door and walked out.

Tim's friend Pete rang him a few days later. He said the story had recently crossed the news desk. An unusual tragedy. Police were investigating a double murder in Scotland. They said it was some kind of bizarre shoot-out. Pete said that he had spoken to Sanjay's family. They told him not a single person from London had been to see them.

"Tim, Janice's parents live just outside Leeds. We're going up there next weekend. I thought it might be nice if someone from here paid their respects."

Pete and Tim drove to a large house on the outskirts of town. The door was opened by a man in his thirties. Slimmer than Sanjay, darker. He had a moustache. But the same face.

He explained that the cremation could not take place until the coroner had released the body. They had set up part of the house as a shrine. Pete and Tim took off their shoes. They were led into a room. At one end was a large picture, Sanjay as a teenager. There were flowers, garlands, incense candles. A few people sat silently on cushions dotted around.

Later they were introduced to an old man. He said he was honoured that they had travelled this great distance. He asked them if they knew Sanjay well, and Pete said he had known him years ago when they were students. Tim said that he also had been at university with Sanjay, but that he had got to know him again more recently. Sanjay had been wealthy and successful.

His father insisted they stay. The man's sister, the boy's aunt, would prepare food. The old people fussed.

Later, Sanjay's brother took them aside. They sat, the three of them, alone in a basement. He poured three glasses of scotch.

"I shouldn't really be doing this," he said.

He looked at Tim and sighed. "So you're Tim." He stared for a minute. The conversation ran in stops and starts. "My brother hardly ever spoke much about his friends at uni. But he mentioned you a few times."

"What did he say?"

"I'm glad we can finally meet face to face."

They sipped their drinks. It seemed that something lay between them, beyond even their shared loss, some source of great disquiet, silencing them. Tim could tell Sanjay's brother was not a drinker. Perhaps for a second the alcohol made him bold.

"It's the way it all ended for him. Alone. At the hands of that madman. That's what's so... troubling."

As if he had reached for a different word, and then drawn back. And Tim could hardly bear to keep silent. But he did.

Pete spoke softly. "Try not to... to imagine the worst."

Tim nodded. And then he said something. "I think ... I know... he would have been at peace. At the end." Pete looked across at him. "Remember, I saw him, many times, over the last few months. Perhaps... perhaps, it wasn't the way you think."

"Tell me," Sanjay's brother said. "What did you talk about? The last time you met."

Tim looked down.

"Please. Try to remember."

"He talked about his family."

"Really?" There was silence. "I wish I could believe you. I really do."

Another pause.

"Somewhere it all went wrong," Sanjay's brother said. "Perhaps it was me. I stopped looking out for him."

And Tim said, "I swear to you it's true. I remember it with absolute clarity. His last words were about his family."

They looked at each other.

"Thanks for that, Tim. Thank you so much."

"Tim, there's something I have to say..."

"Sanjay, why don't you hand me the gun?"

"Tim, I must say it now."

"Let's have it."

"We never really talked about it. I don't know why."

"What?"

"That time years ago, when we drove back from Oxford. You remember. Afterwards."

"Let's forget it. It's in the past."

"No. Tim. We must talk now."

Tim leant forward. Sanjay whispered.

"That time, years ago. Afterwards. We cleaned up the car, I hid it away. You were so ill, you had to stay in bed. But I went back that day. I went back to the place where it all happened. I looked round, I even asked a few of the old tramps. After an hour I found an old guy, squatting in a cardboard box in a corner somewhere, and there was something hidden under a load of old rags at his side. He scowled at me, he told me to get lost, but I persisted and hassled him, and eventually he said someone had killed his dog, the body was there at his side. This thing, the only thing he had ever loved, and it was dead. Run over. And he was shouting and swearing at me, until I couldn't stand it, and I left.

"Tim. You remember that day. You never killed anyone." And Sanjay began to weep.

"I don't know why I never said anything before. I just... I just don't know. No, I do know. I hated you all. I despised you. Everything I knew about you that you didn't, it was a kind of power over you. Something I could use. One day."

Tim listened. He said nothing.
"And I was right."

Tim spent the next day with Pete and Janice and the children. He delighted in their company. They took his hand as they walked. They sang and told him secrets. After lunch, as Janice took the kids for a stroll, he and Pete talked.

"Tim, you remember that guy you were asking about? Last time we met?"

"Who's that?"

"The businessman? Michael Palmer?"

"Yes."

"He's been in the news. Apparently the police have been talking to him."

"Oh?"

"A string of suspicious deaths. This business with Sanjay." Pete looked at him. "You knew that, didn't you? The connection between those two."

Tim said nothing.

"And then, the other day. A profile in the FT. Glowing. One of the new movers and shakers, they say."

Tim drank his coffee.

"Interesting, that. Wouldn't you say?"

In London, the next night, Tim tried the number he had in California. The tour manager. Again. He told Tim there was a performance later in the evening. She was rehearsing. Tim insisted. He was told to ring the following day.

He did. The exact same time. Secretaries, voice mail extensions. He waited. And then.

"Hello?"

Tim did not know what to say for a few seconds.

"Hi. It's me."

Another pause. Words stilted, cut short. Scraps, formalities, hesitations. And then Tim took a deep breath.

"Imogen, I have some news. Some bad news. Sanjay, he's... he's dead."

"My God... how...?" He heard her swallow. "Tim, I'm so sorry. I..." And for a second he hated himself, because he knew and hoped that the telling might open a door.

"Are you OK?" Imogen said.

"I'm fine. I saw the family. They're coping."

"How did it...?"

"There was an accident. Up north. It's in the papers."

Then, tentatively, quietly. "Do you want to talk about it?"

He thought, *One day, I will tell her. One day, not now.* He clasped the receiver to his ear and listened. "Perhaps, another time." For the slightest sound of relief.

"But you," he said after a moment. "How are you?"

"Tim..."

He waited.

"Tim, I've been thinking of staying here for a while. After the tour's finished."

"I see."

"It's just, I've met so many people.."

"Imogen..."

"It's so lovely here, the weather.."

"Imogen. I need to know something..." An imagined balance, in his favour. A tragedy revealed, a confidence owed.

"There are so many opportunities..."

"Imogen. Please, you must tell me..."

Silence. Once more.

Then he said it. "Is it mine?"

"It?"

"He? She?" He waited. A heartbeat's fear that he had miscalculated.

"Tim. I've got to go."

"Imogen. Please." His voice, pinched. "You can't."

"Call me tomorrow."

Tim swore silently. "When?"

"Same time. Yes. Call me then. Yes. That would be nice."

"Same time?"

"Call me then, Tim. I've got to go, I've just got to go now..."

He wanted to stay up all night, then sleep during the morning and somehow align his day, his perception of time, his whole sensibility, with hers, so that he might experience the first cup of coffee, the opening of the curtains and the first glimpse of the sky, the whole rhythm of the day, exactly as she would six thousand miles to the west. And he did find it difficult to sleep that night. But he was awake at seven, London time. He fretted the whole day.

At the hour, daylight long gone, he sat at his desk in front of the phone.

"Hi."

"Hiya."

And he wondered whether she would tell him, whether he had been right to ask the previous night. It sounded so wrong now as he thought about it, the way he had phrased it. But she talked about other things. Her music, her new friends. Places she had stayed at, people she had met.

She talked about an exhibition she had seen.

"A gallery, it was here in San Francisco. Old stone buildings. Wooden floors, white walls. Contemporary American portraits or something.

"There was a painting in one room, a triptych, three sketches, the same person. Soft colours, contours, kind of ... splashed, not quite blurred. A sensibility, almost, I don't know, Victorian. Three moods, it said. Each one set against the landscape of the coast north of here. We sat there, a group of us, on a bench in the centre of the room. There was something in her face, an expression in all three pictures. We all just sat there. And stared....

"I checked out the painter and the name was familiar. *Grace Bradberry.* I couldn't figure out why. And then, an hour later, it came to me. It was you. You told me about her. Years ago.

290

"And, Tim, I went back to those paintings, and I thought how beautiful they were, how sad, how..." She paused. "I spoke to the gallery owner later. Apparently she lives close by. She's sometimes here, kind of artist in residence. I left my number."

Tim waited.

"Why didn't any of you come out here, Tim? Not one of you?"

"Imogen, I was a kid."

"Your brothers, your father..."

"I was so confused, it was... Imogen, it was traumatic."

"It's all wrong. There's something about your whole family, Tim, something." She paused. "I'm sorry, I shouldn't have said that."

He waited. She never did tell him what he wanted to know. They talked of other things. They agreed to speak again. The next day. Same time.

twenty three

Tim went to visit his father. He left early morning. Two hours out of London, he pulled in to a service station to call ahead. He waited eight, ten, twelve rings.

"Hello?" An unsteady voice at the other end of the line.

He shouted. "It's Tim!"

"Hello? Hello?"

He looked at his phone. It went dead. He sighed and got back in the car. It was about eleven when he passed through the suburbs of Cambridge. In the driveway of the family home, he saw his father's old Ford. He noticed a wing mirror was missing.

Tim had a key. He rang the bell, and then walked through into the hall. The heating was full on. He shouted as he went.

"It's me! Dad! It's me."

His father was sitting on a settee, arms neatly at his side. He was staring straight ahead. He remained that way for a few moments, and then turned to look at Tim. The flash of a smile, sudden, somehow sheepish, almost involuntary. His father raised himself up and extended a hand. Tim took it awkwardly.

"Don't get up."

His father fussed. "Tim. My dear boy." He grabbed his stick. "My dear, dear boy."

He led Tim into the kitchen.

"I'll prepare the tea," Tim said.

His father shooed him away. "Don't tell me I ignore my guests," he said. He struggled to reach the tea bags and the milk.

Tim waited until the old man had settled on a chair at the kitchen table. He wanted to look around. He said he needed the loo. He bounded up the stairs. Afterwards he checked the bedrooms. Doors and cupboards all closed, surfaces cold, dusty, beds un-slept-in. The heating was off. He lingered in his old room for a few moments.

Downstairs, he helped his father with the tray back into the living room.

"Dad, where are you sleeping these days?"

His father pointed a stick towards the second room.

"Mind if I take a peek?" The furniture had been cleared out. A single bed was made up, with a small table set beside it. A few books. He saw a copy of the Times, folded to reveal the crossword on the back page. He glanced at it. As a teenager he had always struggled with this particular intellectual challenge, one that his father and brothers seemed to accomplish so effortlessly. A few clues had been attempted. One word trailed off after three or four spidery letters. Tim looked more closely. With a sense of shock he realised that the answers were wrong. Dead wrong. Not even close. He sat on the bed, chin in hand, checking clues.

His father poured tea.

"Dad, has something happened?"

"What kind of thing?"

Tim let it go. He asked his father about himself. The old man talked about the health visitor, his winter flu jab. The cleaner who came twice a week. He said Julian and Brian were very good to him. He dribbled as he spoke.

"Here, Dad. let me help." Tim got a roll of kitchen towels.

His father cursed softly. "I'm all right, son," he said. "I'm all right."

In the afternoon Tim took his father for a drive. They went through the centre of town. At a stretch of green, his father asked him to stop.

"Your mother loved this park," he said. "She brought Julian and Brian here when they were young."

They watched couples strolling.

"Dad, did you ever...?" Tim began to frame a question. He waited for his father to prompt him, but the old man said nothing.

After a few minutes he tried again.

"Dad, after Mum left, did you ever meet anyone? Did you ever think ... afterwards... about someone else perhaps?"

A toddler chased after a flock of pigeons. Screams. Wings flapping.

"She loved it here."

They drove on. There was silence, and Tim became afraid. He sensed something, a discontinuity. He thought of his father at the wedding. He thought of him now.

At home he prepared some lunch. Afterwards his father drank more tea. Tim looked at photographs on the mantelpiece.

"Dad, I have something to tell you," Tim said.

He picked up a picture of Julian and Brian.

"It's something I've done," he said without turning.

There was a clink of cup against saucer behind him. He heard his father slurping. He waited. He passed a finger over the dark, varnished surface of a bookcase. On a shelf above there was a clock ticking. It was wrong.

And then, his father speaking. "In this family we don't break promises."

Tim felt a moment of panic.

"In my day it was for life. When your mother and I met, we made a vow to each other. For life."

Tim was struck by the beauty of the antique finish, the stained brown of the wood, a hint of succulence in its depth and sheen. A hinge on the glass cover was loose. He looked at the titles inside. Hardbacks, cracked spines, yellowed pages. He traced a fingernail over the panelling, the ornamentation, the curve of the wood. He was suddenly mesmerised by the detail he saw in the craftsmanship. The care and attention, the lost skills.

"It wasn't a religious thing. It wasn't a Christian thing. It was a declaration. To the world, to oneself. That you were incomplete, somehow diminished, unless you had your partner at your side, this person whom you would care for and cherish for the rest of your days. It was an affirmation to the woman you loved.

And also the completion of a kind of journey. To find out the kind of chap you really were.

"That day. It was such a beautiful service. We had it in a church. Her parents, they insisted, they would have been so hurt. And we were all moved. Despite everything. Even my friends, atheists, rationalists, every one of them. But that day we saw the centuries of ritual for what they were, a statement of trust between man and woman, not man and god. The truth was a human one, not supernatural. The moment we saw that, that was the moment we made our promise to each other. Our vow.

"And your mother that day. Sparkling, so captivating. With her beauty, her style.

"It was a special time. A unique day. How could one ever repeat it?"

Tim turned back to his father. He noticed his right hand was shaking. He sat by him. After a while he took his hand in his own. He saw a single tear forming on his father's cheek.

Why didn't you fight to win her back? he thought. *Why didn't you go straight out there and plead with her to come home?*

He made more tea. His father was better. His hands were steady. Tim got up. He found a tin of biscuits in the kitchen. He spread them out on a plate beside the teapot. He felt better as well. And somehow grateful. As if the sky had cleared for a moment.

And then, more.

"Julian arrived a couple of years later." His father was talking again. "It's strange for the man. For the husband. He's just a spectator, the woman's done all the hard work. And yet, when I saw that little bundle in the nurse's arms, when she handed him to me, even I, who had devoted my life to studying the processes and the mechanics of these things, even I found myself experiencing something strange. One thinks for a moment that the future lies there, in one's hands, to mould, to

295

create, as best as one can. Of course, it's nonsense, there are a thousand generations of genetic material swimming around in every cell of that body. I should know, as well as anyone. But for a second, the illusion is there, the thought that the secret of creation is in front of you, a kind of power, to build and shape and control.

"And looking down at him, I began to understand the nature of goodness, of my own morality, the essence of what I should try to be and do. I had lived all my life by the light of my reason, but it would be driven, I now knew, by the emotions of those few seconds. Looking at that young life, I understood, almost for the first time, the actual meaning of words like duty, responsibility. Care. Even love."

His father paused. Tim waited for him to say more, but his eyes were already dimming. He picked up a biscuit. He offered one to Tim. Tim shook his head. His father's eyelids began to droop. After a few minutes Tim got up from the sofa. His father started at the movement

"Brian said he would pop round this evening. With Sarah. Have you ever met her?"

"Yes, Dad. The wedding. You remember?"

Tim read to him for a while. Later his father asked him if he was staying. He said he had to leave.

"When will I see you next?" his father said.

"Dad, I'm going away for a while."

"Oh? Where to?"

"To America."

And Tim thought his father appeared to crumple in his seat.

"For ever? Not for ever, I hope."

Tim put his arm around his father's shoulder. "No. Not forever."

Tim prepared to go. He picked up his things. His father struggled to his feet.

"When will you be back? Please tell me."

"Soon, Dad," Tim said, as he stood at the front door. "I promise. Soon."

He flew to Switzerland the next day. At a bank in Zurich, he asked for a statement for his account.

He asked them to prepare five banker's drafts, each for fifty thousand pounds, made payable to charities he had selected at random. He drew out ten thousand dollars in cash, and then asked for a withdrawal facility to be made available in London and California.

Later he looked at the cheques. *He had a son,* Tim thought. *I said I could trace him. Perhaps one day I will.* He tore up one of the cheques.

He flew back in the evening. He posted four letters.

The following day he booked a flight to San Francisco.

twenty four

Tim boarded the aircraft. He had his book, his ipod, his newspaper. He had his mementoes, his letters and photographs. It was a long flight.

He sat at the window. Seats filled slowly, it looked as if the plane would be half empty.

A woman and her three children walked down the aisle. Loud voices, strong American accents. They stopped at the row of seats in front of him. She was weighted down, she carried bags and books, toys and plastic bottles. She told the children to move along. They argued over who was going to sit where. She bawled. A stewardess asked her if she needed help. For what seemed an age, they fussed and fidgeted. Other passengers waited patiently.

The flight attendants went through the safety routines. He watched idly. The child in front of him was standing on her seat gazing at him.

"Hello," Tim said.

She giggled, turned away, and then looked back at him. Two other faces appeared.

"Hey, you kids, don't you go bothering the man."

Tim grinned conspiratorially. "I'm Tim," he said. "What are your names?"

They were shy.

An hour later the plane was airborne and the seat belt sign was off. Tim put on his headphones and sat back. He thought of the city he was leaving behind. Of his life there, and then the events of the last few months. Their beginnings, their endings, their sequence. And a faint unease began to twist and coil inside him, oddly reflected in a subtle tremor that seemed to pass through the cabin as they hit a spot of turbulence. He leaned forward and

298

looked out the window. He stared at the cloud until it cleared, and saw suddenly a coastline beneath, a strip of sand five miles below, separating the land of his birth from a dark expanse of deep blue. The sense of distance, the stark purity of the colour, and then, something about the straight-line precision he saw in the form and design of the plane's fuselage and wing, all these seemed to calm him. He breathed out and felt his tension finally evaporate. This land below. Now behind him. He floated far above it all, and for a moment was overcome by the dizzying vertical geometry of his new viewpoint. This experience so commonplace in modern times, yet unknown to a hundred generations of mankind before him, until men from his father's grandfather's time had miraculously re-shaped the laws of the world to their own purposes. But he thought some more and knew also that it was not a miracle at all, but rather the exact opposite, it was the demonstration of the primacy of the powers of rationality over superstition, the proof that insight into the mechanics of how things worked, this dry application of the intelligence, was the alchemy that would raise this construction of steel into the sky. In a manner quite contrary to the suppositions of intuition or common sense.

He wondered whether he could ever explain this to the children seated in front of him. But they were too pre-occupied with magic, the magic of the button that tilted their seats, the magic of the toys in their laps, of the cartoons on the screen in front of them. He asked them why they were so excited, and they said they were excited because they were going home. They told him about their dad, about their cousins and grandparents, about the new and the old friends they would meet at school. The magic of the undiscovered, and the rediscovered.

They asked him where he was going.

To discover my future, and my past, he thought, and for a second the same excitement washed through him.

He felt exhilarated by its warmth.

A gray room. A gray table. A sheaf of photographs. He sees a holiday cottage, picturesque, remote. Then a figure lying on the floor. Another, seated. Eyes staring into space, mouths open.

"We think there was a third person."

A man in a pinstripe suit sitting to Michael Palmer's right leans over and whispers into his ear, but he brushes him away. "It's OK," he says, and he looks up at the two policemen opposite.

He stares at them and he thinks about his wife, his children, and the perfume that Lily seems to exude from the space between her legs, and he begins to wonder what it is these men want. What it is they think they are doing, what they think they are defending. This London, this shit hole of theirs, this place which that notice on the wall signed by both Police Chief and Mayor declares they will protect, this fantasy world of good citizens, porcine bureaucrats, compliant neighbours. Of tourists, students, mothers. Anodyne, its history stripped of its blood and pain, its culture flaccid, gutless, inoffensive. Like those fucking brochures. He stares across the table. He knows that that place does not exist.

The other London, the real London, this skull-like horror beneath the make-up, this is his town, another place, primitive, violent, which its civilised exterior just can't cover up. A place where nothing seems to work, a place as much third world as first, yet which seems to suck dry even the rich of every last penny. With its mass of humanity, and the chaos and corruption slithering in its wake. A hundred races and creeds. As many faultlines of irreconcilable hatred. The squalor, the knives on the street, the carjackings, the shootings. The new terror, that each plane or train journey will end in sudden fire, white light and death. A place where half the world's terrorists seem to fester on welfare in their midst. And the asinine mixture of panic and paralysis with which the authorities respond. A million cameras, on every corner, spies in the sky, a city staring at itself, waiting for the beast that it will spawn from its bowels. "Do us all a favour," one of his Special Branch guys loves to say. "I'll give you a list of names. Think of it as charity." Mick always laughs. "Just make 'em disappear."

His London. These detectives don't have a clue.

The two men held open the swing doors for him. Outside, bright winter sun fell across the steps in front of the station.

"I still don't get it," one of the policemen said.

Michael Palmer unfolded a pair of dark glasses.

"Good family, high-powered job. Girlfriend." The policeman chatted.

Michael Palmer rubbed his neck and scanned the street below.

"It just doesn't make sense."

A black car slowed as it approached.

"Do you understand it, sir? Unless... as you say..." the policeman mused "...there was something between them. Him and Mr Roy. Something from their past. Their student days."

Michael Palmer raised a gloved hand. He waited.

"You know, Mr Palmer, my old man was a copper. The way he talks. It was so simple in his day. So black and white. You knew who the good guys were. Who the bad. It was all so different."

He took off his sunglasses and then his right glove. He turned.

"But this ... this fellow Scott," the policeman said. He laughed. "Back then, you could always tell. You could just look at someone. And you could tell. Every time."

Michael Palmer shook hands with one, then the other.

"Perhaps that's just it," he said. "Perhaps these days, you just can't."